THE BIG BAD CITY

ALSO BY ED McBAIN

THE 87TH PRECINCT NOVELS

Cop Hater • The Mugger • The Pusher (1956) The Con Man • Killer's Choice (1957) Killer's Payoff • Killer's Wedge • Lady Killer (1958) Til Death • King's Ransom (1959) Give the Boys a Great Big Hand • The Heckler • See Them Die • (1960) Lady, Lady, I Did It! (1961) The Empty Hours • Like Love (1962) Ten Plus One (1963) Ax (1964) He Who Hesitates • Doll (1965) Eighty Million Eyes (1966) Fuzz (1968) Shotgun (1969) Jigsaw (1970) Hail, Hail, the Gang's All Here (1971) Sadie When She Died • Let's Hear It for the Deaf Man (1972) Hail to the Chief (1973) Bread (1974) Blood Relatives (1975) So Long As You Both Shall Live (1976) Long Time, No See (1977) Calypso (1979) Ghosts (1980) Heat (1981) Ice (1983) Lightning (1984) Eight Black Horses (1985) Poison • Tricks (1987) Lullaby (1989) Vespers (1990) Widows (1991) Kiss (1992) Mischief (1993) And All Through the House (1994) Romance (1995) Nocturne (1997)

THE MATTHEW HOPE NOVELS

Goldilocks (1978) Rumpelstiltskin (1981) Beauty & the Beast (1982) Jack & the Beanstalk (1984) Snow White & Rose Red (1985) Cinderella (1986) Puss in Boots (1987) The House That Jack Built (1988) Three Blind Mice (1990) Mary, Mary (1993) There Was a Little Girl (1994) Gladly the Cross-Eyed Bear (1996) The Last Best Hope (1998)

OTHER NOVELS

The Sentries (1965) Where There's Smoke • Doors (1975) Guns (1976) Another Part of the City (1986) Downtown (1991)

AND AS EVAN HUNTER

NOVELS

The Blackboard Jungle (1954) Second Ending (1956) Strangers When We Meet (1958) A Matter of Conviction (1959) Mothers and Daughters (1961) Buddwing (1964) The Paper Dragon (1966) A Horse's Head (1967) Last Summer (1968) Sons (1969) Nobody Knew They Were There (1971) Every Little Crook and Nanny (1972) Come Winter (1973) Streets of Gold (1974) The Chisholms (1976) Love, Dad (1981) Far from the Sea (1983) Lizzie (1985) Criminal Conversation (1994) Privileged Conversation (1996)

SHORT STORY COLLECTIONS

Happy New Year, Herbie (1963) The Easter Man (1972)

CHILDREN'S BOOKS

Find the Feathered Serpent (1952) The Remarkable Harry (1959) The Wonderful Button (1961) Me and Mr. Stenner (1976)

SCREENPLAYS

Strangers When We Meet (1959) The Birds (1962) Fuzz (1972) Walk Proud (1979)

TELEPLAYS

The Chisholms (1979) The Legend of Walks Far Woman (1980) Dream West (1986)

THE BIG BAD CITY

A novel of the 87th Precinct

Ed McBain

Hodder & Stoughton

First published in Great Britain in 1999 by Hodder and Stoughton
A division of Hodder Headline PLC
First published in paperback in 1999 by Hodder and Stoughton

10 9 8 7 6 5 4 3 2 1

British Library Cataloguing in Publication Data
A CIP catalogue record for this title is available from the British Library

ISBN 0 340 75007 3

Printed and bound in Great Britain by
Caledonian International Book Manufacturing Ltd, Glasgow

Hodder and Stoughton
A division of Hodder Headline PLC
338 Euston Road
London NW1 3BH

This, again, is for my wife—
Dragica Dimitrijević-Hunter

The city in these pages is imaginary. The people, the places are all fictitious. Only the police routine is based on established investigatory technique.

THE BIG BAD CITY

1.

THE DETECTIVES HADN'T EVEN KNOWN THE TWO MEN WERE ACQUAINTED. ONE OF THE MEN WAS IN THE HOLDING CELL because he'd inconsiderately shot a little Korean grocer who'd resisted his attempts to empty the store's cash register. The other one was just being led into the cell. He'd been caught running from the scene of a liquor store holdup on Culver and Twelfth.

Aside from their occupations, the two men had nothing in common. One was white, the other was black. One was tall, the other was short. One had blue eyes, the other had brown eyes. One had the body of a weight lifter, possibly because he'd spent two years upstate on a prior felony. The one being led into the cell was somewhat plump. Sometimes, the plump ones were the ones to watch.

"Inside, let's move it," Andy Parker said and nudged him into the cell. Parker would later tell anyone who'd listen that he'd automatically figured the arresting blues had frisked the perp at the scene. "How was I to know he had a knife tucked into his crack?" he would ask the air.

In this instance, "crack" was not a controlled substance. Detective Parker was referring to the wedge between the man's ample buttocks, from which hiding place he had drawn a sling-blade knife the instant he spotted the body builder slouching and sulking in the far corner of the cage. What Parker did the minute he saw the plump little magician pull a knife out of his ass was slam the cell door shut and turn the key. At that very moment, Steve Carella and Artie Brown were together leading nine handcuffed basketball players into the squadroom. Both detectives smelled trouble at once.

The trouble was not that any policeman was in danger from the chubby little knife-wielding man in the cage. But the body builder was in police custody, and presumably under police protection as well, and every cop in that room conjured up visions of monumental lawsuits against the city for allowing a black man—*black*, no less—to be carved up while in a locked cell—*locked*, no less—with a fat white assassin who kept slashing the air with the knife and repeating over and over again, "Oh, yeah? Oh, yeah? Oh, yeah?"

Carella fired a shot at the ceiling.

"A minute before I was about to," Parker would later claim.

"You!" Carella yelled, sprinting toward the cage.

"Don't get any ideas," Brown warned the nine basketball players, who, although they were not lawyers, were already spouting learned Supreme Court decisions on false arrest and civil rights and such. Just in case one of them decided to drag the rest of his handcuffed buddies after him into the corridor, Brown drew his own gun and stood massively and menacingly between the players and the slatted wooden railing that separated the squadroom from the hallway outside.

"Oh, yeah?" the knifer in the cage said again, and slashed the air. The body builder kept backing away, hands circling the air in front of him. He had seen a few knife-wielders in his time, this dude, and he was waiting for the next gunshot from outside the cage, hoping the cops would help distract this crazy fat bastard who kept coming at him with the knife and yelling "Oh, yeah?" as if he was supposed to know what it meant. "Oh, yeah?" the corpulent little shit said again and again came at him.

"You hear me?" Carella shouted from just outside the cage now. "Throw that knife down! Now!"

"Juke him, man!" one of the basketball players shouted.

"Oh, yeah?" the fat man yelled, and lunged again, and this time drew blood.

The body builder yanked back his right hand as if a searing line of fire had scorched the palm, which in fact was exactly what the knife slash had felt like. His face went ashen when he turned his palm up and saw the deep cut spurting from pinkie to thumb. By then, the knifer, smelling blood, smelling fear, was closing in for the kill.

Parker, standing outside the cage with his gun in his hand, Carella standing alongside him with his own gun in his hand, had to decide in the next ten seconds whether they would be justified within the guidelines to drop the man in his tracks. They were both certain that a man pulling a knife while in police custody was reason enough for them to have drawn their weapons and shouted a warning. They both shouted warnings again, "Drop the knife!" from Carella, "Freeze!" from Parker, but the fat little man was neither freezing nor dropping the knife.

He simply kept moving closer and closer to the black body builder whose palm was steadily and alarmingly gushing blood, the knife swinging in the air ahead of him as he advanced, muttering, "Oh, yeah? Oh, yeah?"

"You crazy sumbitch, what's *wrong* with you?" the black man yelled, but the knifer kept coming on like a tank in the streets, the knife swinging,"Oh, yeah? Oh, yeah?"

"Steve?" Parker asked.

"Drop him," Carella said, and fired the first shot, hitting the knifer in the right thigh, collapsing him to his knees. Parker fired an instant later, taking the man in the right forearm, causing him to release his grip on the knife. As it clattered to the cell floor, the black man lunged for it.

"Don't," Carella said very softly.

THE REASON THERE WERE ONLY *nine* basketball players in the squadroom—rather than the customary ten, five to a team—was that the forward on one of the teams had been shot while running downcourt for a basket. Presumably, one of the remaining nine players had fired the shot, since this had been a practice game without spectators, on a deserted playground court, on a sizzling Friday evening in August.

The oppressive heat notwithstanding, the pair of blues riding Adam Four knew the sound of a gunshot when they heard one. Two, in fact. In rapid succession. Bang, bang, like in the comics. They rolled up outside the cyclone fence in time to stop nine youths from dispersing fast, as was the usual case in this neighborhood whenever the music of gunfire filled the air.

The kids ranged in age from seventeen to twenty-four, twenty-five, the blues guessed, all of them wearing T-shirts and what one of the Adam Four cops described as "droopy shorts," which meant they hung down below the knees. The white team was wearing white T-shirts. The blue team was wearing blue T-shirts. The kid lying on the ground with two bullet holes in his chest was—or had been—a member of the white team, but his T-shirt was now stained a bright red.

The Adam Four cops found a .32 Smith & Wesson revolver in the weeds lining the dilapidated court. None of the nine knew anything at all about the gun or how Jabez Courtney happened to have got himself shot with it. All of them—presumably including the one who'd shot young Jabez—complained that they were being rounded up and herded to the cop shop simply because they were black, the O. J. legacy.

Now, at ten minutes to eight, Carella and Brown started doing their paperwork. In this city, the tempo in August slowed down to what Lieutenant Byrnes had once described as "summertime," not quite the equivalent of "ragtime," a slow-motion rhythm that leisurely waltzed the relieving team into the sometimes frantic pace of police work. There were three eight-hour shifts in any working day. First came the day shift, from eight in the morning to four in the afternoon. Next came the night shift, from four to midnight. Lastly, and least desirably, came the morning shift, from midnight to eight A.M. Usually, the teams were relieved at a quarter to the hour, but not during the month of August. In August, a good third of the squad was on vacation, and many of the detectives were pulling overtime working double shifts. Which perhaps explained why Carella and Brown, who had both clocked in at a quarter to eight this morning, were still here more than twelve hours later.

At this hour, there was a sort of languid tranquility to the squadroom. Despite the clamor of the nine ballplayers and their arriving attorneys, all armed to the teeth with arguments pertaining to mass and indiscriminate roundups of suspects, all prepared to summon the spectres of the Holocaust and the World War II Japanese-American concentration camps . . .

Despite the arrival of a paramedic team, all urgency and haste in earnest imitation of the actors on *ER*, rushing the bleeding body builder onto a stretcher and down the iron-runged steps to the waiting ambulance even though the patient kept protesting he could *walk*, damn it, wasn't nothin wrong with his *legs* . . .

Despite the arrival of a *second* team of paramedics, no less skilled in TV emulation than the first, who briskly and efficiently lifted the plump little former knifer onto another stretcher, bleeding from forearm and thigh and shouting to his benefactors that the man he'd stabbed had stolen his wife from him, an accusation dismissed by one of the paramedics with the consolation, "Cool it, *amigo*," though the knifer wasn't Hispanic . . .

Despite the arrival of two detectives from Internal Affairs who wanted to know what the hell had happened up here, how come a man in custody had been wounded by another man in custody, and how come sidearms had been drawn and fired, and all that bullshit, which Parker and Carella—and even Brown, who'd innocently been riding herd on the nine ballplayers—had to address before they could call it a day . . .

Despite the arrival of a man and his helper from what was euphemistically called the police department's Maintenance and Repair Division, here to fix the building's decrepit air-conditioning system, which of course was malfunctioning on a day with a high of ninety-two Fahrenheit, thirty-three Celsius . . .

Despite what to a disinterested observer might have appeared merely excessive motion and commotion, but which to the detectives coming and going was simply the usual ambience of the place in which they worked, give or take a few warm bodies . . .

Despite all this, there was a sort of familiar serenity.

As Carella and Parker and Brown reeled off guideline chapter and verse to the two shooflies eager to earn points with the Mayor's office by exposing yet more use of excessive force by yet another trio of brutal police officers . . .

As Carella and Brown together typed up their Detective Division report in triplicate on the nine ballplayers still protesting innocence in separate interrogations although almost certainly one of them had been the shooter and Jabez Courtney nonetheless lay stone-cold dead on a stainless-steel table at the St. Mary Boniface Mortuary . . .

As Parker kept complaining vociferously, first to the shooflies, and next to his fellow detectives, that the goddamn blues in Adam Four should have frisked the fat little bastard before cuffing him and bringing him up here for interrogation . . .

As Meyer and Kling came in from the field where they'd been interrogating a pawnbroker about a burglar they'd nicknamed The Cookie Boy, real life imitating art once again in that every cheap thief in every crime novel, movie, or television show was colorfully nicknamed by either newspersons or cops, fiction copying reality, the fake then feeding the actual in endless cyclical rotation . . .

"Leaves a platter of chocolate chip cookies just inside the front door," Meyer told Brown.

"Yeah?" Brown said, unimpressed.

"Better than shitting in the vic's shoes," Parker said.

"Which lots of them do," Kling agreed.

"You missed all the fun up here," Carella said.

"Looks like you're *still* having fun," Meyer said cheerfully.

As telephones rang, and voices overlapped and intertwined, Carella became aware of the summer sounds of August filtering up through the screened and open windows of the squadroom. There was a stickball game in progress under the glow of the side-street lampposts. On Grover Avenue, he could hear the clopping of horses drawing carriages into the park. Suddenly, there was the liquid trickle of a girl's laughter. He did not know how long ago he'd read the story, nor could he calculate how many times it had been brought to mind on how many separate summer days. But hearing the girl's lilting laughter, he thought again of Irwin Shaw's girls in their flimsy summer frocks, and smiled knowingly. Yellow. The laughing girl somewhere on the street below would be wearing a yellow dress.

Still smiling, he went to the wooden In-Out board—admittedly an old-fashioned way of tracking in this day and age of E-mail and computer technology, but still serviceable and accessible at a glance—and was about to move his hanging name tag from the In column to the Out column because finally, at ten minutes to nine on a long hot summer's day—thirteen hours after he'd moved the tag in the opposite direction—he was ready to go home.

The door to Lieutenant Byrnes's office opened.

"Steve? Artie?" he called. "Glad I caught you."

THE DEAD GIRL LAY SPRAWLED in front of a bench in Grover Park, not seven blocks from the station house, on a gravel footpath only yards off Grover Avenue. She was wearing a white blouse and pale blue slacks, white socks and scuffed Reeboks. Flies were already buzzing around her. Not a sign of blood anywhere, but flies were already sipping at her wide-open eyes. Didn't need a medical examiner to tell them she'd been strangled. The bruise marks on her throat corroborated their immediate surmise.

"Touch anything?" Carella asked.

"No, *sir!*" one of the blues answered, sounding offended.

"This just the way you found her?" Brown asked.

He was thinking he didn't see a handbag anywhere around. Carella was thinking the same thing. The two men stood side by side in the dim light cast by a lamppost some five feet from the bench on the winding gravel path. Brown was the color of his name, six feet two inches tall and built like a cargo ship. Carella was a white man standing an even six feet tall and weighing a hundred and eighty-five in a good week. Summertime, with all the junk food, he usually shot up to a hundred-ninety, two hundred at the outside. The men had been working out of the Eight-Seven for a long time, partnered together more often than not. They could almost read each other's minds.

The assistant medical examiner arrived some five minutes later, complaining about summertime traffic, greeting the detectives, whom he'd met before at other crime scenes, and then getting to work while the blues stretched their yellow tapes and kept the forming crowd back. Nothing the residents of this city liked better than a good sidewalk show, especially in the summertime. Brown asked the blues how they'd come upon the body. The younger of the two uniformed cops said a female pedestrian had flagged their car and told them a woman was lying on the park path here, either sick or dead or something.

"Did you detain her?" Brown asked.

"Sure did, sir. She's standing right over there."

"Did you talk to her?" Carella asked.

"Few questions, is all."

"Did she see anyone?"

"No, sir. Just walkin through the park, came upon the vic, sir."

Carella and Brown glanced over toward where a woman was standing under the light of the lamppost.

"What's her name?" Carella asked.

"Susan . . . uh . . . just a second, it's an Italian name," he said, and took out his notebook. Anything ending in a vowel always threw them. Carella waited. "Androtti," the officer said. "That's a double *t*."

"Thanks," Carella said, and looked over at the woman again. She seemed to be in her late forties or thereabouts, a tall, thin woman with her arms folded across her bosom, hugging herself as if trying to retain body warmth, though the temperature still hovered in the low eighties. The detectives walked over to her.

"Miss Androtti?" Carella said.

"Yes?"

There was a stunned look on her face. It was not a pretty face to begin with, but the shock of having stumbled across a corpse had robbed it of all expression. They had seen this look before. They did not think Susan Androtti would sleep well tonight.

"We have to ask you some questions, ma'am, we're sorry," Carella said.

"That's okay," she said.

Her voice was low, toneless.

"Can you tell us what time you found the body, ma'am?"

"It must've been eight o'clock or so," she said. "It was so hot in the apartment, I came down for a walk."

"Here in the park," Brown said.

"Yes."

"Saw her lying there on the path, is that it?"

"Yes. I didn't know what it was at first. I thought it was . . . forgive me, I thought it was a bundle of clothes or something. Then I realized it was a woman."

"What'd you do then?"

"I guess I screamed."

"Uh-huh."

"And ran out of the park, looking for a call box. A police call box. When I saw the patrol car, I flagged it down and showed the officers where the . . . the body was."

"Ma'am, when you came upon her, did you see anyone else in the vicinity?"

"No. Just her."

"Hear anything in the vicinity?"

"No."

"Any noise in the bushes . . ."

"No."

"Sound of anyone running off . . ."

"No. Nothing."

"Where'd you enter the park, ma'am?"

"At the transverse road on Larson."

"Meet anyone coming toward you on the path?"

"No."

"See anyone going *away* from you on the path?"

"No one."

"How long did it take you to walk from Larson to where you discovered the body?"

"Five minutes? A little less?"

"See anyone at all during that time?"

"No one."

"Okay, miss, thank you," Carella said.

"We know this is upsetting," Brown said.

"It is."

"We know."

"We have your address, we'll contact you if we have any further questions," Carella said. "Meanwhile, try to put it out of your mind."

"I will, thank you."

"Goodnight, miss," Brown said.

She did not move.

"Miss?" Carella said.

Still she did not move.

"What is it?" he asked.

She shook her head.

Kept shaking it.

"Miss?"

"I'm afraid," she said.

And he realized she'd been hugging herself to keep from trembling.

"I'll ask the officers to drive you home," he said.

"Thank you," she said.

"Well, well, what have we here?" someone said, and they turned to see Monoghan and Monroe waddling toward the bench. In this city, the presence of Homicide Division detectives was mandatory at the scene of any murder or suicide. Even though the actual case belonged to the precinct detectives catching the squeal, Homicide was always there in a supervisory and advisory capacity. Didn't used to be that way in the old days, when Homicide cops were considered elite and precinct detectives were thought of as mere general practitioners in a world of police department specialists. But that was then and this was now, and in today's Cop Land the arrival of Homicide detectives was greeted without enthusiasm by the precinct cops actually working the case. The ME had his stethoscope inside the dead girl's blouse now. Monoghan looked somehow offended. So did Monroe.

"What is she, eighteen?" he said.

"Nineteen?" Monoghan said.

"Barbarian takeover," Monroe said, and glanced at the girl's face. "What do you think, Doc?"

"My immediate guess is strangulation," the ME said.

"Was she raped?" Monroe asked.

"Can't tell you that till we get her downtown."

"Guys who strangle teenagers usually rape them first," Monroe said. "Hello, Carella."

"Hello," Carella said.

Brown noticed that neither of the Homicide detectives ever said hello to him, but maybe he was being overly sensitive. "Has that been your experience?" he asked. "That strangled teenagers are usually rape victims as well?"

"That has been my experience, yes," Monroe said. "Most strangled teenagers have been violated first."

"Violated, huh?"

"Violated, yes."

"How many strangled-teenager cases have you investigated?" Brown asked.

Carella tried to keep from smiling.

"A few in my time, kiddo," Monroe said.

"Nothing's hard and fast in homicide cases, of course," Monoghan said, defending his partner. "But as a general rule, you can say strangled teenagers have usually been violated first."

"Be interesting to find out," the ME murmured, almost to himself. "Besides, she looks older."

"I'd appreciate your letting us know," Monroe said.

"How old would you say?" Monoghan asked.

"In her twenties, easily," the ME said.

The two Homicide detectives were wearing black on this hot summer night, black being the color of death and therefore their color of choice. Black was the traditional color of all Homicide detectives in this city. Black suits and black hats. In this city, the Homicide detectives needed only sunglasses to make them look like the Blues Brothers. Or like the two alien-chasers in the movie *Men in Black*. But one of those two had been black, and Brown had never seen a black Homicide cop in his life, except on television. He wondered how these dressed-in-black, lily-white guys felt, drawing down salaries for virtually nonexistent jobs. Supervisory and advisory, my ass, he thought. This was featherbedding of the highest order. Worst part of it was, they *earned* more than either he or Carella did. And it still rankled that they never said hello.

"Any witnesses to this?" Monroe asked.

"No," Carella said.

"How'd she happen to turn up?" Monoghan asked.

"Woman out for a stroll found her."

"Talk to the woman?"

"Few minutes ago. Saw no one, heard no one."

"Any idea who she is?"

"Her name is Susan Androtti."

"The dead girl?"

"No, the woman who . . ."

"I meant the girl."

"No ID that we could see. You find anything?" he asked the ME.

"Like what?" the ME said, looking up.

"Anything around her neck, or her wrists? Any kind of identification at all?"

"Nothing."

"Jane Doe," Brown said.

"*Mrs.* Jane Doe," Monroe said. "That's a wedding band, isn't it?"

The men all looked down at the slender gold band on the third finger of her left hand.

"Child bride," Monroe said.

"Nice knockers on her, though," Monoghan couldn't help observing.

"You got this?" Monroe asked.

"We've got it."

"Send us copies."

"In triplicate."

Brown wondered if they'd say goodbye to him.

"So long, Carella," Monroe said.

Monoghan said nothing. He followed his partner off, two black suits disappearing into the blackness of the night. The ME sighed, snapped his bag shut, and stood up. "I'm done here," he said. "She's yours."

"Okay to remove the wedding band?" Carella asked.

"She's no child bride," the ME said, as if Monroe's earlier remark had just registered. "Maybe twenty-two, twenty-three."

"Okay?" Carella asked again.

"Sure, go right ahead."

"Tell the paramedics I'll need a few minutes."

"Take your time," the ME said, and walked toward where a man and a woman in hospital gear were leaning against the ambulance. There was the incessant chatter of invisible insects on the soft night air. Carella knelt beside the dead girl.

Rings were often difficult to remove in the summertime, but this one came off with very little effort. He held it up to the light. There were three initials engraved inside the band: IHS.

"She's a nun," he almost whispered.

*   *   *

"THING YOU GOT TO REMEMBER," Juju was saying, "is this man never gonna get you out of his mind."

"Mm-huh."

"I wouldn't be sprised he the one set you up."

"You mean this time?"

"I mean now, right here and now, set you up for the fall got you behine bars again, man."

"This is shit time," Sonny said. "I be out of here soon's my lawyer meets bail."

"And right back *in* again, long as this man's on your case."

"I don't think he had nothin to do with this one, Juje, I mean it. Wasn't even his part of the city. This is a big city, man."

"Things happenin all over it, you right. But they have ways."

"What you mean, ways?"

"*Cop* ways. They get on your case, they know where you are every minute of the day and night. This man's on your case, Sonny."

"Yeah, well."

"I'm tellin you. This man prolly thinks about you all the time. Can't *sleep* from thinkin about you. Man, you offed his *papa*. He ain't . . ."

"Shhhh."

"He ain't about to forget that," Juju said, lowering his voice. "He ain't about to *forgive* it neither."

The holding cells were noisy, really no need to whisper, wasn't nobody goan hear them, anyway. This was nine-thirty at night, lights out would be at ten, everybody was still wide awake and clamoring for a lawyer, nothin closer to a zoo than a city jail. Sonny had been arrested earlier tonight for beating up a hooker called him nigger trash, herself black as a sewer. Funny thing was, he'd robbed a grocery store two nights before but nobody was bothering him about that cause nobody knew he was the one done it. Instead, he was here on a bullshit assault charge, which would go away three, four months from now when it came to trial, he hoped. Or be dismissed even beforehand, who paid any attention to strung-out black hookers? Otherwise, there was a sister out there gonna rue the day she was born. Meanwhile, soon as his lawyer got here with the fuckin bail, he'd be out on the street again.

"Another thing," Juju said, "this man ain't goan be satisfied juss lockin you up, man."

Juju was one of the people he'd met since he come to this city, funny how you ran into the same people in different lockups over and over again. It was a small community, really, what they called the criminal justice system. Some kind of justice when a two-bit whore could blow the whistle and they booked you for assault, hardly even *touched* the bitch. Might pay her a little visit even if this thing went up in smoke, teach her who she messin with here.

"He coulda killed me," Sonny said. "He had the chance."

"Who you talkin bout?"

"The cop. Carella. You know. The one whose father."

"Coulda killed you?"

"We was all alone in a dark hallway, man. Him, me, and another brother."

"What kinda brother?"

"Another cop."

"A cop ain't no brother, man, don't kid yourself."

"Kept tellin him to do it. I can still hear him whisperin in that hallway. 'Do it. We all alone here. Do it.'"

"But he didn't."

"Which is what makes me think he ain't sweatin this."

"Man, you kill *my* father, I be sweatin it day and night, believe me. Waitin for the chance to get at you."

"Then why didn't he do it when he coulda?"

"There was a witness there," Juju said.

"The witness was another cop, I tole you."

"Cops testify against other cops all the time."

"I don't think he's the kind to seek revenge," Sonny said.

"You're positive about that, huh?"

"I just don't think he's that kinda man."

"Mm-huh."

"Else he woulda done me when he coulda."

"Mm-huh."

"Is what I think," Sonny said.

"Long as you're dead certain," Juju said. "Cause if you ain't, you goan have to look over your shoulder every step you take. He won't let you breathe, man. He be after you, man. He be your *nemesis*. And when he fine you . . ."

Sonny was listening hard now.

"Why, he goan kill you, man," Juju said.

Sonny nodded.

"You want my advice? Do him fore he does you. And do it clean, man, cause you the first one they goan come lookin for. Clean piece, no partners, in, out, been nice to know you."

Juju looked him dead in the eye.

"And forget we ever had this conversation," he said.

IHS.

Carella first saw those initials on a statue of Christ hanging from the cross in the church he'd attended as a boy. The initials were lettered onto a banner above Christ's thorn-crowned head. When he asked his grandmother what they stood for, she said, "I Have Suffered."

Carella felt fairly certain they didn't mean "I Have Suffered" because that was an English sentence, and what they spoke in Jerusalem was either Latin or Hebrew. So he'd asked Sister Helen, the nun who was teaching him catechism three afternoons a week in preparation for his first Holy Communion, and she said the letters were a monogram of our Lord's name and that they stood for *Jesus Hominum Salvator,* which meant "Jesus, the Savior of Men." He was only ten years old but he asked her whether Jesus didn't save *women,* too, and she said he most certainly did and told him to go sit in the back pew of the church.

Several weeks after that, on a rainy Saturday when only two

other kids showed up for catechism, Sister Helen took him aside
and told him she was a virgin consecrated to God. And as lightning crashed overhead, illuminating the tall stained-glass windows, she removed a slender gold band from the third finger of
her left hand, showed him the letters IHS engraved inside, and
reverently whispered that she wore the ring in memory of her be-
trothal to her heavenly spouse.

Carella hadn't known what a virgin was.

It wasn't until he was sixteen or seventeen and knew what vir-
gins were and weren't that he began wondering again about those
initials IHS. This was after he'd already stopped going to church
and rarely wondered about holy matters anymore, but he kept seeing the letters over Christ's head whenever he wandered past any
shop selling religious items. He hated mysteries as much back
then as he did now, so he went to the library and began digging.
He discovered that the *nomina sacra*—as the various names of Jesus
Christ were called—were very often shortened or abbreviated and
that one of the monograms was the Greek IHΣ for IHΣΟΣ, usually
followed by ΧΡΣ for ΧΡΙΣΤΟΣ, which made about as much sense
to him as had Sister Helen's *Jesus Hominum Salvator.* So he dug a bit
further and learned that the Greek spelling IHΣΟΣ ΧΡΙΣΤΟΣ
translated as *Iesous Christos,* or Jesus Christ, and IHΣ was IHS, or
the Greek abbreviation for Jesus.

Jesus, he had cracked the code!

Now, almost thirty years later, he found the initials IHS engraved on the inside of a gold wedding band worn by a murdered
woman, and remembered Sister Helen again and the initials inside *her* ring, and he knew without question that the woman lying
beside that Grover Park bench was a nun.

Carella's desk copy of the current "Official Catholic Directory
of the City's Archdiocese" listed six hundred and thirty-seven nuns
living in thirty-five convents and residences. There were forty-four
other convents statewide and Carella chose not to count the number of sisters living in those, thank you very much.

He called the number he had for the archdiocese and spoke to a priest there who listened to his question and said he had no way of knowing whether any of the convents had reported a missing nun. He suggested that Carella try calling each of the convents individually, but . . .

"I'm sure you know, Detective . . . or perhaps you don't."

"What's that, Father?"

"Well . . . in this day and age, not all nuns live in convents. Many of them take up residence close to their work. They'll either rent an apartment or a small house with another nun or nuns, or else they'll live alone."

"Is there another listing?" Carella asked.

"Sorry?"

"Of these other residences."

"I'm afraid not. Sisters go where they're needed and where they're sent. Their mother houses would know where they are at all times, but then again . . . if you don't know who the nun is, you won't know her mother house, either, will you?"

"Do you know which orders still wear wedding bands?" Carella asked.

"Wedding bands?"

"Symbolizing the marriage to . . ."

"Oh. No. I'm sorry. I don't."

Well, Carella could have spent the next week and a half zeroing in on the orders that still wore wedding bands with the initials IHS engraved inside, or he could have spent the next *month* and a half calling every convent in the directory—none of which had listed phone numbers, he noticed, another plus—but there was an easier way.

A surefire American way.

He went directly to the media.

2. S

"**S**UPPOSE YOU GET ON A BUS, AND THE DRIVER IS DUSTIN HOFFMAN? I MEAN, THERE'S THIS GUY SITTING BEHIND THE wheel, and he looks just like Dustin Hoffman and everything, but you know he isn't Dustin Hoffman because there aren't any cameras around, they're not shooting a movie or anything on the bus. This is just a normal bus and a normal bus driver who happens to look just like Dustin Hoffman. Do you understand me?"

"Uh-huh," Carella said.

"That's the way I felt when I saw that police sketch of Mary on the front page of the newspaper. I thought 'That isn't Mary, it can't be Mary.' Same as I would think 'That isn't Dustin Hoffman, it's just a bus driver.' *Is* it Mary?"

"You'll have to tell us," Carella said.

"I mean, I just saw her *yesterday*, and everything."

They were in the Chevy sedan Carella and Brown drove whenever their preferred car was in for service, as it was today. The girl's name—they thought of her as a girl because she was still in her early twenties—was Helen Daniels, and she was sitting on the back seat, smoking. She was a nurse, but she was smoking. She had told them on the phone that the woman on the front page of that morning's tabloid was Sister Mary Vincent. It was now close to noon on a steamy Saturday, the twenty-second day of August, and they were driving her to the morgue.

"When yesterday?" Brown asked.

"At the hospital."

Which answered *where* yesterday, but not *when*.

They waited.

"We worked the same shift. Seven in the morning to three in the afternoon."

"Was she a nurse?"

"An LPN. St. Margaret's is one of the hospitals run by her order. She worked with the terminally ill. Cancer patients mostly."

"What's an LPN?" Brown asked.

"A licensed practical nurse. But she was better than any RN *I* know, believe me."

"Was that the last time you saw her? Yesterday at three? When the shift . . ."

"Yes. Well, not three. We went for coffee together after the shift broke."

"Then what?"

"I went to the subway."

"Where'd *she* go?"

"I don't know."

"Didn't say where she was going?"

"I guessed she was going home. It was already four, four-thirty."

"How long have you known her?" Carella asked.

"Be six months in September. That's when she started working at St. Margaret's."

"How'd she get along there?"

"Fine."

"Good worker?"

"Oh, yes."

"Got along with the other nuns?"

"Yes."

"Nurses?"

"Yes, of course."

"Doctors?"

"Yes."

"While you were having coffee . . . ," Brown said. "Where was this, by the way?"

"Deli across the street from the hospital."

"See anybody watching her?"

"Paying unusual attention to her?"

"No, I can't think of anyone."

"Anyone follow you out of the deli?"

"I don't think so."

"When you left each other, was she walking, or did she catch a cab, or what?"

"She was walking."

"In which direction?"

"She turned the corner and headed crosstown."

"Toward the park?"

"Yes. Toward the park."

Helen Daniels was a nurse, and so she did not display any squeamishness at being inside a morgue. This was not the hospital for which she worked, but it was nonetheless familiar territory. She followed the detectives into the stainless-steel chamber with its stainless-steel dissecting tables and stainless-steel drawers, and watched while the attendant on duty rolled out the drawer with the unidentified corpse on it, and she looked down at the face and said, "Yes, that's Mary Vincent," and went outside to vomit.

FIRST THING YOU HAD TO UNDERSTAND about this city was that it was big. It was difficult to explain to someone who came from Overall Patches, Indiana, that you could take his entire *town* and tuck it into one tiny corner of the smallest of the city's five separate sectors and still have room left over for the entire bustling municipalities of Two Trees, Wyoming, and Sleepy Sheep, South Dakota.

This city was dangerous, too. That was the next thing you had to know about it. Never mind the reassuring bulletins from the Mayor's office. Ask the Mayor to take an unescorted two A.M. stroll through any of the city's barren moonscapes and then interview him in his hospital bed the next morning to ask him about lower crime rates and improved police patrols. Or just watch the first ten minutes of the eleven o'clock news every night and you'll learn in the wink of an eye exactly what the people of this city were capable of doing to other people in this city. It was on last night's eleven o'clock news that the story of the unidentified dead nun had first been broadcast to a populace accustomed to news of dead people turning up in Dumpsters or abandoned bathtubs. Bad things happened in this city every hour of the day or night, and they happened all *over* the city.

So if you came here thinking, Gee, there's going to be a neat little murder takes place in a town house and some blue-haired lady will solve it in her spare time when she isn't tending her rose garden, then you came to the wrong city at the wrong time of the year. In this city, you had to pay attention. In this city, things were happening all the time, all over the place, and you didn't have to be a detective to smell evil in the wind.

S HE HAD COME HOME FROM WORK yesterday evening to find that her apartment had been "robbed," as she'd put it when she phoned the police. The two responding uniformed cops informed her that the correct expression was "burglarized," as if that made a damn bit of difference, and then asked her a lot of dumb questions about "access" and "vulnerability," which she supposed meant Who has a key to the front door and Which window opens onto a fire escape? And now—only a day late and a dollar short—here were two plainclothes detectives asking the same dumb questions. Her best friend, Sylvia, whose apartment had been broken into last year around this time, told her that there wasn't a single recorded instance in this city of the cops ever catching who did it or ever recovering the stolen goods, it was all a waste of time and taxpayers' money. But here they were at twenty minutes to one on the day after the burglary, when she had a hundred Saturday afternoon errands to run.

"We're sorry to bother you," the bald one was saying. She was sure he'd introduced himself as Meyer Meyer, but that couldn't be a person's *name*, could it? He was a tall, burly man wearing pale blue trousers and a lightweight sports jacket, the collar of his shirt open and worn *outside* the jacket collar, the way teenagers in America used to wear it in the forties and the way Russian gangsters wore it today, from pictures she had seen in *Life* magazine.

"What time did you get home from work last night?" the blond one asked. He was very good-looking, if you cared for apple pie and chocolate milk midwestern shit-kicking looks, an inch or so taller than his partner, just as wide in the shoulders, both of them in their mid- to late thirties, she supposed, which made them both too young for her, not that she was interested. Annie Kearnes was forty-two years old, almost to the day, since her birthday had been last Tuesday, August eighteenth, a Leo as she was proud of telling first dates. Annie went on a lot of first dates. She wondered if either of these two boring gentlemen was married, though police work seemed an extraordinarily dangerous occupation.

"I get home most nights a little before six," she said.

"And last night?"

"The same."

Did they think she was telling them she got home most nights a little before six because *last* night she'd got home at seven? What kind of mentality was that? Or was this just cops zeroing in on the facts, ma'am, as if she herself was the one who'd robbed her own apartment, burglarized it, *whatever* the hell. Where she worked was R&R Ribbons, which manufactured the shiny little red and blue and green and gold bows you peeled the backs off and stuck to all sorts of presents. August was the busiest time of the year for R&R, which stood for Rosen and Riley. August was when all the Christmas orders came in. October was when they shipped. What she really needed was a friggin *robber* breaking into her apartment yesterday.

"How'd the place look?" Meyer asked.

"Excuse me, but did you say Meyer *Meyer?*" Annie asked.

"Yes, ma'am, that's correct," Meyer said.

"That's unusual," she said.

"Yes, it is," he agreed.

Nice gentle manner, like a dentist who treated mostly kids. She wondered again if he was married. Too bad he *wasn't* a dentist. Bring a cop home to her mother, oh boy, what a scene *that* would be. The blond one was looking at a framed picture on the wall, which showed Mr. Rosen and his wife in her mink coat sticking a giant bow onto a giant package outside the city's biggest department store seven Christmases ago, while it was snowing very hard. It hadn't snowed at all this past Christmas. Nor even this entire winter, for that matter. People had been grateful it was such a mild winter. Boy, are we *lucky*, people were saying all over the place. Now it was so hot you could melt in your panties and everybody was in the streets on their hands and knees, *praying* for a stray breeze, it just goes to show, she thought.

"That's Mr. Rosen," she said to him, by way of flirtation. "He's one of my bosses."

"Nice," he said.

Typical big dumb cop remark.

Nice.

Bert Kling his name was. A name to match his obvious intelligence.

"So how'd the apartment look when you walked in?" Meyer asked.

"Same as always," she said.

If you're so curious about how the apartment *looked,* she thought, why didn't you come around last night, so you could see it right after it was robbed? No wonder you never catch anybody, she thought.

"Was there a mess or anything?" Kling asked.

"No. Neat as a pin," Annie said.

"When did you realize someone had been in here?"

"When I found the bag of cookies."

"On the bed?" Meyer asked.

Mind reader, she thought. Or had the two Keystone Kops from yesterday submitted a report on what she'd told them?

"On the pillow, yes. Chocolate chip cookies."

The cookies still infuriated her. The goddamn *nerve!* Guy breaks in, steals all her jewelry and a red-fox jacket that had cost her two thousand dollars wholesale and then he had the audacity to leave a box of chocolate chip cookies on her *pillow?* Like spitting in her eye, wasn't it? Did he expect her to *eat* the damn cookies? Who knew what was in those cookies, what kind of poison he'd put inside them, the friggin lunatic?

"We just want to make sure it's the same person," Meyer said. "He's been getting some play in the papers and on TV, he might be inspiring copycats."

"Did they give you the list?" Annie asked.

"The officers who responded? Yes, they did. Thank you. We're working on it now."

"They're calling him The Cookie Boy," Kling said.

"Cute," she said, and pulled a face. "You ever catch him, *I'll* give him cookies." She hesitated for just an instant, and then she said, "*Will* you catch him?"

"We'll try," Meyer said.

"Yes, but *will* you?"

"We'll be circulating the list to pawnshops all over the city, maybe we'll get a call, who knows?" Kling asked the air.

"Also," Meyer said, "we make a lot of unrelated arrests every day of the week. Someone we pull in may drop something about him, who knows?"

"What do you mean?"

"Thieves talk to each other, they learn things they sometimes use to bargain with us."

"Like what?"

"Like this guy leaves cookies on the pillow, he mentioned he was in an apartment on South Twentieth two days ago, like that," Kling said.

"You actually had someone tell you this?"

"No, I'm just giving you an example."

"So what you're saying is it's all a matter of luck, is what you're saying."

"No, not at all," Kling said.

"Not at all," Meyer said.

"Must be an echo in here," Annie said. "Then what is it, if not luck? You send a list to pawnshops, you hope some pawnbroker'll spot my sapphire ring and give you a call. Or you arrest some rapist or whatever, some bank robber, and you hope he'll turn in his best friend, who happens to be The Cookie Burglar . . ."

"The Cookie Boy."

"Cute," she said again, and again pulled a face. "What's that if it isn't luck?"

"Well, there *is* a certain amount of luck involved," Meyer agreed. The good dentist.

"But we'll be doing a lot of investigative work as well," Kling said.

"Like what?"

"Well, it would take all day to explain."

I'll bet, she thought.

"What it looks like to me," she said, "is I can kiss my stuff good-bye, right?"

"We may surprise you," Kling said, and smiled.

"Surprise Mr. *Cookie* instead," she said.

THE MESSAGE FROM A WOMAN NAMED Annette Ryan was waiting on Carella's desk when they got back to the squadroom. It said that she could identify the dead nun whose picture she had seen on television this morning, and asked that he please call her. When he reached her at two that afternoon, he discovered that Annette Ryan was *Sister* Annette Ryan, who told him she'd been Mary Vincent's spiritual director ever since she'd come to this city from the order's mother house in San Diego. Carella asked if he might come to see her, and she gave him the address of her convent in Riverhead. He put the phone back on its receiver, and turned to where Brown was settling in behind his own desk.

"Don't get too comfortable," he suggested.

*   *   *

THE HONDA SONNY COLE WAS DRIVING had been loaned to him by a nineteen-year-old girl he'd met three months ago. He'd been seein her on and off the past month or so, movies and such, all that datin shit. She was willin to slobber the Johnson when her mama wasn't home, but fearful of doing the major push, fraid she'd get pregnant. So much easier with hookers, you didn't have to go through none of this courtship bullshit, none of these restrictions. One thing Sonny hated was restrictions.

"Why do you need to follow this man?" Coral had asked him. The whole name put on her by her Southern mama was Coralee, but she'd shortened it to Coral the minute she got to be fifteen and learned where it was at. Coral was a sophomore at Ramsey University, studying to be a television broadcaster. Clean as a baby's first tooth. *Do it clean, man, cause you the first one they goan come lookin for. Clean piece, no partners, in, out, been nice to know you.*

"He owes me money," Sonny said. "He knows I'm after him, he'll skip town."

"So you need to follow him in my car."

"*Any* car, actually. Be nice if you lent me yours, though."

"Why don't you just go up to him and *ask* him for the money?" Coral asked.

"Doesn't work that way, honey," he said.

"Why does he owe you this money, anyway?"

So Sonny had wrote a whole big story out of thin air, told her how the man was a police officer married to his first cousin . . .

"Your cousin's married to a *cop?*" Coral said.

"Was. They split up three months ago."

"Gee," Coral said.

What it was, Sonny explained to her, his cousin had been in the hospital needing a costly operation and Sonny had gone to his bank and withdrawn practically his entire life savings to lend to the husband cause he'd saved his life out there in the desert during the fracas in the Gulf, all bullshit, and now the girl had recovered, Sonny's first cousin, and Sonny had asked him for the money back because he had a large business opportunity looming, but the man had since separated from her and Sonny was now trying to find out where he'd moved, or his cousin either, for that matter, because last time he'd gone to their apartment the landlady told him they'd both left for God knew where, all of it bullshit, which is why he was following him so he could maybe find where his *cousin* was, you see, the one had the thing done on her kidney, cost twenty thousand dollars of Sonny's hard-earned cash, maybe plead on her kindness to intercede with her husband, who Sonny thought until now was one of his closest friends on earth, all of which was merely blowin smoke up Coral's skirt.

But it had got him the loan of the car.

Sonny was a good driver. Stayed nailed to the blue Chevy sedan up ahead, but at the same time kept a respectable distance behind. Next few days he'd learn the whereabouts and wherewithals of every move Carella made. Find a place he could lay in wait and cold-cock him. Had to catch him alone. Bang him from behind. Goodbye nemesis, which in the dictionary said, "A person who inflicts relentless vengeance or destruction"—he'd looked it up the minute his lawyer paid the bail and popped him.

Meanwhile, careful was the thing. Slow and easy. These were cops he was following, so presumably they knew all about tails. Oreo pair again, he noticed. Did the police department deliberately team up brothers and honkies to keep the peace? He had nothing but contempt for brothers who joined the enemy camp.

Where the hell were they *going*, anyway?

THE CONVENT OF THE ORDER of the Sisters of Christ's Mercy was located on a tree-lined street in a section of Riverhead that could easily have passed for a small New England village. On this hot summer afternoon late in August, butterflies floated above the flowers lining the path that led to the arched wooden door of the modest stone building where Sister Annette Ryan and eleven other nuns made their home. There was a cemetery on one side of the convent, and on the other a smaller stone building. A nun in habit was a rare sight these days, but the sister who answered their ring was at least seventy years old, and she was wearing the simple black-and-white habit of the order, a wooden crucifix hanging around her neck, a slender gold band on the third finger of her left hand. She led them down a hushed unadorned corridor and knocked discreetly on the arched door at its end.

"Yes, come in, please," a woman's voice said.

Sister Annette Ryan . . .

"Please call me Annette," she said at once.

. . . was a tall, slender woman in her late fifties, Carella guessed, wearing tailored slacks, a pale blue cotton sweater, and low-heeled walking shoes. She had high cheekbones and a generous mouth, graying red hair cut close, eyes that matched the patch of lawn sparkling in the cloister beyond the arched and leaded windows of her study. She introduced the nun who'd answered the door as *Sister* Beryl, possibly in deference to her age, and then offered the detectives tea.

"Yes, please," Brown said.

"Please," Carella said.

"How do you take it?" Sister Beryl asked. "Milk? Lemon? Sugar?"

"Just milk in mine," Brown said.

"Lemon, please," Carella said.

Sister Beryl smiled graciously and scurried off. To Carella, nuns in habit always seemed to be moving fast, like windup toys. Perhaps because their means of locomotion was hidden by the long voluminous skirt. The door whispered shut behind her. The book-lined study went still again. Outside, Carella could hear the sound of a sprinkler tirelessly watering the lawn.

"Not good news," Annette said, and shook her head in disbelief.

"Not good," he agreed.

"Do you have anything yet?"

"Nothing."

"How can I help?"

"Well, we know where she worked . . . ," Carella said.

"That's recent, you know."

Brown was already consulting his notebook.

"Six months, we have. From a nurse named Helen Daniels."

"Yes, that's correct. St. Margaret's is one of the three hospitals conducted by the sisters. Our order was founded expressly for the care of the sick, you see, especially the impoverished sick. That was a long time ago, of course. 1837, in fact, in Paris. The charism has changed somewhat over the years . . ."

Charism, Carella wondered, but did not ask.

". . . to include teaching of the handicapped. We run a school for the deaf next door, for example, and another for the blind, in Calm's Point."

Carella wondered if he should mention that his wife was deaf and that he did not consider her handicapped. He let the moment pass.

"Mary was working with terminally ill patients. She was marvelous with the sick."

"So we understand," Carella said.

"A prayerful nun," Annette said. "And a unique individual. She was only twenty-seven, you know, but so mature, so compassionate."

She turned her head aside for an instant, perhaps to mask a tear, her gaze falling blindly on the open leaded window beyond which the sprinkler persisted. There was a knock at the door. Sister Beryl came in bearing a tray, which she set on a low table.

"There we go," she said, sounding remarkably sprightly for a woman her age. "Enjoy."

"Thank you, Sister Beryl."

The old nun nodded, surveyed the table as if she had not only made the tea but the tray upon which it sat. Pleased with what she saw, she nodded again, and hurried out of the room, the skirt of her black habit whispering along the stone floor.

"Where had Mary worked before?" Carella asked. "You said the job was recent . . ."

"Yes, she'd just come here from San Diego. That's where our

mother house is. Actually, just outside San Diego. A town named San Luis Elizario."

"So then you've only known her since she came east," Brown said.

"Yes. We met in March. Our major superior called me from San Diego and asked that I help get Mary settled here."

"Your major . . . ?"

"What we used to call *mother* superior. Times have changed, you know, *oh* how they've changed. Well, Vatican Two," she said, and rolled her eyes as if mere mention of the words would conjure up for them the sweeping reform that had swept the church in the sixties. "Even major superior is a bit outdated. Some communities have gone back to calling her the prioress. But she's also called the president and the provincial and the superior general and the provincial superior and the delegate superior or even simply the administrator. It can get confusing."

"Was Mary Vincent living here?"

"You mean here at the convent? No, no. There are only twelve of us here."

"Then where *did* she live?" Brown asked.

"She was renting a small apartment near the hospital."

"Are nuns *allowed* to do that?"

Annette suppressed a smile.

"It's different nowadays," she said. "The focus today is less on the group than it is on the individual."

"Can you let us have that address?" he asked.

"Of course," she said.

"And the name and phone number of the major superior in San Diego."

"Yes, certainly," Annette said.

"When you say you were Mary's spiritual director," Brown said, "what do you mean?"

"Her advisor, her guide, her friend. Everyone needs someone to talk to occasionally. Women religious have problems, too, you know. We're human, you know."

Women religious, Carella wondered, but again did not ask.

"When's the last time you talked?" he said.

"The day before yesterday."

"This past Thursday?" Brown said, surprised.

"Yes."

Both detectives were thinking she'd come to see her spiritual director on the day before she was killed. Both detectives were wondering why. Brown picked up the ball.

"Was she having a problem?" he asked.

"No, no. She just felt like talking. We saw each other every few weeks. Either she'd come here to the convent for dinner or I'd meet her in the city."

"So this wasn't an unusual visit."

"Not at all."

"Nothing specific on her mind."

"Nothing."

"No spiritual problems."

"None that she mentioned."

"Did anything at *all* seem to be troubling her?"

"She seemed her usual self."

"Mention any threatening phone calls . . . ?"

"No."

"Or letters?"

"No."

"Anyone lurking about the building where she lived?"

"No."

"Anyone unhappy with the nursing care she was giving?"

"No."

"Perhaps a relative or friend of someone she was treating."

"Nothing like that."

"Anyone with a minor grievance . . ."

"She didn't mention anyone like that."

". . . or petty annoyance?"

"No one."

"Any idea what she was doing in Grover Park yesterday?"

"No."

"Did she mention she might be going to the park?"

"No."

"Was it a usual thing for her to do?"

"I don't know."

"Walk all the way crosstown to the park? Sit on a bench there?"

"I can't imagine her doing that."

"She didn't say she went there to *pray* or anything, did she?" Brown asked. "Or meditate? Anything like that?"

"No, she prayed at home in the morning. For half an hour to forty-five minutes, before leaving for the hospital. And she went to mass once or twice a week."

"Where would that be?"

"The church?"

"Yes."

"Our Lady of Flowers. I'll give you the address there as well, if you like. And the name of the parish priest."

"Please," Carella said.

Annette rose majestically and swept across the room just as if she were still wearing the habit. She opened the drawer on a long rectory table, and removed from it a leather-bound address book. Over her shoulder, as she began leafing through the book, she said, "Please find who did it, won't you?"

It sounded almost like a prayer.

IT WAS FIVE MINUTES PAST THREE when they got back to the squadroom and called the mother house in San Luis Elizario. The woman to whom they spoke identified herself as Sister Frances Kelleher, assistant to the major superior. She was shocked and dismayed to learn of Mary Vincent's death, and apologized for the absence of Sister Carmelita, who was in Rome at the moment.

"She's expected back in three days, if you'd like to try again," she said.

Carella marked the date on his calendar: August 25.

"Actually," he said, "we're trying to locate a next of kin we can notify. Would you have any information regarding her family?"

"I'm sure we do," Sister Frances said. "Let me transfer you to the records office."

The nun in the records office answered the phone with a cheerful, "Louise Tracht, good morning," and then immediately said, "Oops, it's ten past noon already."

"Good afternoon then," Carella said, and identified himself, and gave her much the same information he'd given Sister Frances. Again, there was the shocked reaction, though Sister Louise admitted she hadn't known Mary all that well. "Let me check her file," she said, and was gone from the phone for perhaps two or three minutes. When she returned, she said, "Both her parents are dead, but I have an address and phone number for a brother in Philadelphia, if you'd like that."

"Please," Carella said.

VINCENT COCHRAN WAS ASLEEP WHEN Carella reached him at three forty-five that Saturday afternoon. He told Carella at once that he was a stand-up comic and that he didn't get to bed till sometimes seven, eight in the morning . . .

"So what's this about?" he asked.

The man sounded annoyed and cranky. This was perhaps not the most opportune moment to tell him about his sister's murder. Carella took a deep breath.

"Mr. Cochran," he said, "I hate to be bringing you this kind of news, but . . ."

"Has something happened to Anna?" Cochran asked at once.

Carella didn't know who Anna was.

"No, it's your sister," he said, and plunged ahead. "She was murdered last night in Grover Park here." Silence on the other end of the line. "We were able to make positive identification only this morning." The silence lengthened. "We got your name and phone number from her mother house in San Diego. I'm sorry to bring you such news."

Silence.

"Am I speaking to her brother, sir?"

"Once upon a time," Cochran said.

"Sir?"

"When she was still Kate Cochran, yes. I was her brother before she became Sister Mary Vincent."

"Sir?"

"Before she became a nun."

There was another silence on the line.

"Mr. Cochran," Carella said, "your sister's remains are currently at the Buena Vista morgue here in Isola. If you'd like to make funeral arrangements . . ."

"Why would I?" Cochran said. "The last time I even *talked* to her was four years ago. Why would I want to see her now?"

"Well, sir . . ."

"Tell her beloved *church* to bury her," he said. "Maybe that way she'll get to heaven sooner."

There was a click on the line.

Carella looked at the phone receiver.

"Is he coming up?" Brown asked.

"I don't think so," Carella said.

CARL BLANEY HAD VIOLET EYES, somewhat too exotic for a medical examiner, perhaps, but there they were nonetheless, neither blue nor gray but as violet as Elizabeth Taylor's eyes were supposed to be. Rather sad eyes as well, as if they'd seen far too many internal organs in far too many degrees of trauma.

He greeted Carella in the mortuary at ten to five that Saturday afternoon and had the decency not to mention that he was almost three hours late, their scheduled meeting having been for two. Carella instantly explained that he'd had to shlepp all the way up to Riverhead in ninety-degree heat on clogged roadways, and then had to make some phone calls when he finally got back to the squadroom, all of which impressed Blaney not a whit.

He told Carella that nobody here at the morgue was in any

hurry, anyway, and besides he'd only just finished the autopsy on the woman who'd come into the morgue as an unidentified Jane Doe, had immediately been dubbed Jane Nun, and then Jane *None*, after a mortuary wag discovered she *still* hadn't been identified—a situation now rectified, or so Carella informed him.

Even Blaney's initial examination had revealed the extensive bruising characteristic of manual strangulation. The bluish-black fingertip bruises, oval in shape, somewhat pale and blurred. The crescent-shaped fingernail marks. But he had then raised the shoulders on a head block, eviscerated the body, and removed the brain, allowing the blood to drain from the base of the skull. When the blood flow from the chest also stopped, Blaney began his examination of the intact neck organs. He made his first incision just below the chin, allowing him clear and unobstructed scrutiny without the necessity of handling the organs before dissection.

"In manual strangulation," he explained, "fractures of the larynx are common. I was searching for the horns because those are particularly weak parts of the thyroid cartilage and therefore . . ."

"The horns?"

"The ends of the hyoid bone. We'll sometimes find fractures of calcified hyoid bone in old people who've suffered a fatal fall or some sort of accidental blow to the neck. But usually the bone and cartilage fractures we see are caused by strangulation. That's not to say we don't get *old* people who've been strangled. Or even strangled and raped. Your nun was how old?"

"Twenty-seven."

"Sure. Of course, fractures can happen during dissection, but then we don't find focal bleeding. However slight, hemorrhaging of the tissues adjacent to a laryngeal fracture indicates it occurred while the victim was still alive. We found blood. She was strangled, Steve, no question."

"Was she also raped?"

"Whenever a strangulation victim is female, we routinely check the genitalia. That entails a search for sperm in the vaginal vault, and acid phostase determinations on vaginal washings. She wasn't raped, Steve."

"I'll tell Homicide."

"Incidentally . . ."

Carella looked at him.

"Are you sure she's a nun?"

"Why?" Carella asked. "What else did you find?"

"Breast implants," Blaney said.

3.

"THEN SHE'S NOT A NUN," CARELLA'S MOTHER SAID.

"DON'T BE SO OLD-FASHIONED," HIS sister said.

"What's old-fashioned got to do with it? A nun doesn't get herself breast implants, Angela. That's all there is to it."

Carella expected her to cross her fingers and spit on them, the way she used to when he was a kid. The trouble with sign language, he thought, is that fingers can't whisper. Last night after dinner, he had told Teddy all about Blaney's discovery, little knowing that the twins—presumably playing Monopoly across the room, on the floor beneath the imitation Tiffany lamp—had been eavesdropping, each of them fascinated in a separate boy-girl way by the topic under discussion.

According to Blaney, before 1992 there had been three types of fillings for the implant: silicone gel, saline, or a combination of both, where saline was contained in one compartment of an elastomer shell and silicone gel in another. When it was discovered that the gel could bleed through the envelope and migrate to other parts of the body, potentially causing cancer, silicone gel implants were banned.

Sister Mary Vincent's implants were saline.

This did not necessarily mean they'd been inserted *since* 1992; saline implants had been on the market for more than a decade before the ban on silicone gel. But a good reason to suspect the implants had been recent was the fact that the shell had not yet turned from clear to cloudy. Apparently, when the shell was in

49

place for any amount of time, the body's oxidizing compounds attacked it, causing discoloration. This had not yet happened in Mary's instance. Given the fact that Mary was only twenty-seven, given the longevity of the silicone gel ban, given as well the fact that the envelope was still clear, Blaney was willing to guess that the implants could not have been more than three or four years old.

All of this the prepubescent twins had overheard and felt compelled to repeat to their grandmother the moment they were all assembled on her backyard lawn for the big outdoor barbecue. Judging from previous Sunday afternoon feasts at his mother's house all throughout his childhood and beyond, he would not get home till eight tonight, by which time *Sixty Minutes* would have come and gone, oh well.

The indiscretion of the twins was compounded by the presence at the barbecue of Angela's new boyfriend, an assistant district attorney named Henry Lowell, who had merely allowed the man who'd killed Carella's father to walk out of a courtroom scot-free. He now had the balls to say, "That's privileged information, isn't it, Steve?" to which Carella replied, "Only if it's revealed by *me*, Henry," to which the asshole replied, "Who else was privy to it?" to which Carella replied, "Mark and April. They're twelve."

"Oh, let it go," Angela said.

The men were standing at the barbecue, Carella turning steaks, Lowell placing chicken breasts on the grill for anyone who preferred white meat. Teddy was just coming out of the house, carrying a bowl of pasta that had been warming on the big stove in the kitchen. The screen door slammed shut behind her, the sound signaling dappled sunlight, capturing her in stuttered gold. Depending on which degree of political correctness you wished to accept, Teddy Carella was either a deaf mute, a hearing-and-speech impaired woman, or an aurally and vocally challenged person. Or else she was simply Carella's wife and the most beautiful woman in the world, dark-haired and dark-eyed, moving with elegance and grace as she carried the steaming bowl to the wooden picnic table and set it down. Carella watched her. He loved to watch her. She caught him. Threw a brazen hip at him. He smiled. On the table, his mother's good red sauce immediately attracted bees. Teddy ripped plastic wrap from a roll, shooed the bees, covered the steaming bowl.

"Angela, the salad!" his mother called. "The bread!"

"Getting it now, Mom!"

Angela slammed into the house, followed by her three-year-old twins. Bang, bang, and bang again, the screen door went. Twins ran in the family. There were two sets here today, his sister's and Carella's own. Plus Angela's seven-year-old, Tess.

"April! Mark! Dinner! Cindy! Mindy! Everybody! Henry! Come on! Tess! Dinner!" his mother called, though this wasn't quite dinner at two in the afternoon, nor was it lunch, either, just your garden-variety, eat-till-you-bust Italian-style Sunday get-together.

He could remember hiding under the dining room table with his sister when they were kids. Now her estranged husband was a goddamn drug addict, and her boyfriend had let their father's killer walk, my how the time does fly.

His mother would not let go of the breasts, so to speak.

Kept rattling on and on about it being impossible for the woman in the park to be a nun because nuns simply didn't need or want breast implants. Sometimes she gave him a pain in the ass. Well, he guessed she was a little better nowadays, didn't as often fall into those long moments of deep silence, when she retreated to whatever private space she continued to share with her dead husband. My father, too, don't forget, Carella thought. My dead *father*. I mean, Mom, we *all* lost Pop, you know. But I don't retreat, I dare not retreat, oh dear God I would burst into tears.

Today it wasn't one of her deep meaningful silences. Instead, it was the nun and the Catholic Church, his mother seemingly having forgotten that she herself hadn't been to church for, what was it, twenty years? And, listen, don't even *mention* confession! On and on about the nun who had to be an impostor, while Henry Lowell sat across the table fretting over a detective's family knowing the intimate details of a case the detective was investigating, well, gee, pardon me all to hell, Henry!

Carella would be forty years old in October.

Oh, yes, no more thirtysomething, forget it. He had read someplace that when Hollywood studios wanted to do a movie about a twelve-year-old, they hired a twelve-year-old to write the script. That was because a forty-year-old writer had never been twelve. Which meant that a seventy-year-old writer had never been forty, though a Hollywood studio would never hire a seventy-year-old to do anything but *star* in a movie opposite a thirty-four-year-old girl, the theory being that the gonads remembered what the heart and the head had long ago forgotten.

He sometimes watched old ladies plodding heavily across city streets where buses threatened, and knew for certain that inside those shrunken bodies were the shining faces of fourteen-year-olds.

Angela's three-year-olds were babbling in their own secret code, he remembered Mark and April when they were that age, inseparable, a gang in miniature. Twelve years old now. April blossoming into a young woman, already taller than her brother, Mark, who was essentially still a boy. Sunrise, sunset, where had the time flown? Mark favored his father, poor kid. April was the image of Teddy, who was now signing to Angela—and Angela was trying to understand—that her court appearance was scheduled for tomorrow morning at nine, and she was scared to death they'd find her guilty and send her to jail.

"They won't, Mom," Mark said at once, forgetting to sign, and then tapped her arm, and when she turned, reassured her in the language that had been in his hands from when he was a small boy.

"No one's going to find you guilty," Carella said aloud, simultaneously signing it, even though he knew this was no mere bullshit violation. Assault Three was a misdemeanor for which Teddy could spend a year in jail if she was convicted. The accident leading to the assault charge had occurred so long ago that neither of them could remember exactly when, but court calendars being what they were, it was only coming to trial tomorrow morning.

"Who's the judge?" Lowell asked.

"Man named Franklin Roosevelt Pierson, do you know him?"

"Yes. He's fair and honest. What's this all about, anyway?"

Teddy began signing, and Carella began talking at the same time, so she yielded to him for the sake of expediency since Lowell didn't understand sign language at all.

What had happened was that a woman had backed her red Buick station wagon into the grille of Teddy's little red Geo. The district attorney was insisting that a) Teddy had caused the accident, and b) Teddy had kicked the woman, and c) Teddy had taken advantage of her husband's position as a police detective to intimidate the arresting officer at the scene. The only truth to any of this was that Teddy had, in fact, kicked the woman, but only after she'd taken Teddy by the shoulders and shaken her the way some nannies do with infants.

April had heard all this before, so she turned to her aunt and asked her if she knew about this new nail polish that dried in ninety seconds flat. If this were a sitcom, Mark would have told her she was too young to wear nail polish, and April would have warned him to shut up, brat. But this was real life here on Grandma's lawn, and Teddy had let her daughter wear lip gloss for the occasion and Mark said, "Yeah, that's cool, Sis, I saw it on television."

Carella knew that it could go badly for Teddy tomorrow morning because the plaintiff was a black woman and so was the judge, and nobody in this city liked to see a person of color pushed around by a white cop, even if it was only a white cop's white wife. He did not mention a word of this to Teddy. He planned to be at the trial tomorrow morning, dead nun or not. Even in police work, there were priorities.

"Who's representing you?" Lowell asked.

Proper nouns were the most difficult words to sign. Especially when your listener couldn't read your fingers. Teddy turned helplessly to Carella.

"Jerry Flanagan," he said.

"Good lawyer," Lowell said.

Unlike you, Carella thought.

Maybe it made a person cranky—twelve years old, or going on forty, or well over the hill at seventy—to be sitting opposite the district attorney who with an ironclad chain of evidence on the murder weapon had allowed a man to walk, had so bungled the case that a jury had let a murderer walk out of that courtroom, the man who'd killed Carella's father, well, listen, who the hell cared?

Could you just imagine sitting at a dinner party with Carella on your right, and he's telling you all about how justice had not been served in the case of his father's murder, a killer had been allowed to walk free, oh, what a delightful dinner companion *this* would be, are all police detectives as entertaining as you?

Maybe it had to do with getting to be forty.

Or maybe it had to do with guilt.

Carella himself had *arrested* the son of a bitch, you see, Carella could have blown the man's brains out in a deserted hallway with no one to witness except another cop who was urging him to pull the trigger, Do it, *do* it, but he had not done it, he had not killed the man who'd killed his father because he'd felt somewhere deep inside him that *becoming* a beast of prey was tantamount to having *been* that beast all along.

And now the guilt.

In the guilt game, Italians were second only to Jews. He never thought of himself as Italian, however, because, gee, you see, he'd been *born* here in these United States of America, you see, and an Italian was somebody who lived in Rome, or was he mistaken? He never thought of himself as an Italian-American, either, because that was someone who'd come to this country from Italy, correct? An immigrant? As, for example, his father's father, whom he'd never met because the man had died before Carella was born. *He* was the Italian-American, the hyphenate, the man who'd come all those miles from a walled mountaintop village midway between Bari and Naples, Italian at the start of his long journey, Italian when he'd reached these shores and this big bad city, becoming

Italian-*American* only after he'd recited the pledge of allegiance under oath.

Carella's father was an American, born and bred in this country. And the man who'd killed him was American as well. Whatever his distant heritage had been, he'd been born here, and raised here, and he'd acquired his gun here in this land of the free and home of the brave, but only when you had a pistol in your hand. This American had learned to use his pistol here, and he had used it on Carella's father, another American, bang, bang, you're dead.

I should have killed him, Carella thought.

Because this is the way it turns out.

You are here on a sweltering Sunday in August, and your sister has brought to the table the man who let your father's murderer walk, and she is sleeping with this man, she is *fucking* him in the dead of night, and all your mother can talk about is a nun with fake tits.

He guessed he was getting to be forty.

He wondered if he'd suddenly start chasing nineteen-year-old girls.

He looked across at his wife.

She winked at him.

He winked back.

He would kill himself first.

SUNDAY EVENING TURNED A ROSY PINK and then a deeper blush and then a reddish-lavender-blue and then purple and black, the golden day succumbing at last to night.

It was time to go buy a gun.

Stringent laws or not, it was as easy to buy a gun here in this city as it was in the state of Florida. That's because laws were made for honest people. Honest people knew that if you wanted to purchase a handgun in this city, you first had to get a permit from the police department's Pistol Licensing Division. The PLD issued four different types of permits. Owners of businesses that had been robbed, or persons who made night deposits at banks could apply for a "carry" permit. A "premise" permit could be issued for keeping a gun in a home or a business location. "Special" permits could be granted to out-of-state residents, and "target" permits to gun-club members. In this city, it was illegal to own or carry a handgun without a permit. But the police estimated that there were at least two million handguns out there—despite the fact that fewer than fifty thousand permits had been issued. Thieves didn't need permits. Thieves knew a hundred and one ways to buy an illegal piece.

One of those ways was Little Nicholas.

At eleven o'clock that Sunday night, Sonny went to see him.

LITTLE NICHOLAS DID BUSINESS in the rear of a laundromat he owned and operated on Lyons and South Thirty-fifth. The washing and drying machines closed down at ten-thirty, which is why Sonny didn't go by until eleven. He had called ahead, and he was expected. Even so, Little Nicholas was extremely cautious about opening the back door of the Soapy Suds until he'd turned on the outside floods and ascertained through a peephole that his visitor was indeed Samson Wilbur Cole.

"Hey, man," he said, and instantly closed and double-locked the door behind Sonny. The two men shook hands. Little Nicholas's grip was thick and sweaty. He was wearing a white tank-top undershirt and shorts roomy enough to accommodate *two* men his size, a length of clothesline threaded through the loops and tied at the gathered waist. Sonny guessed he was about five-eight and weighed in at three-fifty.

"Got some nice new merchandise up from Georgia yesterday," Little Nicholas said. "One of my mules made a quick run down there and back. Picked up a silver-plated Mac-ll, a pair of Glock-17s, a 5.56 semi, a Colt .45 with a laser scope, and four .25-caliber Ravens. What are you looking for?"

"Got to do me some hunting," Sonny said.

"Then you need stopping power," Nicholas said. "We're talk-ing a nine. Your nine is anything that uses a .357 or a 9-millimeter cartridge."

"I know what a nine is."

Was a nine stopped Carella's father.

"So show me," Sonny said.

Part of the ritual here was who could outlip who. The price of-ten rose or fell on who had the biggest mouth.

"Your nine did three hundred and two homicides in this city, last year alone," Nicholas said.

"Nobody's thinking of any homicide here."

"Course not. Just thought you'd like to know. How much money are we talking here?"

"Money's no object."

"I heard that tune before. Till I state the price."

"State it."

"I got nines ranging from seven hundred to a thou. Your uglies are more expensive. The Cobray M-11 and the Tec-9'll run you around twelve, fifteen hundred, depending. But you can't hide an ugly, cept under an overcoat, and you're not about to wear a coat in this heat, are you? Or did you plan to go huntin after it cools down a little?"

"I'll be needin the gun now."

"So you want somethin you can tuck in your waistband or a holster, am I right?"

"Yes," Sonny said.

"But not one of your junk guns, cost you a low of fifty, a high of two-fifty."

"You talking your Raven and such?"

"Your Raven, your Jennings weapons, all the cheap Saturday-night specials."

"I want a gun can do the job."

"Your junk gun'll give you control but not much else."

"Show me what you got in a nine."

"Happy to," Nicholas said, and waddled over to a wall covered with half a dozen cabinet doors. "You got anything against Jews?" he asked.

"No more'n against any other man."

"You got a quarrel with the state of Israel?"

"None a'tall."

"Cause I have some real fine Israeli nines, if you're interested. You ain't an Arab, are you?"

"Can't you tell?" Sonny said, and Nicholas chuckled.

"These are kosher weapons, man," he said, and threw open one of the cabinet doors. From one of the shelves, he picked up a pistol that looked like a Buck Rogers ray gun. "This is your Uzi nine," he said. "Shorter and lighter version of the Uzi sub. Take it in your hand, man, go ahead."

"Feels clunky," Sonny said.

"By comparison with your Beretta, yeah. I got the 1951 Model Ber, you want to see it. But the piece you're holdin has a mag capacity of twenty rounds. Your Ber don't even come close."

"I just don't like the look of it," Sonny said.

"You plan to fuck the gun or shoot it?"

"How much is it, anyway?"

"I can let you have this beautiful weapon for eleven hundred dollars, what do you say?"

"I say what else have you got?"

"I even mention the name, you goan wet your pants."

"Try me."

"The Desert Eagle."

"I'm still dry," Sonny said.

"You crack me up," Nicholas said, chuckling again. He opened another cabinet door, and reached in for what looked to Sonny like a Colt .45 with a longer barrel. "Ten and a half inches long," Nicholas said, handing the gun to him. "Man, this is one fuckin burner."

Sonny turned it over and over in his hands.

"Check out the balance, man."

Sonny hefted the gun.

"Weighs less than four pounds," Nicholas said. "Light, but one of the biggest motherfuckin semis there is."

Sonny gripped the gun, held it at arm's length, sighting along the barrel.

"Comes in three popular calibers," Nicholas said. "The fifty fires a cartridge half an inch in diameter. That is one fuckin bone-cruncher, man."

Sonny went "P-kuh, p-kuh, p-kuh," like a kid with a toy pistol.

"You want to, you could knock down a elephant with that piece. If that's what you plan on huntin."

Sonny turned the gun on Nicholas, and went "P-kuh, p-kuh, p-kuh" again.

"Leaves an entry wound the size of a lemon," Nicholas said, "exit wound looks like a cantaloupe. You can mount this fuckin piece on a *tank,* it'd feel right at home."

"What does the magazine hold?"

"Seven, eight, or nine rounds, depending on the caliber. Your fifty holds seven. What do you think?"

"It's okay, I guess," Sonny said.

"Okay, my ass, it's a fuckin *Lexus!*"

"How much you askin for it?"

"I can let it go for fourteen large."

"I can do better retail."

"Okay, thirteen-fifty, but that's it."

"Eleven," Sonny said.

"Twelve-fifty. And I'll throw in a box of fifties. Twenty rounds to a box, soft point or hollow point, take your choice."

"Twelve and the ammo."

"I'm losing money."

"Take it or leave it," Sonny said.

"Cause I love you," Nicholas said, and the men shook hands on a done deal.

It was already ten minutes past midnight on Monday morning, the twenty-fourth day of August.

*   *   *

TEDDY CARELLA WAS EATING like a wolf.

Sitting opposite Carella at a table in a small Italian restaurant not far from one of the criminal courts buildings where they'd spent all morning, she could not stop eating. Nor could she stop talking about the trial. Carella sat watching her moving mouth and flying fingers, amazed by how she managed to combine a feeding frenzy with a continuous narrative stream, the fork in her right hand never skipping a beat while the fingers of her left hand sloppily signed the story of their day in court this morning, no small feat.

I love that judge, Teddy signed.

"Me, too," Carella said, watching her flying fingers.

Judge Pierson happened to have been brought up in Diamondback, right here in the big bad city. He'd escaped the ghetto by busting his ass in a white man's world, never currying favor or demanding sympathy, never once in his entire life playing the race card, something he suspected the district attorney was doing here in his courtroom today—or such was the way Teddy had read the dynamics of what had happened this morning. Pierson had dismissed the charges, telling the plaintiff to drive more carefully in the future and actually suggesting that she might live longer if she quit being so darned angry, didn't she know stress was the primary contributing factor to heart attacks?

The D.A. got on his high horse and informed Judge Pierson that he planned to appeal, but Pierson just shook his head and said, "Go on, make a federal case of this one, counselor. Because we don't have any *important* causes to fight just now, do we?" Meaning "we" collectively, black people, we who have suffered, we who are still suffering, go make a federal case out of this petty grievance, was what Teddy thought she'd read in the judge's words, and saw in his eyes.

"We were lucky," Carella said.

I know.

"It could just as easily have gone the other way. I might have been bringing you cigarettes in jail today."

I don't smoke.

"Neither do I," he said. "Wanna go out sometime?"

Oh, sir, I'm married, she signed, and lowered her eyes like a virgin.

He wanted to scoop her into his arms that very moment, crowded restaurant or no, shower her face with kisses, tell her she was his moon and his stars and his very essence. Instead he observed her unobserved, her eyes still lowered, dark head bent over her plate, the delicate oval of her face, the generous mouth and long dark lashes, she raised her eyes and he melted in the dark-brown laser beam of her steady gaze.

She said nothing.

She could not speak, of course, but she could have signed. Instead, she remained essentially silent, her eyes saying all there was to say. He reached across the table and covered her hand with his own. They were both grinning like high school sweethearts, which they'd never been. He was thinking he wished he didn't have to go meet Brown. She was thinking the same thing. He looked up at the clock. She did, too. It was almost two. He signaled for the check. Teddy went off toward the ladies' room. The air conditioner thrummed a noisy accompaniment to the flirty swing of her skirt, the easy sway of her hips. He watched her until she was out of sight.

There was the busy sound of chatter, the clatter of silverware against china, the clink of ice cubes in frosted glasses, the lilting laughter of a black woman at another table. The diners here in this "moderately priced Northern Italian" —as Zagat had defined it—were a random mix of ethnic types. This was a city of contrasts, black and white, yellow and brown, khaki and teak, ochre and dust. In the wintertime, the days were chillingly gray, the nights inky and bleak. Summer's colors were softer, the longer days golden, the nights purple.

He paid the check and waited for Teddy to return.

He missed her whenever she was gone from him, and often became alarmed when she was gone for too long a time. He knew she could not cry for help if ever the need arose; a voice had been denied her at birth. Nor could she easily detect, as hearing people could, the warning signs of danger. In her silent world, in this city of predators, Teddy was easy prey.

When at last he saw her coming back to the table, he shoved back his chair, and went to her, and took her hand.

HAS TO BE HIS GIRLFRIEND, Sonny was thinking, cause there ain't no man on earth looks at his wife the way Carella was lookin at this woman right this minute. This was the first time he'd really got a good look at the man since he'd sat opposite him in court at his father's trial. Standin on the sidewalk across the street now, just outside the restaurant, holding both her hands in his, and leanin down to kiss her. His jacket was open, Sonny could see the butt of what looked like a nine sticking up out of a holster. Woman walking off now, Carella watching her. Kept watching her till she was out of sight. Then he turned and began walking toward where he'd parked the Chevy.

Sonny gave it a minute, and then started his own car.

4. THE BUILDING MARY VINCENT HAD LIVED IN WAS ON YARROW AVENUE, CORNER OF FABER STREET, NOT A MILE FROM THE hospital, a brief ten-minute ride by subway. Why she'd gone to Grover Park last Thursday instead of heading directly home was a question of some importance to the detectives. There was a good-size park alongside the hospital and bordering the River Dix. If she'd felt like taking the air, she could have gone there. Instead, on one of the hottest days of the year, she had walked seven long crosstown blocks to the park—the equivalent of fourteen uptown-downtown blocks—and then had walked the width of the park itself to a park bench on its farther side. Why?

Carella met Brown downstairs at a quarter past two, told him the judge had dismissed Teddy's case . . .

"Yay," Brown said.

. . . apologized for being late, and asked if Brown had located the super of the building yet. Brown said he'd just got there a minute ago himself, and they went to look for him together. They found him out back, trying to repair the pulley on a clothesline that had fallen down, dropping clean white sheets all over the backyard. The super was enormously uncomfortable in this humid heat. "I'm from Montana," he told them. "We get breezes there." It was unusual for people from Montana to end up in this city unless they were seeking fame and fortune in television or on the stage. You didn't get many building superintendents from Montana riding their horses in the streets here. Come to think of it, Carella had never met a single person from Montana in his entire life.

Neither had Brown. Carella wasn't even sure he knew where Montana *was*. Neither was Brown.

Nathan Harding was a man in his early sixties, they guessed, burly and balding, sweating profusely in a striped T-shirt and blue jeans. He had difficulty recalling exactly which of his tenants was Mary Vincent even though there were only twenty-four apartments in the entire building. When they pointed out that she was a nun working at St. Margaret's Hospital, he said he didn't know where that was, which wasn't exactly answering the question. They told him Mary Vincent was twenty-seven years old, a nun in the Order of the Sisters of Christ's Mercy. He said he had three or four girls that age in the building, but he didn't remember any of them looking like nuns. Neither Carella nor Brown were enjoying this damn heat, either, and the man was beginning to give them a Monday afternoon pain in the ass.

"Haven't you got a tenant list someplace?" Brown asked.

"What's this about?" Harding asked.

"It's about a murder," Carella said.

Harding looked at him.

"Can we see that tenant list?" Brown said.

"Sure," Harding said, and led them into his apartment on the ground floor. The building was what they called a non-doorman walk-up, which meant there was no security and no elevator. Harding's apartment looked as if the Cambodian army had recently camped there. He rummaged around in a small desk in a small cluttered office just off the kitchen and found a typewritten list that showed a Mary Vincent living in apartment 6C.

"Want to open it for us?" Brown said.

"A *nun* killed somebody?" Harding said.

"The other way around," Carella said, and watched Harding's face. Nothing showed there. The man merely nodded.

"Guess it'll be okay," he said.

It damn well better be, Brown thought, but did not say.

Both detectives were out of breath when they reached the sixth-floor landing. Harding was from Montana, he took the climb in stride. There were three other apartments on the floor, but this was two-thirty in the afternoon, and the building was virtually silent, almost all the tenants off to work.

"How long was she living here?" Carella asked.

"She the one I think she is," Harding said, "she moved in around six months ago." He was searching his ring of keys for the one to 6C.

"Live here alone?"

"I couldn't say."

The detectives exchanged a glance. It was hotter here in the building than it was on the street outside, all of yesterday's heat contained in this narrow sixth-floor hallway just under the roof. They waited patiently. Brown was just about ready to snatch the goddamn ring away from him, when Harding finally found the key. He tried it on the keyway. It slid in easily. He twisted it, unlocked the door, and opened it wide. A wave of hotter air rolled heavily into the hallway.

Carella went in first.

This was not a crime scene, but he pulled on a pair of cotton gloves, anyway, before opening one of the windows. Only slightly cooler air sifted in from the street outside. There was the sound of an ambulance siren bruising the comparative mid-morning stillness.

"Studio?" he asked.

Harding nodded.

This was a particularly small studio apartment. Single bed against one wall, phone on a night table beside it. On the other side of the room, there was a bookcase, an easy chair, a standing floor lamp, and an unpainted dresser. A locked window alongside the dresser opened onto a backyard fire escape. The kitchen was the size of a closet. Refrigerator with two oranges in it, a container of skim milk, a loaf of seven-grain bread, a package of organic greens, and a tub of margarine. The freezer compartment contained six frozen yogurt bars and a bottle of vodka. The bathroom was small and immaculate. A glistening white tub, sink, and toilet bowl. Over the sink, there was a mirrored cabinet containing several prescription drugs that appeared to be antibiotics, and the usual array of over-the-counter pain and cough medications one could find in any medicine cabinet in this city. That was it. Not a painting or a photograph anywhere. The place was featureless, colorless, drab, and depressing.

Brown opened the door to the single closet in the room. There were three skirts, four pairs of slacks, two dresses, a woolen winter coat, a raincoat, several pairs of sensible shoes. Carella opened the top dresser drawer. Cotton panties and bras. White pantyhose. Socks. Darker pantyhose. Blouses in the middle drawer. Scarves. Sweaters in the bottom drawer. Not a piece of jewelry. Not a hint of anything truly personal.

In the night-table drawer, they found an address book, an appointment calendar, and a budget-aid spiral notebook.

"We'd like to take these with us," Carella said, leafing through the appointment calendar.

"Nope," Harding said.

Both detectives looked at him.

"We'll give you a receipt," Brown said.

"Nope," Harding said.

The detectives looked at each other.

"That stuff ain't mine," Harding said. "I got no right to let you take it."

Carella gave the man a look that could have melted Greenland. He sat in the easy chair, took out his pad, and began copying Mary Vincent's appointments for the two weeks preceding her murder. Then he went back to the night table, put all three books into the drawer again, gave Harding another look, and said, "We'll be back."

IN THE CAR AGAIN, BROWN SAID, "Son of a bitch is forcing us to get a warrant."

"Well, I guess he's right," Carella said.

"Most people would've accepted a receipt."

"People don't like cops, is what it is. We remind them of storm troopers."

"You and me?"

"All of us."

"He probably understands sheriffs better," Brown said.

"Probably."

"Want to run downtown for it now?"

"Doctor said he'd be leaving at four."

"We don't hurry, we may miss a judge," Brown said.

"Let's do the doctor and the priest, save the cowboy for last. What do you think?"

"Sure. Either way, we have to drive half an hour downtown, the son of a bitch."

Neither of the men noticed the little green Honda following them some six car lengths behind.

THE DOCTOR IN CHARGE of what was euphemistically called the Extensive Care Ward at St. Margaret's Hospital was named Winston Hall, which made him sound like a college dormitory. The detectives supposed he was somewhere in his forties, a tall, sun-tanned, angular man with an infectious smile and a pleasant, soft-spoken manner. He was wearing a rumpled wheat-colored linen jacket over sand-colored slacks, a pale blue shirt, and a delicately hued blue-and-yellow-striped cotton tie. Sitting behind his third-floor desk at a quarter past three that Monday afternoon, he seemed dressed more for a boat ride around the island than a day at the office.

He explained that there were forty beds on the floor, most of them occupied by patients who required long-term nursing, many of whom, in fact, belonged in nursing homes rather than a hospital.

"The homes 911 'em out to us the minute there's a serious problem, hoping we'll keep them forever. Sometimes we do, but with many of our patients forever is a short-term probability."

"What kind of patients was Mary treating?"

"We've got all kinds on this floor," Hall said. "COPD, terminal cancer, Alzheimer's . . ."

"What's COPD?"

"Chronic Obstructional Pulmonary Disease. Asthma, emphysema, chronic bronchitis. Most of them are on oxygen. We've also got a woman with Whipple's Disease, she's been dying for the past three years, refuses to let go. She's got a PEG tube sutured into her belly, that's how we feed her and administer medi . . ."

"What's a peg tube?" Brown asked.

"P, E, G, all caps," Hall said. "It's an acronym for Percutaneous Endoscopic Gastrostomy. The woman with Whipple's has a PEG in her belly and a permanent catheter in her chest wall. She has no control of her extremities, no teeth, she's balding at the back of her head because no matter how many times we turn her, she ends up on her back. She really should be a DNR, but she refuses to sign the permission forms."

"What's that?" Brown asked.

"DNR? Do Not Resuscitate. Big sign at the foot of the bed, DNR. Essentially, it means let 'em die."

Carella was thinking he wouldn't do this kind of work for five million dollars.

"One of our patients has prostate cancer that metastasized to bone," Hall said. "Another has *lung* cancer that metastasized to bone and brain. We've got a bilateral amputee on the ward, he's incontinent of stool, his skin's broken down, and he's got a permanent trache tube in his throat."

Not for *ten* million dollars, Carella thought.

"This isn't a fun ward," Hall said.

Mind reader, Carella thought.

"Mary began working for me six months ago. Transferred here from a hospice in San Diego, which is where her mother house is. I believe she spoke to the major superior there, who referred her to the director of ministry. I'm glad they sent her here, believe me. Quite often, as was the case with Mary, a woman religious can be more devoted than the most dedicated doctor."

Carella, quick study that he was, figured that "woman religious" was the politically correct term for nun. Somehow, he preferred nun. Same way he preferred cop to police officer.

"We have a hundred and ten beds here at St. Margaret's," Hall said. "Four hundred people on the staff, including the Christ's Mercy nuns. The other hospital run by the order is even smaller. The government's cutting back on funds, you know, and some seventy percent of our patients are either welfare or Medicaid recipients. The sisters are just scraping by, but they're really committed to serving the poor. Last year St. Margaret's had close to twenty-five-hundred admissions. There were twelve hundred clinic visits every month, nine hundred emergency-room visits, four hundred outpatient surgeries. This is a poor neighborhood. We're much needed here. I'll miss Mary sorely, I can tell you that. She was a thorough professional, and a wonderful person."

"Know anyone who may have felt otherwise?" Carella asked.

"Not a soul. I've worked with nuns for the past ten years now, and they're as different one from the other as any other women. I'm sure some of them may, in fact, be *exactly* like the childish little creatures or strict disciplinarians we see portrayed on television, giggling as they carry in the sheaves or snarling as they crack a ruler over the knuckles of a schoolboy. But I've never personally met a nun who fits the stereotype. For the most part, they are complex, intelligent women who share only one trait—their complete devotion to God. Mary considered her work here a divinely inspired gift. The nuns call it charism, you know, the work chosen for them by God. Mary's work was particularly difficult. She labored for God tirelessly, dutifully, and cheerfully. I'd sometimes hear her . . ."

His voice broke.

"She'd . . . sometimes sing to the patients on the ward, she had a beautiful voice. There wasn't anyone who didn't feel enlightened and encouraged by her very presence. Everyone here will miss her."

"Were you working here last Friday, Doctor?" Carella asked.

"Yes, I was."

"Did Mary seem her usual self?"

"Yes, her same sweet self." He considered this a moment, nodded, and said, "We worked on and off together all through the day. I saw no difference in her behavior."

"Nothing strange or . . ."

"Nothing at all. She was her usual sweet self. I'm sorry to keep using that word. 'Sweet' can sometimes be misconstrued as insipid. But Mary had a manner that somehow soothed and at the same time cheered. A certain . . . sweetness, yes. In her smile, in her eyes. She seemed to be a completely realized human being, and as such she spread joy as if it were an infection. I'm sorry," he said, and turned his face away for a moment. "I was very fond of her. We all were."

He pulled a tissue from the box on his desk, dabbed at his eyes, blew his nose. The detectives waited.

"I'm sorry," he said again.

"Dr. Hall," Brown said, "did she happen to mention where she might be going after work last Friday?"

"No, she didn't."

"When was the last time you saw her that day?"

"Let me think."

They waited.

"Just before the shift ended, I would suppose."

"What time would that have been?"

Helen Daniels had told them she and Mary had left the hospital together at a little past three. They were merely attempting to verify this now.

"Two-thirty?" Hall said. "A quarter to three?"

"Leaving the hospital, did you say?"

"No, no. The shift ends at three. This would have been a little before then."

"Where'd you see her?"

"Just outside the women's locker room. Talking to one of the nurses."

"Which one? Would you remember?"

"I'm sorry," Hall said. "Her back was to me."

"How many nurses were on that shift?" Brown asked.

"It varies from day to day."

"Would you have a record of who was here?"

"Yes, certainly."

"Could we have it, please? Doctors, too," Carella said.

Hall looked at him.

"Doctors, too, of course," he said.

WHAT SONNY COULDN'T FIGURE OUT was why Carella and his partner—he assumed the big black dude with him was his partner and not his goddamn chauffeur—kept shuttling back and forth between St. Margaret's Hospital and all these places had to do with religion. Saturday it was the convent up there in Riverhead. Now, at four in the afternoon, it was this church here on Yarrow, not too distant from the walk-up apartment building they'd gone to. Our Lady of Flowers it said in the letters chiseled over the arched front doors.

You'd think the fuckin pope had got himself shot or something.

FATHER FRANK CLEMENTE WAS A MAN IN HIS FIFTIES, wearing a black cotton sweater over black slacks and a black T-shirt. He looked a lot like a priest, Carella supposed, but he could have passed as well for any cool dude enjoying a cappuccino at an outdoor table on Jefferson Avenue. Instead, he and the two detectives sat on wrought-iron chairs as black as his attire, around a wide stone tabletop set on a stone pilaster, sipping lemonade the good father had himself made.

"Mary was here for mass last week," he said. "She . . ."

"When last week?" Carella asked.

"Tuesday night."

Three days before she was killed, Carella thought.

"We had a drink together afterward."

Bottle of vodka in her fridge, Brown thought.

"She seemed troubled," Father Frank said. "She was normally so cheerful and outgoing, but that night . . ."

He finds her somehow distant on this Tuesday night, the eighteenth day of August. It's almost as if there's a weight on her shoulders she wishes to share and yet is reluctant to reveal. He has known her since she came to this city in February, a prayerful nun who comes to mass at his church at least once, sometimes twice a week. He knows of her difficult ministry at St. Margaret's, and he thinks at first she may have lost a patient today, so many of them are terminally ill. But no, it isn't that, she assures him everything is fine at the hospital, everything just fine, Frank, thank you for your concern.

Some nuns have drinking problems; some priests as well, for that matter. It is not an easy path they've chosen, and sometimes the hardships of the religious life can seem overwhelming. The church has programs for those unfortunates who need help, but Mary isn't one of them, and neither is he.

He keeps a bottle of twelve-year-old scotch in a cabinet in his study, and it is there that he mixes the drink for her. Two fingers of scotch in a tall Venetian glass Father Frank brought back from Italy when he had his audience with Pope John last summer. Three ice cubes. Fill the glass to the rim with soda. The same for himself. They carry the drinks out to the garden, and they sit here at this very same stone table he now shares with the detectives.

The summer insects are noisy tonight.

They listen to the night all around them.

"Is something troubling you?" he asks at last.

"No, Frank."

"You seem . . . I don't know. Withdrawn."

"No, no."

"If it's something, please tell me. Perhaps I can help."

"Do you ever feel . . . ?" she asks, and hesitates.

He waits. He knows better than to press her. If she wishes to share whatever this is, she will of her own accord. He has heard her confession every week since she came to this city. She knows she can trust him. He waits.

"That the past and the present . . . ," she starts again, and again stops.

The noise of the insects seems suddenly deafening. He wishes there were a volume control, wishes he could tune out the sounds of the universe and peer directly into Mary's mind, find there whatever it is that has cast this pall over her, help her to reveal it to him, reveal it to God for His understanding and mercy, His forgiveness if in fact there is anything to forgive.

Yet he waits.

Takes another sip of his drink.

Waits.

The insects are rowdy.

"What I mean . . . ," she says. "Frank, do you ever feel that the past is *determined* by the present?"

"You've got that reversed, haven't you?" he says.

"Not at all."

"You're saying the *present* determines . . . ?"

"Yes, the past. What we do *today* determines what already happened *yesterday*."

"Are we about to get into a discussion of free will?"

"I hope not."

"Determinism? Predestination?"

"That's not what . . ."

"*Double* predestination? Calvinism? Am I back at the seminary?"

"I'm not joking, Frank."

"How can you seriously suggest that the *future* determines . . . ?"

"Not the future. The *present*."

"In the past, Mary, the present *is* the future."

"Yes, but I'm talking about *now*. The *immediate* present."

"Can you give me a concrete example?" he says, thinking that if he can move her from the abstract to the specific, then perhaps he can get her to talk about what's *really* troubling her. For surely, a metaphysical discussion isn't what she . . .

"Let's say, for example . . ."

She sips slowly at the drink.

"Let's say we're sitting here enjoying our scotch . . ."

"Which, in fact, we are doing."

"Here in the present. This moment is the present."

"It most certainly is."

"I'm sorry you think this is funny, Frank."

"Forgive me."

"What I'm trying to *say* is . . . do you think that our drinking this scotch, here and now in the present, somehow induced you to *buy* the scotch whenever you bought it?"

"No, I don't."

"Why not?"

"Because I *didn't* buy it. It was a gift from Charles. He brought it back from Glasgow."

"Then was *his* buying it, whenever that was . . ."

"Three months ago."

"Was *his* act influenced by our drinking the scotch right this minute? Did he somehow *know* back then, three months ago in Glasgow, that you and I would be sitting here in your garden tonight . . . what's today's date?"

"The eighteenth."

"July, June, May," she says, counting backward. "On *May* eighteenth, did Father Charles *know,* or discern, or even prognosticate that tonight we'd be drinking the scotch he was at that moment buying in Glasgow? Did the present . . . *tonight,* August eighteenth, at . . . what time is it?"

"Nine-thirty."

"Did *this* hour and *this* minute in *this* garden on *this* night determine his buying *this* scotch three *months* ago?"

"I didn't think it was *that* strong," he says, and looks into his glass as if searching the drink for hidden potency.

"I'm serious, Frank. Suppose, for example . . . well, just *suppose* a decision I made two Sundays ago . . . here at mass, in fact . . ."

"What decision was that?" he asks at once.

"It doesn't matter. A decision. Let's say a spiritual decision."

"All right."

"Do you feel my decision could have determined the contents of a letter written the day after I'd *made* the decision?"

Frank looks at her.

"What letter?" he asks.

Even the insects seem suddenly still.

"This is all supposition," she says.

"I realize that. A letter from whom?"

"I told you. I'm theorizing."

"Did you receive a letter, Mary?"

"This is all so silly, isn't it?" she says. "Let's talk about the *real* world, shall we?"

The moment passes.

The topic changes.

He has lost her.

She leaves the church at a little before ten, thanking him for the drink and telling him she'll be here for mass again on Sunday.

"But, of course . . . by Sunday, she was dead."

The garden was as still now as it must have been last Tuesday, when she came so close to telling him what was troubling her.

"Had she *really* received a letter?" Carella asked.

"I have no idea."

THIS TIME, they went equipped with a court order authorizing them to seize Sister Mary Vincent's appointment calendar, her address book, and her budgeting notebook. The warrant also allowed them to search for and to similarly seize any correspondence addressed to her.

Harding was not happy to see them again.

He'd apparently been checking with a friend who was a cop or a lawyer or merely a student, and he'd been informed that the nun's apartment was not a crime scene and the cops had no right bothering him every ten minutes to ask him to unlock the door for them.

"That's right," Carella said. "You want us to kick it in?"

"You got no right—"

"Listen, mister, are you defying a court order?"

Harding looked at him. "I'll take you up," he said grudgingly.

Behind him, they labored up the steps to the sixth floor. Outside the door to 6C, they waited patiently while he fumbled with his key ring again. At last, he unlocked the door, opened it, and said, "Mind if I see that warrant you mentioned?"

Carella showed it to him. Harding read it carefully, word for word, and then handed it back, and stepped aside for the detectives to enter the apartment.

Someone had beat them to it.

The place was a shambles.

The refrigerator door was open, its contents swept out onto the kitchen floor. They could see into the bathroom, where the intruder had searched the medicine cabinet and the toilet tank, leaving the lid on the seat. The bed had been stripped. The closet door was open, Mary's meager belongings strewn everywhere. The dresser drawers . . .

"Window's open here," Brown said.

The window was on the wall beside the dresser. It was locked the last time they were here. Now it was wide open. Several clay pots of blooming flowers were on the fire escape outside. One of the pots had been overturned in the intruder's haste to leave.

"See anybody in the backyard late this afternoon?" Carella asked.

"Wasn't *in* the backyard late this afternoon," Harding said.

"Would've been sometime after three," Brown said.

"Why then?"

"That's when we left here."

"Didn't see anybody *anytime* cause I wasn't *in* the backyard after I fixed that pulley."

"You got a hair across your ass, mister?" Brown said.

"I don't like cops shoving their weight around, that's all," Harding said.

"Maybe you'd like to come to the station house, answer some questions there," Brown said heatedly. "Would you like to do that, sir?"

"You got no reason to detain me," Harding said.

"Try obstructing the progress of a murder investi . . ."

"Let it go, Artie," Carella said.

"Man's beginning to annoy me! A woman's been *killed* here, he's acting like . . ."

"Let it go," Carella said again. "Let's see if we can find that letter."

Harding stood just inside the door while they searched, his arms folded across his chest, a smug look on his face. Brown wanted to smack the bastard. In the night-table drawer, they found the various books they'd tried to remove from the apartment earlier . . .

"We'll be taking these now," Carella said.

Harding nodded.

. . . but they did not find the letter Mary Vincent had mentioned to Father Clemente.

Or any letter at all, for that matter.

Not in the night table or anywhere else.

"If you're finished here," Harding said, "I got work to do."

Brown was thinking of all the fire-department and building-code violations he'd noticed on the arduous climb up to the sixth floor: the burnt-out lightbulb on the first-floor landing, the air-shaft window painted shut on the third floor, the exposed electrical wiring on the fifth floor, the stacked cardboard cartons obstructing passage on the sixth floor.

He smiled like a Buddha.

*   *   *

IF MARY VINCENT'S APPOINTMENT CALENDAR was a true indicator of her social life, the nun had been fairly busy during the two weeks preceding her death. The calendar listed:

August 11: 6:30 P.M.
            Felicia @ CM.
August 14: 7:00 P.M.
            Jenna and Rene
            Here.
August 15: 7:30 P.M.
            Michael @ Med
August 18: 6:00 P.M.
            Frank @ OLF
August 20: 5:00 P.M.
            Annette @ CM

They had already talked to Father Frank Clemente at Our Lady of Flowers and Sister Annette Ryan at the Christ's Mercy convent. A check of first names in Mary's address book came up with the information that Felicia Locasta was a nun at Christ's Mercy, Jenna DiSalvo and Rene Schneider were both registered nurses at St. Margaret's, and Dr. Michael Paine was a physician at the hospital.

It was still relatively early on Monday night.

They hit the phones.

5. "She was upset about her budget," Sister Felicia Locasta said. "I think that's why she came to see me that night. I was a math major in college before I joined the order. We often talked about money matters."

The detectives were back in Riverhead again, at the Convent of the Sisters of Christ's Mercy, at the crack of dawn, and they were sitting in a little room off the chapel, where there was a coffee machine, a refrigerator, and a sink.

"Please call me just Felicia, okay?" she said. "I mean, I know there are nuns who dig the sister bit, but they're all a hundred years old."

Felicia was in her mid-thirties, a dark-eyed woman with curly black hair fastened at the back of her head with a simple ribbon. She was wearing jeans, loafers without socks, and a white T-shirt lettered with the words SISTERS OF CHRIST'S MERCY . . .

". . . which Sister Carmelita might not find *appropriate*," she said, hitting the word hard, "but she's in San Diego, and I'm here. Anyway, I *am* a Sister of Christ's Mercy and I only wear this around here before I go to work, what time is it, anyway?"

It was seven A.M. on August twenty-fifth, a blistering-hot Tuesday with the sun barely risen, an exaggeration, but, man, it was *hot!* Felicia had told them last night that she had to be at work by nine sharp, so if they wanted to talk to her they had to be at the convent by seven *latest.* Her work was teaching mathematics to the little deaf kids at the school next door, so if they could be out of here by eight, she could shower and dress like a proper nun before she faced the day.

Carella wondered if he should mention that his wife was deaf.
Funny, but he never thought of her as deaf.

He let the moment pass.

"Mary always had trouble making ends meet," Felicia said, "I don't know why, I kept telling her to ask Sister Carmelita to move her up here to the convent. We pool our resources here and I know it's a lot cheaper than living alone in the city. But she said she wanted to be near the hospital. 'You never know what's going to happen,' she used to say. 'One of my patients might need me.' She was very conscientious, you know. I was with her one night when she'd lost a patient and she was virtually inconsolable."

"Did she come up here often?"

"Or I'd take the train into the city. We were close friends. I mean, we're *all* united in Christ, all the sisters in the order, but you naturally gravitate to some people more than you do others. We became friends shortly after she came here from San Diego. We met through Annette. Her spiritual advisor? Have you talked to Annette?"

"Yes, we have," Carella said. "This would've been in February sometime, is that it? When you met Mary?"

"February, March, along about then."

"How often did you see her?"

"We got together for dinner every three weeks or so. Usually she came here, sometimes we met in the city."

"According to this," Brown said, consulting Mary's calendar, "she was here at the convent on the eleventh. That would've been a Tuesday night. She has you listed for six-thirty."

"Yes, that's when we have supper here at the convent. Right after vespers. The evening prayer. You have to understand . . . this will sound terrible, I know, but, well, I'm sorry, but it's the way it is. You see, we take vows of poverty, charity, and obedience. We *are* poor, we don't simply *pretend* to be poor. So whenever Mary came here for supper . . . well . . . it was an extra mouth to feed, you see. We have a budget, too. So she chipped in for the meal. And we gratefully accepted whatever she could offer. Whatever her budget would allow."

"How about when you went out to eat together?"

"Oh, we never went to anyplace fancy. You'd be surprised how many inexpensive little places there are in the city. We usually had pasta and a salad, a glass of wine. There are places that will let you sit and talk. We knew a *lot* of them," she said, her eyes twinkling as if she were in possession of a state secret. "And in the spring and summer months, we'd walk. It was a gorgeous spring this year. There are a lot of very poor people in this city, you know. And not many of them had a choice in the matter. We *chose* this life. You must never forget that."

"When you say she was upset about her budget . . ."

"Well, yes."

"Was that why she came to see you?"

"Yes. I mean, we were good friends, she also wanted to spend some time with me and the other sisters. But the budget was on her mind, yes."

"Did you talk about anything *but* her budget that night?" Brown asked.

"It was on her mind," Felicia said. "That's what we talked about mostly."

"Just you and Mary? Or did the other sisters join in?"

"Just the two of us."

"And you say she was upset."

"Yes."

"Only about the budget?"

"That's all she told me about."

"Did she mention receiving a letter from anyone?" Carella asked.

"No."

"Did she mention some kind of decision she'd made a few weeks ago?"

"No."

"You just talked about her budget."

"Mostly. The difficulty she was having making ends meet. The trouble she was having with the vow."

"Of poverty, do you mean?"

"Of poverty, yes. I'm not sure why it should suddenly have been such a burden. She'd been a nun for . . ."

"Did she owe anyone money?" Brown asked.

"No. Well, I'm sure she didn't."

"How can you be sure?"

"I'm sorry, but such a thing would never occur to me."

"She didn't drink, did she?"

"Not to excess, no. No. Of course not."

"Hadn't developed any bad habits, had she?"

"Is that a pun, Detective?"

"Huh? Oh. No. I'm talking about bad habits like gambling or dope, your everyday bad habits."

The room went silent.

"She *was* a nun, you know," Felicia said.

"We have to ask," Brown said.

"Do you?"

She looked up at the wall clock. Brown figured he'd blown it. He waited for Carella to ask the next question. Carella was thinking he'd have a tough time pulling this one out of the fire. Felicia looked up at the wall clock again. He decided to bite the bullet, what the hell.

"How much was she living on?" he asked. "Would you know?"

"She got by."

"But she complained."

"Only to me. I was her closest friend. You can't complain to God, gentlemen, but you *can* complain to friends. I told her she should have been used to it by now, what did she think poverty meant, champagne and caviar? I told her I could understand this if she'd just entered the order. But six *years?* Why did she take her final vows if she still had doubts? Why did she accept the gold ring of profession . . . ?"

"Did she *say* she had doubts?"

"No, she simply said it was very difficult."

"All at once."

"I don't know if it was all at once. Maybe she'd been thinking about it for some time. This was the first *I'd* heard of it."

"But you said you often talked about money matters."

"There is not a nun on earth who doesn't talk about money matters."

"Had she ever *complained* about money matters before?"

"Never."

"Why now?" Carella asked.

"I don't know why. A nun for *six* years," Felicia said, shaking her head. "Entered the order straight from college. Brown University, I think. So all of a sudden she hasn't got enough money to spend? Can *you* understand that? I certainly can't."

THERE HAD BEEN MENTION OF HIM last night on the eleven o'clock news, but he didn't like them referring to him as The Cookie Boy, which made him sound like some kind of fat little Pillsbury Doughboy you poked your finger in his belly and he giggled. He was not only a grown man—twenty-seven years old—but he was also tall and slender and quite good-looking if he said so himself. A skilled burglar besides. A *professional* burglar, mind you, who'd been entering apartments unobtrusively since he was twenty-two when he'd been discharged from the armed forces of the United States of America, in which he'd served honorably and nobly, go ask Mom. Not a single arrest in five years, either, and never *hoped* to get busted, thank you very much.

The Cookie Boy.

Didn't like that name at all.

Sort of diminished the whole point of what he was doing. Demeaned it somehow. This wasn't some kind of dumb *gimmick*, this was a genuine attempt to transmute victims—he *hated* that word—into honest-to-God recipients. He was trying to create some sort of *exchange* here. No hard feelings, you understand? I know I've been in your apartment, I know I've taken with me some of your precious belongings, once very near and dear to you, but, alas, now gone. I want you to understand, however, that no malice was intended. This is what I do for a living, in much the same way that you're a stockbroker or a nurse, a lawyer or a waitress. I am a burglar, and I want you to respect what I do, just as I respect what you do, just as I've shown respect for all your possessions while inside your apartment. I haven't thrown things all over the floor, I haven't left any kind of mess here, have I? I've left the place just the way I found it, except for taking a few things with me. And in return, because I truly *don't* want you harboring any feelings of resentment or anger, I leave you these chocolate chip cookies I baked myself. Not as payment for your goods, I don't want you to misinterpret the gesture. This is not an act of commerce. Rather, I think of it as an exchange of gifts. I thank you for your belongings, and I humbly offer this gift of my own, these delicious chocolate chip cookies baked by yours truly, from my own recipe, and offered with all my love. Low fat, no less.

The windows were wide open because it was another hot morning—he did all his baking in the morning—and he was preheating the oven to three hundred and seventy-five degrees. Whenever he baked, which was every day except Sunday, he imagined people all over the neighborhood poking their heads out of similarly opened windows to sniff in the good, sweet aroma of his cookies wafting out on the still summer air. All of his ingredients were laid out on the kitchen table, his sugars and his margarine, his flour and baking soda, his vanilla and salt, his egg white and his chocolate chips. The oven was almost ready. He began mixing.

First the half cup of granulated sugar and next the quarter cup of brown sugar. Then the quarter cup of softened margarine and the teaspoon of vanilla. All in a large bowl, mixed with a wooden spoon, his hand moving in circles, a smile on his face, oh how he loved doing this! Now he stirred in a cup of flour and a quarter teaspoon of salt, and then he dropped in his semisweet chocolate chips, a half cup of them, dribbling them in bit by bit, watching them fall like punctuation marks into the white mix, stirring them in, sniffing the air, smiling, opening the oven and feeling the good heat on his face, oh my. Onto an ungreased cookie sheet, he dropped his tea-spoon-size bits of dough, spacing them about two inches apart, and then sliding the sheet into the oven, and setting the timer for ten minutes. The recipe was good for about fifty cookies.

Smiling, sitting at the kitchen table now and drinking a cup of decaffeinated coffee, he imagined he could see, actually *see*, wave after wave of aroma rolling from the oven to the open windows across the room and out into the courtyard, drifting on the air, through the open windows across the way, above and below, float-ing into the apartments of grateful neighbors who could only won-der who on earth was baking these glorious treats, never once imagining that the baker was The Cookie Boy himself.

This afternoon, in whichever apartment he burglarized, he would leave a dozen chocolate chip cookies in a little white box on the bed, resting on whichever pillow he supposed the lady of the house placed her head upon. A gift from The Cookie Boy, madam.

A name he rather fancied, after all, now that he played it over and again in his mind.

WHEN THEY GOT TO ST. MARGARET'S at nine-thirty that morning, the head nurse told them Rene Schneider and Jenna DiSalvo were in with a patient. They went down the hall to the visitors' waiting room, and took chairs in a windowed corner overlooking the park-ing lot. Brown seemed unusually silent.

"What are you thinking?" Carella asked.

"Nothing."

"You still upset?"

"Yes, you want to know. I didn't handle it right, I realize that. But I have to tell you, Steve, I don't really *care* if they're nuns or priests or whatever the hell they are, the mother superior, the pope himself. Somebody got *killed* here!"

"Take it easy, Artie."

"I'm sorry, but what did I say that was so damn outrageous, can you please tell me? Is it impossible for a nun to have a drinking problem? Last night, Father Clemente *said* there were nuns who did."

"He also said Mary wasn't one of them."

"Yeah, well, my mother told me it never hurts to ask the same question twice."

"She must've known *my* mother."

"I have to look at this person like a human being. And human beings borrow money. So what'd Sister Felicia get so upset about? Did I spit on her crucifix or something? I asked if Mary owed anybody money, big deal! She tells me Oh, gee, I'm terribly sorry, but such a thing would never *occur* to me! Why not? Mary all at once needs money, why's it impossible that she *owed* somebody?"

"She was a nun, Artie."

"So what? Can't a nun bet on the horses? Can't she buy crack on the street corner? Can't she go play poker with *other* nuns? She lived in an apartment all by herself, Steve. Nobody was checking on her."

"God was checking on her."

"Oh, come on. Do you believe that?"

"No. But I'm sure she did."

"Okay, why do *you* think she suddenly needed more money?"

"Why do you?"

"Blackmail," Brown said.

"Excuse me?"

They both turned toward the entrance door. Two uniformed nurses were standing there, one of them blonde, the other dark-haired.

"You wanted to see us?" the blonde said.

The detectives rose. The nurses came into the room.

"I'm Jenna DiSalvo," the blonde said.

"I'm Rene Schneider," the brunette said.

The detectives introduced themselves. The nurses apologized for the delay and told them they'd been doing a wet-to-dry dressing on a patient with a decubitus ulcer on his coccyx . . .

"A pressure sore," Jenna explained.

"On his tailbone," Rene explained.

. . . which had taken two of them because he was too weak to keep himself rolled over on his side, and one of them had to hold him while the other one cleaned the two-inch hole with saline, and then packed the wound with saline-soaked gauze, and then put dry gauze and an ABD pad over that, and then paper-taped it. The whole dressing change had taken about fifteen minutes, which was why they were late, and again they apologized.

Not for a *hundred* million dollars, Carella thought.

The nurses, crisp and white in their pristine uniforms, looked unruffled but enormously wary. They knew that in police work a mandatory suspect was anyone who'd had contact with the victim in the proximate period before a murder. They'd also seen too many tabloid television shows about mistaken arrests and police brutality. The detectives were both wearing Dacron suits, rumpled in this heat, damp button-down shirts, silk ties that needed pressing. They looked tough. When Brown asked if they might talk to each of the women separately, the nurses knew positively that they'd both end up in a state penitentiary where they'd be sodomized by hardened criminals and sadistic guards.

Jenna led Carella down the hall to the nurses' lounge.

Brown stayed here with Rene in the visitors' waiting room.

Because she got the black cop, Rene figured she'd end up in the electric chair. She happened to be Jewish, and she knew blacks, the ingrates, didn't like Jews. Because Jenna got the cop with the Italian name, she figured she'd get the electric chair, too. She happened to be of Italian descent herself, and she knew Italians didn't trust other Italians.

"Have a seat," Brown said, as if the waiting room were his own living room. Rene took a seat on the sofa. Brown sat in an easy chair facing her. Rene cleared her throat and folded her hands in her lap. She was the prettier of the two women, and she knew it. But that wasn't going to save her from the electric chair. Brown took a notebook from the inside pocket of his jacket.

"August fourteenth," he said. "That would've been the Friday a week before Mary Vincent was murdered."

*   *   *

"YOU'RE LISTED IN HER CALENDAR for seven o'clock that night,"
Carella said. "You met at her apartment, is that right?"

"Yes," Jenna said. "For drinks."

"WE WENT OUT to dinner afterward," Rene said.

"How much did she drink?" Brown asked.

Never hurt to ask the same question *three* times, either.

"She had a single glass of wine."

"Got there at seven, did you?"

"*I* did. Jenna got there a bit later. We went separately."

"WHERE'D YOU GO after you had your drinks?"

"To a Chinese restaurant nearby."

"Would you remember the name of it?"

"Ah Fong," Jenna said.

"AH WONG," Rene said.

"Who paid for dinner?"

"We split the check."

"WE WENT DUTCH."

"Was that Mary's suggestion?"

"No, we always worked it that way. Whenever we went out together."

"How often was that?"

"Every two weeks," Jenna said.

"ONCE A MONTH," Rene said.

"Did Mary mention anything about money?"

"Money?"

"About the bill? It being too expensive. Anything like that?"

"No, why would she?"

"I<small>T CAME TO SOMETHING LIKE</small> nine dollars each. Including tip. Why would she think that was expensive?"

"Well, she was on a tight budget, wasn't she?"

"How would I know?"

"N<small>EVER SAID ANYTHING ABOUT HOW</small> hard it was to make ends meet?"

"No. Why would she? She was earning a good salary."

"H<small>OW MUCH WAS SHE EARNING,</small> do you know?"

"Twenty-two dollars an hour, same as us. I think. No, wait a minute, it might have been less. Rene and I are RNs. Mary was an LPN."

"S<small>HE WAS PROBABLY GETTING FIFTEEN,</small> sixteen bucks an hour," Rene said. "But how is that pertinent?"

"We've been told she was worried about money."

"What's that got to do with how much money *we* earn? How much money do *you* earn, okay?"

"D<small>ID SHE MENTION</small> any threatening telephone calls or letters?"

"No."

"Would you know if she owed money to anyone?"

"Yes," Jenna said. "She owed me a buck seventy-five for bus fare. Her transit card gave out, so I ran her through on mine."

*　　　*　　　*

LATER, RENE TOLD HER MOTHER that the *shvartzeh* had grilled her like a common criminal.

"It's what we get," her mother said.

Jenna later asked her boyfriend, who was a lawyer, if she could sue Carella for treating her like a common streetwalker.

"How were you sitting?" her boyfriend asked.

6.

COOKIE BOY NEVER WENT FOR THE BIG SCORE. HE FIGURED THAT WAS FOR AMATEURS. EVERYBODY WAS IN THE BUSINESS for money, sure, but amateurs were also in it for the glamour and the thrill, the goddamn glory. Amateurs thought of themselves as movie stars. Get past security in a luxury high-rise overlooking the park, pick the lock on the door, crack the safe behind the framed Rembrandt on the wall, walk off with a fortune. Thank you, thank, you, this is an honor. I also want to thank my mother, my drama coach, and my police dog.

Amateurs.

America was a nation of lucky amateurs.

Cookie Boy never even *thought* of the big score. He'd see a lady in a sable coat that dusted her ankles, strutting out of a luxury building, doorman whistling for a cab, holding an umbrella for her, whisking her inside the taxi, Cookie Boy walked right on by. Sure, you managed to get in her pad you'd find a couple more furs, loads of diamonds, priceless artwork, whatever. Which you had to get *out* with, don't forget. Even if you got past security once, going in, you still had to get past them a *second* time, going out. Not only going out, but going out with a shitpot full of stolen goods, try explaining *that* to the members of the Academy, thank you all, I love you all so very much, this is such a great honor.

What Cookie Boy had learned early on in his career was that even poor people had treasures. Whether it was a locket that used to be Grandma's they kept in a candy tin, or five hundred bucks hidden in the bottom rail of a venetian blind, everybody had something. Well, not everybody. He didn't go into tenement apartments in Diamondback, for example, where he wouldn't find anything but cockroaches and empty crack vials.

Cookie Boy chose to walk the middle ground.

He considered himself a moderate.

He knew there were people in the profession who felt that if you were going to take the chance of going in at all, then you might as well go for the big one. You were looking at the same time whether you walked off with Grandma's locket or the rich lady's sable. It was all burglary. Well, there were different *degrees* of burglary, depending on whether you went in armed—he *never* went in armed, that was foolish—or whether it was the daytime or the nighttime or whether it was a dwelling or a place of business, or whether the place was occupied at the time or not. All of these factors determined how long you could stay in prison, where Cookie Boy had never been, and where he never intended to go, thank you very much.

But the amateur thinking went: If you're looking at five, ten, twenty, whatever, depending on the particular circumstances, God forbid you should *kill* somebody during the commission, which made it a felony murder and you were looking at the long one, baby—

But the amateur thinking went: Suppose you were looking at ten in the slammer, that wasn't going to change no matter *what* you stole, the price of admission was ten in the slammer, got it? You wanted to play, you had to understand you were looking at ten down the line if you got caught.

Cookie Boy never intended to get caught.

First of all because he didn't go after the really big scores, that was for amateurs. Second because he was *content* with the smaller hits, didn't go around grumbling or complaining, didn't tell bartenders he coulda been a contenduh, didn't let it bother him that he went home with three, four grand a week instead of five hundred thou on a single hit. Cookie Boy was living well and enjoying himself besides. And every now and then, he'd pop a crib and lo and behold he'd discover a red-fox jacket and a candy tin full of all kinds of baubles and beads. He'd fence the jacket for five hundred and the jewelry for a thou, which gave him a fifteen-hundred-dollar profit for jimmying a window and spending twenty minutes in an apartment.

Sometimes you went in and you found a shithole, what could you do? You could tell at a glance you wouldn't find anything of value in such an apartment, but you tossed it fast, anyway, so it shouldn't be a total loss, and you got out as fast as you came in, no sense looking at time for no reason at all, risks were for amateurs. Never mind leaving any cookies, either, thanks for *nothing*, lady!

What he tried to do was find a well-kept building in a low-crime area, didn't have to be silk stocking. Just your average middle-class neighborhood where you'd find buildings without doormen, some of them walk-ups without elevators, it didn't matter. You were looking for something without security. You walked the neighborhood three or four times, got the feel of it, looked for steps leading down to the backyards, made a few trips behind the buildings. Anybody questioned you, you told them you were a "city inspector," checking "ordinances," and you moved on to another block. If you took no risks, you spent no time upstate.

The backyards were another world.

It was like being inside a piece of modern sculpture back there, a fantastic universe of flapping clotheslines and telephone poles and fire escapes and soot-stained brick and blue sky overhead, all crazy angles, wood and iron and concrete against the soft billowing curves of laundry drying. Another world. Music coming from open windows, television voices blending with real voices, toilets flushing, cooking smells floating out over fences and walls, a private world back here, hidden from the street. Exciting, too, in a way that had nothing to do with risk. Exciting because it was an intimate glimpse. Like catching sight of a girl's panties when she crossed her legs.

In the summertime, you avoided any apartment where a window was open. This usually meant somebody was home trolling for a breath of fresh air. An occupied apartment was the one thing on earth you did not desire, unless you were an amateur who got his kicks scaring sick old ladies in bed. Apartments with air conditioners were tricky because all the windows *had* to be kept closed, and you couldn't tell if anyone was in there or not. So you looked for an apartment with closed windows and fire-escape access, and then you took your chances. Went up, listened outside, you could usually tell if anybody was home or not. Lots of windows were closed but unlocked; people got careless, even in a city like this one. If the window was locked, you jimmied it. If the lock was painted shut, you used a glass cutter, though in such cases it was usually best to meander on by and look for another score. You dropped a piece of glass, the noise of it shattering was the best burglar alarm in the world. Once you had the window open, you took a deep breath and went in.

The apartment he'd chosen today was on the third floor of one of those white-brick buildings that had been all the rage a few decades back. Once they got covered with all the filth and grime of the city, they didn't look so hot anymore, and landlords discovered they cost a fortune to clean, so they just let them revert to the jungle. Some of these buildings still had doormen, but not the one he'd chosen. This one was sandwiched between two red-brick walk-ups. He preferred a building with access to structures on either side, rather than a corner one. When there were adjoining buildings, if ever push came to shove you had rooftop escape routes.

The backyard here was uncommonly still this afternoon.

He thought at first something might be wrong, everything so still. The way a forest went suddenly still whenever a predator approached. He stood in the tunnel leading from the steps into the yard itself, garbage cans already in for the night at three-thirty in the afternoon, lined up along the walls of the tunnel, faint whiff of garbage here, everything so still. He waited. If the super or anyone else was prowling the backyard, he'd do his city-inspector routine and disappear. What he usually did, a building like this one, he went in through the fire escape and then took the elevator on his way out, if there was one. Otherwise, he walked down the stairs and strolled out through the lobby. He never went in with anything but a small suitcase containing his tools and the box of chocolate chip cookies he'd baked that morning. He was holding that suitcase in his right hand now.

He kept waiting.

It was very hot here in the tunnel. He moved to the very end of it where he had a better view of the yard, white sheets hanging limply overhead on a breezeless afternoon. Somewhere a radio was going. He loved the intimacy back here.

Well, he thought, let's boldly go, and stepped out into brilliant sunshine. The yard was empty. The radio was playing an opera, he didn't know which one. He moved swiftly toward the fire escape he had located on his last reconnaissance mission, jumped up for the hanging ladder, pulled it down, and began climbing in almost the same motion. The windows on the first- and second-floor landings were closed. He walked quickly past them, and climbed to the third floor. The tenor was reaching for a high note. It hung on the summer air, liquid and pure, and then fell with a dying grace.

He crouched outside the window, listening intently.

The apartment was still.

He tried the window gently. Like a skilled craftsman, he knew better than to force anything. He always tried it delicately, seeing if it would ease open at a touch. Sometimes, he got lucky. The window slid open under his hands, but an unlocked window didn't mean an apartment was empty. He waited, listening. He had read someplace that professional burglars always went in through a door. Subverted the alarm, picked the lock, went in that way. Burglars who went in windows were supposed to be junkie burglars, your smash-and-grab types. He was not a junkie, but he was most certainly a burglar. In fact, he was a *professional* burglar going in through a window right this very minute, Beam me down, Scottie, he thought, and stepped through and dropped softly to the floor.

He was in a dining room.

The apartment was dim, not a light burning, no sunlight streaming through the east-facing windows at this hour of the day. Still as a tomb. Just what one would expect at three-thirty in the afternoon, occupants off working or shopping, place all to himself. He kept listening. Every minute he was inside, he listened. Never knew when someone might be coming home unexpectedly. He heard an elevator moving up the shaft. Heard a telephone ringing in an apartment somewhere on the floor. Heard the muffled voice of an answering machine picking up. Listened. At last, he took a chamois cloth from the small suitcase, and turned back to the window, and wiped the sill behind him, and the sash inside and out.

He never started in a dining room because he didn't know anything about expensive dinnerware, and silverware was heavy to carry and often difficult to fence. He never stole television sets, either, because that was a sure way of getting a hernia, struggling a heavy TV set out of the building. He waited a moment longer, and then, still carrying the suitcase, he moved toward a closed door at the end of the room. Again, he moved cautiously. Turned the knob slowly and gently, eased the door open, and stepped into a long corridor running left and right from the open door.

To the left were walls bearing framed photographs. At the end of the corridor, there was a closed door. To the right, there was an open door leading into a kitchen. People sometimes hid jewelry in ice cube trays, he wondered if he should give the fridge a shot first. Listened again. Someone turning a water faucet on either next door or above. Off again. Silence again, except for what he long ago learned to identify as ambient room noise.

He decided to try what he guessed was a bedroom behind the closed door at the end of the corridor. The bedroom was where you usually hit the jackpot. This was where the man of the house kept his watches and his cuff links, the lady kept her bracelets and necklaces and rings. Cash, too, you'd find in dresser drawers or even old shoe boxes. Rich people took their valuables to banks and put them in safe-deposit boxes. Bedrooms were the vaults of the lower middle class and the poor.

The photographs on the wall were family pictures, most of them black-and-white, more recent ones in color. A blonde woman and her obvious husband were the framed stars of weddings and graduations and birthday parties and picnics, and other indoor and outdoor events Cookie Boy could not nor did not care to iden-tify. Walking softly past and through the smiling faces on either side of him, he knew he was marching through a history not his own, and one he somehow resented. By the time he reached the door at the end of the hall, he was mildly annoyed, although he could not have clearly explained why to anyone, least of all him-self.

He took the knob in his hand and gently twisted it.

He eased the door open.

A woman was naked and flat on her back on the bed, legs and arms widespread. A man was between her legs, similarly naked.

Cookie Boy's heart leaped into his throat.

He stood unseen in the open doorway, transfixed, scarcely dar-ing to breathe.

He was backing away when the couple decided to change posi-tions. The man rolled off of her, turning as he did. The woman sat up. They both saw Cookie Boy in the very same instant. The woman was the blonde who'd featured so prominently in most of the photographs lining the wall outside. In her late forties, Cookie Boy guessed, with a round face and wide surprised blue eyes. The man, however, was *not* the one in so many of the photos outside, the smiling, dark-eyed, mustached man so obviously her husband. In fact, the man naked in bed with her was hardly a man at all. He was instead a boy of sixteen or seventeen with flaming red hair and a freckled face and eyes as blue and as surprised as the woman's.

Cookie Boy had stumbled into a matinee with the delivery boy. He had walked smack into a burlesque skit, which might have been comical if he hadn't been here to burglarize the apartment.

"Oh my God!" the woman yelled, as well she might have since she'd never seen Cookie Boy in her life and here he was standing in her bedroom door holding a suitcase in his right hand, as if he were checking into a hotel, and here she was in bed with a sweaty kid named Jerry whose last name she didn't even know, while her husband was toiling downtown in the law offices of Hamlin, Gerstein and Konstantine, whose first names she sometimes couldn't remember, like now.

"Don't get nervous," Cookie Boy said. "I'm out of here."

But the delivery boy had other ideas.

Cookie Boy could not later clearly remember the flow of events that followed. He supposed the initial impetus had something to do with the high level of testosterone in teenage boys especially when they got excited. What happened was the kid jumped off the bed like Spider Man himself, hurling himself on Cookie Boy's back just as he was turning to flee.

"Jerry, let him *go!*" the blonde yelled.

"Call the cops, Mrs. Cooper!" the kid yelled. But Mrs. Cooper wasn't about to call any cops because here she was naked in bed with little Jerry here at three-thirty in the afternoon, why the hell would she want *cops* here? Why not sell tickets instead? "Call the cops!" he yelled again, hanging on tight to Cookie Boy, which forced him to ram his elbow backward into the kid's gut. The last thing he wanted here was physical combat of any nature, but Jerry grabbed his shoulder, and spun him around, and brought up his fists in the classic street fighter's pose, naked, however, freckled, and still wearing an erection you might have thought would have disappeared by now, but apparently the fight was keeping him excited.

The blonde hadn't yet screamed. Cookie Boy kept hoping she wouldn't scream. All he wanted to do was get out of this apartment and out the front door and down the steps to the street. But the kid kept swinging as if trying to prove he was Mrs. Cooper's true champion and defender, punching repeatedly at Cookie Boy's face, hurting him now, jabbing at his eyes and his nose, drawing blood from the nose, a torrent of blood, causing Cookie Boy to see red at last, literally. The woman also saw all that blood—and panicked. She didn't scream yet, but she panicked. This was the most dangerous moment, the woman panicking. But Cookie Boy didn't realize this because he was too busy trying to keep the delivery boy out of his face.

Blood was pouring steadily from his nose. Jerry kept jabbing at his eyes, trying to close them. Mrs. Cooper was scrabbling across the bed on her hands and knees now, naked, scooting for the night table beside the bed, but Cookie Boy didn't see this. He kept trying to defend himself from this little prick with the hard-on, but his left eye was already punched shut, and the kid was working steadily on the right. There was a phone on the night table, but Mrs. Cooper wasn't going for the phone. Mrs. Cooper was opening the drawer in the night table. She was taking a gun from the night-table drawer. From his still miraculously open right eye, Cookie Boy saw the gun, and now *he* panicked, because what was supposed to have been a very simple burglary was turning into something quite messy.

"You dumb *fuck!*" he yelled, and flailed out at the kid, moving inside his punishing fists, getting in close, and bringing his knee up sharp and hard into the kid's balls. Like magic, the erection folded and so did the kid. Doubled over, moaning, he backed away, one hand clutching his groin, the other extended in mute supplication. Cookie Boy turned toward the blonde.

"Put down the piece, lady," he said.

The gun was shaking in her hand.

"Put it *down!*" he shouted.

"*Shoot* him!" Jerry yelled, and then began moaning again.

Cookie Boy moved toward the blonde, his hand extended.

"Please," he said. "Give me the gun. Please, lady. No trouble. Please."

He wanted to tell her he'd been on television last night.

"No, trouble, please," he said, and the gun went off.

Cookie Boy ducked, though he didn't need to, turning away from the blast at the same time. The shot missed him by a country mile, but it took Jerry in the center of his chest, slamming him back against the dresser, where he knocked over a framed picture of Mrs. Cooper and her dark-eyed, mustached husband before he slid to the floor. This was Cookie Boy's worst nightmare realized, a burglary gone sour, a kid collapsing to the floor with blood spurting from his chest and his eyes rolling back into his head, a fucking felony *murder* even if he wasn't the one who'd pulled the trigger. He whirled on the woman again, the blonde, Mrs. Cooper, whatever the fuck her name was, and he said, "Give me the gun, lady! *Now!*" but the stupid cunt was on her knees in the center of the bed, her eyes wide, the gun shaking in both hands, the gun pointed right at his head, and he knew if she fired again she would kill him for sure.

He made a flying leap for the bed and the blonde and the gun in her hands, grabbing for both hands, the right hand with her finger inside the trigger guard, the left hand wrapped around it, rolling over onto the bed with his hands covering both hers, the blonde naked, blood from his nose spattering her and the wall behind the bed, a shot went off, knocking plaster from the ceiling. He was almost crying now. The blonde had been caught in bed with a teenager and he was dead across the room now and she didn't know what to do, she didn't know what to do. He dared not let go of her hands because the gun was between them like an uninvited guest and her finger was still inside the trigger guard and her eyes were wild and her mouth was shaking and she was smeared with blood and crazy with fear, and the gun went off again.

He felt her going limp against him.

"Lady?" he said.

And rolled her off of him.

"Lady?" he said again.

And looked into her dead blue eyes.

"Oh shit," he said.

He could not leave the apartment looking like this. There were two dead people here in the bedroom with him and his instinct was to get the hell out of here fast, but if he went into the street covered with blood this way, he'd stop traffic. But suppose the shots had been heard?

He was trembling.

His nose was still bleeding.

He cupped his hand under it to keep the blood from spilling onto the sheets, but they were already covered with blood, his and the blonde's, Mrs. Cooper, he had once known a redhead named Connie Cooper, oh Jesus, how had this gone so wrong?

He kept waiting for a knock on the front door.

Someone surely must have heard the shots.

Wasn't there a super in this building?

But he couldn't go out looking like this.

So he waited.

He could hear a clock ticking someplace in the apartment. He looked at his watch. Ten minutes to four. Was that all it had taken? Twenty minutes? All this blood in only twenty minutes? He had to get out of here before people started coming home from work, the husband with the mustache, Jesus, he had to get out of here!

His nose was still bleeding.

He found the bathroom, and wadded some toilet paper inside his upper lip the way his mother had taught him to do whenever he had a nosebleed, and then he took off all his clothes, dripping blood everywhere, and ran a shower. He washed himself clean and toweled himself off, and then he went back into the bedroom and searched the dresser for a pair of the husband's undershorts, and socks, and a shirt. The kid with the freckles was lying on his back on the floor in front of the dresser. His cock looked all shriveled now. Cookie Boy found a pair of jeans in the closet and put those on, too. There was blood all over his Reeboks, so he borrowed a pair of loafers from the husband, which were too big for him, but that was better than too tight. He packed all his own clothes in the suitcase with his tools and the little white box of chocolate chip cookies.

He knew he could not leave the box behind; it would irrevocably link him to a pair of murders. He wasn't an amateur, he never took foolish risks, he wasn't in this for the goddamn glamour and glory. He took a single cookie from the box, and closed the lid. He bit into the cookie, and then snapped the suitcase shut, and picked it up. It seemed suddenly heavy. As he left the room, he felt he was somehow breaking with tradition, and by so doing erasing a part of his past and therefore a part of himself.

In the hallway outside the bedroom, he bit into the cookie again. Standing there surrounded by family photos recording a past not his own, he munched on the cookie, savoring its texture and flavor, pleased that he had baked it himself, sorry he could not share it. Surrounded by strangers frozen in time, he chewed on the cookie, and finally swallowed the last of it. Without looking back, he walked swiftly to the front door.

His ear to the wood, he listened for several moments. Then he draped the chamois over the knob before opening the door. Pulled the door shut the same way. Wiped the outside knob just for good measure. Went down the stairs, and across the lobby, and into the street.

It was beginning to cool off a little.

He wondered if he'd be on television again tonight.

7.

O NOW THERE WERE *THREE* OF THEM IN THE SPACE OF FIVE DAYS, WHICH IF YOU AVERAGED THEM OUT CAME TO SOMETHING like 219 homicides a year in this precinct alone. This was about right in that some 981 murders were committed in the city the year before, and if the low-crime precincts averaged 15 or 20 a year that was a lot. Which didn't make the boys of the old Eight-Seven any happier.

The first nun joke surfaced at the meeting that Wednesday morning in Lieutenant Byrnes's office. They all knew it would only be a matter of time before the nun jokes started, and they were somehow not surprised that Andy Parker told the first of them. They were all assembled in the loot's office, waiting from him to come back from the toilet down the hall. Perhaps it was the lieutenant's whereabouts that prompted the subject matter of the joke.

"This nun is driving along in her car, and she runs out of gas," Parker said, "have you heard this one?"

Nobody had heard it.

"So she walks half a mile or so to the nearest gas station and buys a gallon of gas, but the gas-station guy hasn't got anything to put it in but a chamber pot. The nun doesn't care, she just wants to get her car going again. So she carries the gas in the chamber pot back to the car, and she takes off the gas cap and is pouring the gas in when a guy passing by stops his car and says, 'I sure wish I had *your* faith, Sister.'"

"I don't get it," Kling said.

"The guy thinks she's pouring piss in the gas tank," Parker said.

"Why does he think that?" Willis asked.

He was the shortest detective on the squad, intense and wiry, here in the lieutenant's office this morning because he and Parker had caught the bloody bedroom squeal the night before.

"Cause she's pouring the gas from a pisspot," Parker said.

"I thought you said a chamber pot," Meyer said.

"That's what a chamber pot *is*, a pisspot," Parker said.

"Let me get this straight," Carella said. "Is this an English joke?"

"It's an *American* joke," Parker said.

"Then why'd you call it a chamber pot?"

"Instead of a pisspot," Kling said, agreeing.

"If it's an English joke," Brown said, "you should have said petrol instead of gas."

"Also," Meyer said, "why didn't she just pee in the tank instead of going all the way to the gas station to get a pisspot to pee in?"

"She *doesn't* pee in the pisspot," Parker said. "The gas station guy puts *gas* in it."

"He farts in it?" Carella said, and Parker finally got it.

"You fuckin animals," he said. "Guy can't even tell an honest joke around here."

"I still don't get it," Kling said.

"Yeah, fuck you," Parker said.

The door opened and Byrnes walked in. "Sorry I kept you waiting," he said.

"Were you down at the gas station?" Brown asked.

"Pissing away a fortune?" Meyer said.

"What's this about?" Byrnes said.

"English humor," Carella said.

"Very funny," Byrnes said, and walked briskly to his desk. He was a burly man with iron-gray hair and an air of impatience, especially when two fresh bodies had shown up in his precinct the night before. "What've we got?" he asked.

"Which case?" Parker asked.

There were three cases on the table this morning. The murders the night before, the nun murder, and the Cookie Boy burglaries.

"You're up, so speak," Byrnes said.

"We figure the lady of the house was making it with the delivery boy from the liquor store up the street," Parker said. "Might've been a three-way, we don't know. Either that, or an intruder. There was a trail of blood going down the hall and all over the bathroom. We've got samples, we ever catch anybody."

"Where was the husband?" Byrnes asked.

If there'd been a third party at the scene, this was the only question to ask.

"At work downtown."

"Witnesses?"

"Hundreds."

"Scratch the husband. What else have you got?"

"Lab should be getting back to us sometime today on the scene sweep. Woman on the third floor told us she heard what she thought were backfires at around three-thirty, four o'clock. Otherwise nobody heard anything or saw anything."

"Stay on the lab," Byrnes said.

"I've already got a call in to them," Willis said.

"What's with Mr. Cookie Boy?" Byrnes asked.

"Quiet yesterday. Maybe he's resting," Kling said.

"We'll be hitting the pawnshops again today," Meyer said. "Some of the stuff on the list is unique . . ."

"Like what?"

"A carved lapis brooch. Lady gave us a good picture of it. Enameled Chinese beads. A wooden snuffbox. Stuff like that. If he's already hocked any of it, we may get lucky."

"Important guy like him, he's probably got a fence," Parker said.

"He's important only because television's making him a hero," Byrnes said. "Otherwise, he's a small-time punk."

"Tell me about it," Meyer said.

"What's with the nun?"

"Andy's got a good nun joke," Carella said. "Tell him your nun joke."

"Yeah, fuck you," Parker said.

"It's an *English* nun joke," Kling said.

"Petrol in a chamber pot," Willis said.

Parker shook his head in disgust.

"The nun," Byrnes prodded.

"She was worried about money," Carella said.

"Who isn't?"

"This is recent."

"How recent?"

"First revealed it to another nun on the eleventh."

"Also, she received some kind of letter," Brown said.

"*What* kind of letter?"

"We don't know."

"Something predicting a decision she'd already made," Carella said.

"Predicting?"

"Well . . . it does sound mystical, I know."

"*What* decision?"

"We don't know."

"Where *is* this letter?"

"We don't know."

"Someone broke into her apartment the day after the murder," Brown said. "Wiped the place out."

"Looking for the letter?"

"Maybe."

"The killer?"

"Maybe."

"How'd you find out about this letter?"

"Priest named Father Clemente mentioned it," Carella said. "She told him about it."

"Where does the priest fit in?"

"He's a friend. She had a lot of friends. We're working them now."

"What's your thinking so far?"

"Blackmail," Brown said.

"*Blackmail?* Why?"

"That's what we're trying to find out."

"What could anyone hope to extort from a nun?" Byrnes asked. "They're *poor,* aren't they?"

"That's the catch," Brown agreed.

"Anyway, you blackmail people only if they've got something to hide," Byrnes said.

"She did have something to hide," Carella said.

"What?"

"Breast implants."

"How do you hide big tits?" Parker asked, and laughed at his own rich humor.

"Is this a joke?" Byrnes said.

"I wish," Carella said.

"Breast implants," Byrnes said, and shook his head. "When did she have 'em done?"

"Blaney thinks within the past three to four years."

"Was she a nun at the time?"

"Been a nun for the past *six.*"

"Working in 'The Vatican Follies,'" Parker said, and laughed again.

"Hit your list of doctors," Byrnes said. "Reach back five, six years, find out who did the job. Find out why a nun wanted bigger tits to begin with. This is just what the archbishop needs, breast implants. He's already screaming up a high mass."

"How wide do you want to go?"

"Stick with the city for now. Where's she from originally?"

"Philadelphia."

"Try there next, see if that's where she bought the tits. Then reach out to wherever she entered the church."

"San Diego."

"But start here, we're not made of money. Andy, Hal, this bloodbath is just what television's been looking for, let's clean it up fast. Meyer, Bert, give them a hand on it. Put The Cookie Boy on the back burner. Small-time punk doesn't deserve our attention right now."

But that was before the lab reported that the dirt and dust they'd vacuumed up from the Cooper bedroom and the hallway outside had included cookie crumbs and several small specks of chocolate.

THERE WERE A HUNDRED AND FIFTY-NINE board-certified plastic surgeons in Isola. Sixteen in Calm's Point. Eleven in Riverhead. Nine in Majesta. Six in Bethtown. They sent out flyers to all of them, requesting information on a woman named either Mary Vincent or Kate Cochran who may have had breast implant surgery performed within the past five years.

Then they sat back to wait.

WEDNESDAY WAS DR. MICHAEL PAINE'S DAY OFF. No hospital, no office hours, just a day of leisure. Until the cops arrived. They found him in the locker room of the Tarleton Hills Country Club, where he'd just showered and changed into street clothes after four sets of tennis. He was now wearing beige linen slacks and a lime green T-shirt, tan Italian loafers, no socks. He seemed annoyed that the detectives had tracked him down here, but he asked nonetheless if they'd like a cup of coffee or something and then led them to the clubhouse overlooking the swimming pool. They sat at a green metal table shaded with a yellow umbrella.

Paine was a good-looking man in his mid-forties, unfortunately named for a doctor, but then again he'd chosen his own profession, and it was a good thing he wasn't a dentist. He asked if they'd rather have a drink instead, and when they declined, he ordered a gin and tonic for himself and two coffees for the gentlemen, please, Betsy. This was eleven o'clock in the morning. The pool at this hour was full of mothers and their screaming little kiddies. Both detectives had children of their own. Indulgently, they raised their voices to shout over the shrieking and splashing from the pool. The yellow umbrella cast a brilliant glow on the green metal tabletop.

"It's nice of you to make time for us on your day off," Carella said.

Paine merely nodded.

"We just have a few questions we want to ask about the evening you spent with Mary Vincent."

"That would've been the fifteenth," Brown said. "A Saturday night."

"Yes," Paine said.

"Six days before she was killed," Carella said.

Betsy arrived with the gin and the two coffees. Paine poured tonic water from the bottle. Brown put two teaspoons of sugar in his coffee, spiked it with milk. Carella drank his black. The kids in the pool were squealing up a symphony.

"Can you tell us what occasioned that meeting?" Carella asked.

"It wasn't a *meeting*. We had dinner together."

"I meant . . ."

"We met at a restaurant called Il Mediterraneo. We went there often. Mary liked it a lot."

"Who paid for the meal?" Brown asked.

"What?"

Nun worried about money, Brown thought, who paid for dinner that night was a pretty good question.

"Did *she* pay? Did *you* pay? Did you *split* the . . ."

"I paid," Paine said. "Whenever we had dinner together, I paid."

"Was having dinner with her a usual thing?"

"We'd see each other . . ." Paine shrugged. "Once a month? Sometimes more often. We were good friends."

"How long have you known her?" Carella asked.

"I met her at St. Margaret's when she first began working there."

"About six months ago, would that be?"

"Yes. More or less."

"How'd you happen to ask her out?" Brown asked.

"Ask her *out?*" Paine said. "She was a nun."

Brown wondered why the good doctor was getting on his high horse. Man took someone to dinner once a month, sometimes more often, what the hell was it if not taking her *out?*

"I'm sorry, sir," he said. "What would you call it?"

"It's the connotation that bothers me," Paine said, and nodded curtly, and sipped at his drink again, and then put the glass down rather too emphatically. "We were working colleagues and good friends. Taking her to dinner was not taking her *out.*"

"How'd you first happen to take her to dinner then?" Brown asked.

Paine looked at him.

"Sir?" Brown said.

"One of her patients, a woman with a stomach CA, was dying and in pain. Mary was having a personal problem with it. We went across the street to the deli, to talk it over."

"And this became a regular thing, is that right?" Carella said. "Having dinner together?"

"Yes. As I said, once or twice a month. Mary was good company. I enjoyed being with her."

"Did you ever talk about *other* things? Aside from your work?"

"Yes, of course."

"On the fifteenth, for example, did she happen to mention . . . was that the *last* time you saw her, doctor?"

"Socially, yes. I saw her at the hospital, of course, whenever I was there."

"Did you see her on the day she was killed?"

"Yes, I did."

"When was this?"

"The twenty-first, wasn't it? When she was killed?"

"Yes. But I meant, did you see her at any specific *time?*"

"Well, *several* times during the day. Doctors and nurses cross paths all the time."

"When's the very *last* time you saw her?" Brown asked.

"Just before the shift ended. She said she was going out for a cup of coffee with Helen, asked if I'd like to join them."

"Helen Daniels, would that be?"

"Yes. One of the nurses at St. Margaret's."

"Did she mention where she might be heading after that?"

"No, she didn't."

"Doctor, if we could, I'd like to get back to that night of the fifteenth. Did Mary say anything about . . . ?"

"You know," Paine said, "I hate to ask this . . . but am I a *suspect* in this thing?"

"No, sir, you're not," Carella said.

"Then why all these questions?"

"Well," Carella said, "either Mary went for a walk in the park and was a random victim of someone who stole her handbag, or else she deliberately went to that park to *meet* the person who killed her. Several people we talked to said she seemed very concerned about . . ."

"What's any of this got to do with me?"

"Nothing, sir. We're only trying . . ."

"I mean, why all these *questions?*"

They didn't know why he was so suddenly agitated. They'd probably questioned ten thousand two-hundred and eighty-eight people in their joint careers as police officers, and they were used to all sorts of guarded responses, but why had Dr. Paine become so defensive all at once? Both detectives were suddenly alert. Bells didn't go off, whistles didn't shrill over the noise of the shrieking kids in the pool. But though neither of them revealed any change in attitude—if anything, they were more solicitous than they had been a moment ago—they nonetheless looked at the man differently now.

"We thought you might be able to expand on what we'd heard from other friends of Mary," Carella said.

"Well, there it is again," Paine said.

Yes, there it is again, Carella thought.

"Sir?" he said.

"The emphasis on the word 'friends.' Is it impossible to believe that a man actually might be *friends* with a woman who's taken vows of chastity?"

"We think that's entirely possible, sir."

"I mean, does it have to be turned into some kind of dirty *joke?*"

"Sir, no one . . ."

"Is this still the 1830s?"

"We're only trying . . ."

"Are nuns still the butt of bad pornography?"

"Sir, we . . ."

"Mary was an attractive woman, there's no denying it. But to suggest . . . I mean . . . look, forget it."

The noise from the pool seemed overwhelming in the sudden silence under the bright yellow umbrella.

"We've been told she was concerned about money," Carella said, changing his approach. He caught a small, almost imperceptible nod of approval from Brown. "Did she mention that to you?"

"No," Paine said.

He had drained the glass of gin, and now he was toying with the lime wedge in it, poking it with the plastic straw, his eyes averted.

"Where'd you go after dinner that night?" Brown asked.

"Back to her place."

"Did she mention anything about money problems while you were there?" Carella said.

"No."

"Or anytime that night?" Brown said.

"No."

"Mention a letter she may have received?"

"No."

"What time did you leave her, Doctor?"

"Around ten."

"Where'd you go?"

"Straight home."

"Dr. Paine, could we go back to that *first* time you had dinner together? You said it was at the deli across the street. Could you tell us a little more about that, please?"

Paine sighed heavily.

"I was at the hospital late one night," he said, "and so was Mary. I ran into her coming out of the nurses' lounge, in tears. I asked her if something was wrong, and she said, 'No, nothing,' but she kept crying so hard I thought she might be hysterical. It was plain to me that *whatever* it was, she didn't want to discuss it there in the hospital, so I suggested we go across the street for a cup of coffee. She readily accepted. Actually, she seemed relieved that she could talk it over with someone. What it was . . ."

. . . there was this elderly woman on the ward, Mrs. Rosenberg, Ruth Rosenberg, I believe it was. She was very seriously ill, a cancer patient, as I told you, who had perhaps two or three weeks to live, it was that bad. She wasn't a very nice person. I didn't know her before she got sick, of course, she may have been an angel, who knows? But she was definitely unpleasant now, moaning every minute of the day, snapping at doctors and nurses alike, a totally obnoxious human being.

You'd stop in her room just to be pleasant, ask how she was doing, for example, and she'd yell "How do you *think* I'm doing? Look at me! Does it look like I'm doing fine?" It was hard to have sympathy for a person like that, even though her situation was grave. Or a nurse would bring in her pain med, and she'd yell "It's about time! Where the hell have you been?" A most difficult woman.

I wasn't the physician who'd prescribed her medication, I'm not quite sure what it was now, probably some sort of morphine derivative, most likely MS Contin every six hours. That would have been usual in such a case, one of the morphine sulfates. When Mary told me about the woman, she said she couldn't stand her shrieks of pain any longer, her moaning all day long, the woman was a human being and one of God's creatures, we should be able to *do* something to ease her suffering. Yes, I remember now. She was on a Duragesic patch as well, absorbing Fentanyl all day long, probably fifty, sixty micrograms an hour, plus the morphine, of course.

Mary thought Mrs. Rosenberg should be getting the morphine dose every *four* hours instead of the prescribed six. She discussed this with the woman's doctor, told him she was in no danger of becoming an addict, she was going to *die* in a few weeks, anyway, couldn't they *please,* in the name of *God,* increase the regularity?

The doctor told Mary he thought Mrs. Rosenberg was going for secondary gain. Wanted them to feel sorry for her. Wanted more attention from them. Mary said, "So why *not?* What's *wrong* with a little attention? Her family's abandoned her, nobody comes to see her, she just lies in bed all day, moaning in pain, begging for medication. What on earth is *wrong* with giving her what she so desperately needs?" Well, the doctor told Mary he might be willing to prescribe an additional milligram in the regular six-hour dose, which of course was minimal, a token gesture. But he flatly refused to medicate the woman every *four* hours. Mary was furious.

"She told all this to me over hamburgers and coffee in the deli. I promised I'd talk to the doctor in the morning, see what I could do."

Paine sighed again.

"But by morning, Mrs. Rosenberg was dead."

"Who was the doctor?" Brown asked.

"I've deliberately avoided using his name," Paine said.

"If Mary harbored any ill feelings . . ."

"I'm sure she didn't, she wasn't that sort of person. In fact, I did finally talk to him about denying medication, which I consider stupid, by the way, and he saw the error of his ways."

"In any case . . ."

"Excuse me, sir."

The waitress who'd brought their beverages was standing by the table again, a leather folder in her hand.

"Whenever you're ready, sir," she said. "And sir?"

"Yes, Betsy?"

"Your wife just called. Said not to forget her racket that was re-strung."

"Thank you, Betsy," Paine said, and signed the check.

The detectives said nothing until he'd handed the leather folder back to her and she'd walked away.

Then Brown said, "The doctor's name, sir?"

"Winston Hall," Paine said.

"So ON THE ONE HAND," Brown said, "we got the man heading the ward *rhapsodizing* about Mary, sweetest woman in the world, oh dear, how I will miss her, spreading light and joy everywhere she walked, singing to all the patients, but he forgets to mention she's breaking his balls about medication! She probably hated his guts for letting Mrs. Rosenberg die in pain."

He was behind the wheel. Whenever he got agitated, he drove somewhat recklessly. Carella hoped he wouldn't run over any old ladies.

"And on the other hand, we got *another* doctor who's seeing a woman not his wife sometimes twice a month," Brown said. "Makes no nevermind to me she's a nun. Far as I'm concerned, he's married and seeing another woman. On a Saturday *night*, the last time! A *married* man!"

"Red light ahead," Carella said.

"I see it. Another thing, he *knew* he went too far," Brown said. "That's why he clammed up all at once."

"It wasn't the place to pursue it, anyway," Carella said.

"I know that. Otherwise I'd've jumped in. Do I look shy?"

"Oh, yes. Timid, in fact. We may have to put him in the box later. Meanwhile, all we've got is a man who found a nun attractive and won't admit it to himself."

"Or to his *wife*, either, I'll bet," Brown said.

"You're beginning to sound like my mother," Carella said.

"And what's the matter with that *Hall* jackass, anyway? How's it any skin off his nose he gives the old lady an extra dose? She's gonna die, anyway, am I right?"

"Watch the road, Artie!"

"Letting an old lady die in pain that way."

"Artie . . ."

"I *see* it. Never once mentioned he and Mary had a little *contre*temps back then, did he? Way he tells it, everything was sweetness and light on the ward, Mary flitting around like Sally Field, never mind she could blow her stack when she wanted to, am I right?"

"Artie, that was a baby carriage."

"That's okay, I didn't hit it, did I?"

"You came damn close."

"We oughta talk to that man again. We also oughta run down to Philly, talk to Mary's brother too damn busy to bury her."

"Philly's closed on Wednesdays," Carella said, making reference to one of the countless Philadelphia jokes in the repertoire, something the stand-up comic Vincent Cochran might have appreciated, provided he wasn't still asleep at twelve-fifteen in the afternoon.

It was nine-fifteen A.M. in California.

Carella wondered what time Sister Carmelita Diaz had got home from Rome yesterday.

"LADY NAMED ANNA HAWLEY waiting upstairs for you," Sergeant Murchison said.

Carella didn't know anybody named Anna Hawley.

"Me?" he said.

"You," Murchison said.

The muster room of the Eight-Seven was unusually quiet that Wednesday afternoon. Murchison sat behind the high mahogany muster desk like a priest behind an altar, reading the morning paper, bored to tears because the phone hadn't rung in ten minutes.

Across the room, a man from Maintenance and Repair—one of the two who'd been here last Friday, when the guy went ape shit in the cage upstairs—was checking out the walkie-talkies on the wall rack because they weren't recharging properly. The air conditioner he and his partner had fixed was now functioning, but barely. Murchison was sweating profusely in his short-sleeved uniform shirt.

"She say about what?" Carella asked.

"The dead nun," Murchison said, and went back to his paper.

It was even hotter upstairs than it had been in the muster room, perhaps because the window units here were older than the ones below. Anna Hawley was a woman in her early twenties, Carella guessed, sitting in a chair alongside his desk in a blue cotton skirt and white blouse, her handbag resting near the In-Out basket. Across the room, Meyer and Kling, in shirtsleeves, were working the phones, contacting pawnshops again now that their burglar might have been a double murderer. The squadroom seemed quieter than usual, too. Carella wondered where the hell everybody was.

"Miss Hawley?" he said.

The woman turned. Short blonde hair, green eyes, apprehensive look. Lipstick a light shade of red. Foot jiggling as if she had to pee.

"Detective Carella," he said. "My partner, Detective Brown."

Carella sat in his own chair behind the desk. Brown pulled one up. They both kept their jackets on, in deference to their visitor. At the windows, the air conditioners clanked noisily.

"I understand you wanted to see us about Mary Vincent," Carella said.

"Well, Kate Cochran, yes," she said.

Soft voice, slight quaver to it. The detectives waited. Her nervousness was apparent, but police stations often did that to people. And yet, she was here voluntarily. Carella gave it a moment longer, and then he said, "Was there something you wanted to tell us about her murder?"

"Well, no, not her murder."

"Then what, Miss Hawley?"

"I wanted to make sure Vincent didn't leave you with the wrong impression."

"Are you talking about Vincent Cochran?" Carella asked.

The stand-up comic in Philadelphia, the brother who no longer cared to see his sister, dead *or* alive, thanks.

"Mary Vincent's brother?"

"Yes," Anna said. "Well, Kate's brother."

"What about him?"

"Well, I know you spoke to him a few days ago . . ."

The twenty-second, according to Carella's notebook.

". . . and I'm afraid you might have got the wrong idea about him. You see, *everybody* was against it."

"Against what?" Brown asked.

"Her becoming a nun. It wasn't just Vincent. *All* of us told her it was a stupid idea. All the family, all her friends."

"And what are you, Miss Hawley? Family or friend?"

"I'm a friend."

"Kate's friend? Or her brother's?"

"Vincent's my *boy*friend," she said.

"But you knew Kate as well, is that it?"

"Yes. We grew up together."

"In Philadelphia?"

"Yes. She went to San Diego only after she joined the order. That was another thing. Her having to go all the way out to California. No one liked that very much, I can tell you."

"Why would we get the wrong idea about Mr. Cochran?" Brown asked.

"What he said to you."

"What'd he say?"

"About letting the church bury her."

"He reported that to you, did he?"

"Yes. Well, he was worried you might think . . . well . . . you might think he didn't love her or something."

"Did he ask you to come here?"

"No. Absolutely not. I come into the city regularly, anyway. I'm a freelance copy editor. I deliver work whenever I'm finished with it."

"So when did Mr. Cochran tell you about our conversation with him?"

"Last Saturday night. At the club. He said you'd called that afternoon. Woke him up, in fact. Which was why he sounded so irritated."

"When you say the club . . ."

"Comedy Riot," Anna said.

"Is that where Mr. Cochran does stand-up?"

"Yes. But it was my idea to come here. I didn't want you to think he was still holding a grudge or anything."

"What kind of grudge, Miss Hawley?"

"Well . . . everything. You know."

"Everything?"

"All of it. From the beginning. From when Kate first told the family she wanted to be a nun. Her parents were still alive then, this was right after she graduated from college. I was there the afternoon she told them. Vincent and I were high school sweethearts, you see. This was in January. More than six years ago. I remember it was a very cold day. There was a fire blazing in the living room fireplace. We were all drinking coffee after dinner, sitting around the fireplace, when Kate dropped her bombshell . . ."

"WHAT THE HELL are you *talking* about?" her father shouts.

It is interesting that he has used the word "hell" when his daughter has just told them she wishes to become a nun in the Roman Catholic Church. To Ronald Cochran, who has been a renegade Catholic since the age of thirteen and who considers entering a convent the equivalent of joining a cult like the Hare Krishnas, the words his daughter has just hurled into the glowing warmth of the living room are tantamount to patricide. Ronald Cochran teaches political science at Temple University. His wife is a psychiatrist with a thriving practice. And now . . . *this?* His daughter wants to become a goddamn *nun?*

"You don't mean this," Vincent says.

He is four years his sister's junior, seventeen years old and a high school senior in that cold January more than six years ago. His sister has just told the family and his girlfriend Anna that she wishes to enter the Order of the Sisters of Christ's Mercy as soon as certain formalities have been consummated, the exact word she uses. She expects to begin her novitiate this coming summer, she tells them now. At the mother house in San Luis Elizario, she tells them. Just outside San Diego, she tells them.

"Who's been brainwashing you?" her mother asks.

Dr. Moira Cochran is a Freudian analyst who remembers all too well that the master himself considered religion a "group-obsessional neurosis." That her daughter has now decided she "has a vocation," that her daughter now wishes to become "a bride of Christ" who will swear vows of poverty, chastity, and obedience once she has completed her postulancy and her novitiate . . .

"Is that what you learned at that goddamn school?" she asks.

That "goddamn school" is one of the most prestigious colleges in the United States, and Kate has been graduated from it with honors and a 3.8 index as a political science major and a psychology minor—so much for the token gesture to the old folks at home. In the meantime, because she has a splendid voice and a true love of music, she has joined a choral group in her sophomore year, and then the church choir in her junior year. It is there that she initially meets a visiting nun named Sister Beatrice Camden of the Order of the Sisters of Christ's Mercy, who comes to instruct the choir in a complicated four-part hymn composed by Jacopone da Todi in the thirteenth century.

Kate is hardly a religious person. With a father like Ronald and a mother like Moira, she could never be considered even *faintly* religious. She is singing in the church choir because she loves to sing, but she is also fascinated by Sister Beatrice, who is the first person who ever suggests to her that her voice is perhaps God-given. Well, bullshit, she thinks, and she admits this to her stunned parents and to her brother and his girlfriend . . .

"I mean, my voice is a result of genetic downloading, am I right? So what's this nonsense about it being God-given?"

. . . and yet the notion is somehow exciting, her voice being a gift from God and therefore something more than a mere *human* voice, something rather more exalted instead. When Sister Beatrice asks Kate to join her and some of the other sisters for dinner one night, she recognizes that a sort of recruiting process is beginning, but she's flattered by all the attention. And besides, she begins to realize she *likes* these people. There's an air of dedication about these young women that seems singularly lacking in the college girls all around Kate. The girls she knows are always talking about getting laid or getting married whereas these women in the Order of the Sisters of Christ's Mercy are talking about lives devoted to serving God by *helping* other people. They are talking about a vocation, a ministry, a charism. They are talking about meaningful lives, they . . .

"Meaningful, my *ass!*" Moira shouts in an outburst rare for a psychiatrist trained to listen patiently and never to comment. "You'll be locking yourself away from the rest of the world! You'll be . . ."

"It isn't . . ."

". . . marching backward into the twelfth century!"

"It isn't like that anymore!"

Kate then goes on to explain, to four sets of ears growing increasingly more deaf, that she was given informational books about the order . . .

"Which the sisters call the OSCM, by the way . . ."

. . . as if it's IBM or TWA, a refreshingly modern way of thinking about themselves that forever dispels for Kate any notions of nuns wearing hair shirts. For the past year now . . .

"Is *that* how long this has been going on?" Vincent yells.

. . . she's spent time with the order's Vocation Director, and she's been visiting with the order's Spiritual Director, taking psychological tests, addressing her finances, meeting as well with the Formation Director . . .

"A goddamn *cult!*" her father shouts.

. . . to set up a system for herself, finally creating an individual program best suited to her talents and her needs.

"I'm going to be a nurse," she says. "It's how I can best help people. It's how I can best serve God. I know I'll be sacrificing a home of my own, a family. I know I'll be sacrificing comfort and independence. But as Christ's bride . . ."

"I can't believe this!" Vincent says.

. . . in union with Christ, she will also be sacrificing herself for the redemption of souls. Like Christ, she will live her life in poverty, simplicity, purity, and chastity. And she will forever offer, as only a spouse can, love and solace to His Sacred Heart.

She tells her parents, and her brother, and Anna Hawley that she'll be leaving for the mother house as soon as certain documents have been signed . . .

"You're signing away your life," her mother says.

"This is totally stupid," Vincent says.

"But it's what I'm going to do," Kate says.

"No, you're *not!*" her father shouts.

"Yes, I am," she says calmly. "It's *my* life," she says. "Not yours."

To which, of course, there is no answer.

ANNA HAWLEY PAUSED.

"There was nothing anyone could do to stop her," she said.

"So she left," Carella said.

"Yes. She left. At the end of May."

Again, Anna hesitated.

"I suppose Vincent might have forgiven her sooner or later. But then, of course, her parents were killed."

At his desk across the room, Meyer said into the telephone, "Just hang on to it, sir, we'll be right there. Thanks a lot."

"Killed?" Carella said.

"How?" Brown said.

"Bert, let's go," Meyer said.

"A car crash," Anna said. "On the Fourth of July, last year. Kate's father was driving. They'd been drinking too much."

"Steve, we're off. Piece of jewelry just surfaced."

"Where's the shop?" Kling asked, and followed him out of the squadroom.

"Vincent could never forgive her after that," Anna said.

"Why's that?"

"He blamed her for the accident. It was only after Kate became a nun that they began drinking heavily, you see."

"That's Vincent's reasoning, huh?" Brown said.

"Yes, and he's right," Anna said. "If she'd stayed home, they'd still be alive."

"Uh-huh."

"It was her fault."

"Uh-huh."

"Which is why he wouldn't come up here to claim the body, right?" Carella said.

"That doesn't mean he killed her," Anna said.

Brown was thinking some people should learn when to keep their big mouths shut.

"Sent you instead, right?" he said. "To tell us all this?"

"No, I had to be in the city, anyway."

"You come in every Wednesday?"

"I come in whenever I'm done."

"Done?"

"With the galleys."

"When's the last time you were in, Miss Hawley?"

"Last Friday," she said.

8.I T WAS VERY HOT HERE IN THIS SMALL SHOP
CLUTTERED WITH THE FLOTSAM AND JET-
SAM OF COUNTLESS LIVES FOUNDERING ON
bad times. Meyer and Kling were wearing lightweight sports jackets on this steamy Wednesday at one P.M., but not because they
wished to appear elegantly dressed. The jackets were there to hide
the shoulder holster each was wearing, lest the populace of this
fair city panicked in the streets. The owner of the shop was wearing a white short-sleeved sports shirt open at the throat. A jeweler's
loupe hung on a black silk cord around his neck.

He introduced himself as Manny Schwartz. The name on his license was Emanuel Schwartz. The license, in a black frame, was
hanging on the wall behind him, together with an accordion, a
saxophone, a trombone, several trumpets, a tambourine, and a
ukulele. Meyer wondered if an entire orchestra had come in here
to hock its instruments.

Schwartz took a ring from the case, and handed it across the
counter. "This is what she brought in," he said. "It's Islamic. Ninth
to eleventh century A.D. Origin is probably Greater Syria."

The square signet was engraved with the drawing of a goat or
possibly some other animal with long ears, it was hard to tell. This
was surrounded by engraved petals or leaves, again it was difficult
to tell exactly which. The tapering shank was engraved on both
sides with a pair of snakes, or perhaps crocodiles, flanking a long-
tailed bird. A pair of engraved fish swam upward from the very bottom of the shank toward the signet. Meyer wished he knew what
the talismanic markings meant. It was a sort of cheerful ring. It

made him wonder why there was so much strife in the Middle East.

"What the caliphs did," Schwartz said, "they brought in artisans trained in the Greek and Roman traditions, had them adapt their work to the needs of Arab patrons. This ring was probably commissioned by an upper-class member of society. It was an expensive ring, even back then. Today, it's worth around twelve grand."

"What'd you pay for it?"

"Three thousand. Little did I know it was stolen. Now I can shove it up my ass, right?"

He was referring to the odd legal distinction between a "bona fide purchaser for value" and "a person in knowing possession of stolen goods." Schwartz had read the list of stolen goods the Eight-Seven had circulated, and he now knew that the Syrian ring was hot property. He could have ignored this, gone on to sell the ring at a profit, pretended he'd never seen the list. But if that ring ever got traced back to him, he was looking at a D-felony and a max of two-and-a-third to seven in the slammer. He'd called the police instead, who would now undoubtedly seize the ring as evidence. Some you win, some you lose.

"Did she give you a name?" Meyer asked.

"Yes. But it probably wasn't her real name."

"What name did she give you?"

"Marilyn Monroe."

"What makes you think that wasn't her real name?" Meyer asked.

"Marilyn Monroe?"

"We once arrested a guy named Ernest Hemingway, he wasn't Ernest Hemingway."

"Who was he?"

"He was Ernest Hemingway. What I mean is, he wasn't *the* Ernest Hemingway, he was just someone who happened to be named Ernest Hemingway."

"Who's that?" Schwartz asked. "Ernest Hemingway."

"I'll bet we look in the phone book right this minute," Meyer said, "we'll find a dozen Marilyn Monroes."

"Which wasn't *her* real name, either," Schwartz said.

"What *was* her real name?" Kling asked.

"The girl who brought the ring in?"

"No. Marilyn Monroe."

"I don't know."

"So what'd this woman look like?" Meyer asked. It bothered him now that he couldn't remember what Marilyn Monroe's real name was. Kling had a habit of bringing up annoying little questions that could bug a man all day long.

"She was maybe thirty, thirty-five years old," Schwartz said. "Five-four, weighed a hundred and ten, brown hair, brown eyes, nice trim figure. Wearing shorts and a T-shirt . . . well, this rotten weather. Sandals. Blue sandals."

"You noticed what she had on her *feet?*"

"Woman in shorts, a nice trim figure, you notice her legs and her feet."

"Did she give you an address?"

"She did. Which is why I figured maybe Marilyn Monroe was her real name, after all. I mean, if a person's going to pick a phony name, why such a famous one?"

"That's right," Meyer said.

"Was what I figured."

"Norma Something," Kling said.

"I don't think so," Meyer said.

"Also, she gave me a phone number."

"Did she show you identification?"

"No. She said it was an heirloom she had to hock because she'd left her wallet in a taxi with a lot of money in it."

"You believed her."

"It could happen. This city, *anything* could happen. Besides, I was getting a twelve-thousand-dollar ring for three thousand."

"Ever occur to you it might be stolen?"

"It occurred. It *also* occurred it might only be *lost*. People don't usually report lost items to the police. So if it wasn't reported, it wouldn't show up on any list, am I right? And if it isn't on a list,

then I don't know it's stolen goods and I'm still a bona fide purchaser for value. Was what I thought."

"Can we have the address and phone number she gave you?"

"Sure. You going to take the ring, right?"

"We have to."

"Sure."

"We'll give you a receipt for it."

"Sure," Schwartz said. "Sometimes I wish I wasn't so honest."

"Jean Something?" Kling said.

IT WAS COOLER HERE IN THE PARK. Gentle breezes from the river
blunted the edge of the afternoon heat, promising eventual relief,
perhaps even rain. Carella sat with his sister on a bench overlooking the distant water. Her twin daughters were on the playground
equipment. Cynthia and Melinda, reduced to Cindy and Mindy, as
Carella had dreaded would happen from the moment she named
them. Her older daughter had fared better. Tess, modern and
sleek, for Teresa, which conjured up cobblestoned streets in a
mountaintop village in Potenza. Tess was supervising the twins
now. Seven years old and looking after the little ones. Cindy and
Mindy had been born on the twenty-eighth of July, eleven days after his father was killed. They reminded him of his own twins when
they were small. It occurred to him that his sister was one of the
few people in the world who knew him when he himself was small.
Forty, he reminded himself. In October, you will be forty.

"It was good of you to meet me," Angela said.

"It's no trouble," he said.

It was four o'clock, and he was on his way home, but he'd have
met his sister whenever, wherever, because he loved her to death.
She had specified the park, it would be cooler than her apartment,
she'd said. We have to talk, she'd said. He waited now for her to
begin. In his profession, he was skilled at waiting for people to begin talking.

"It finally looks as if it's going to be a clean break," she said.

She was talking about her divorce. Married for twelve years, and now a divorce. He would always remember the date of her wedding. He had rushed Teddy to the hospital directly from the reception. Twelve years ago this past June. His twins had turned twelve on the twenty-second. And he would be forty in October. Cut it out, he thought. It's not the end of the world. Oh no? he thought.

"Tommy's moving to California. I think he met a girl who lives out there, he's leaving at the end of the month. It'll be better, Steve, I really think so. It's still painful, you know. I mean, whenever he comes by to pick up Tess and the twins, I remember what it used to be like. It's painful, Steve. Divorce is painful."

People who had twins never referred to them as "the kids" or "the children," they were always "the twins." He wondered what that must be like for twins themselves, always to be referred to as *half* of a whole, like a comedy team. The last time he'd seen his brother-in-law was when Tommy had told him he was entering a rehab program. That was after the marriage was shot, after he'd stolen and hocked virtually everything they'd owned, after he'd hit Angela with a closed fist one night when she tried to stop him from taking the twins' silver teething rings that were a gift from Aunt Josie in Florida, Carella wanted to kill him. So now he was moving to California, and Angela thought it would be for the best, which it probably would—but was that why she'd asked to meet him in the park at four o'clock in the afternoon?

He waited.

He was very good at waiting.

"Steve," she said, and drew a deep breath. "Steve, honey, you're not going to like this."

He knew at once what it was. And he knew he was not going to like it, *already* did not like it. But she was his sister, and when he saw the troubled look on her face, he wanted to take her in his arms and say, Hey, come on, Sis, this is me, how bad can it be, huh? But he knew how bad it could be, knew what she was going to tell him, and wondered how he could possibly handle it.

"I know how you feel about Henry," she said, and drew another deep breath. "I know you think he could have sent Sonny Cole to prison, that somehow he screwed up . . ."

"Angela . . ."

"No, please, Steve, let me finish. I've talked to him a lot about the case, and he really did do his best, Steve, he really *was* surprised by some of the stuff the defense . . ."

"He *shouldn't* have been surprised," Carella said. "His job is *not* to be surprised. Sonny Cole killed Papa! And Lowell let him walk."

"So did you, Steve," she said.

Which she shouldn't have thrown back at him because he'd been talking brother to sister when he'd told her about that night in a deserted hallway with only Sonny Cole and a black cop named Randall Wade who kept whispering "Do it" in his ear. He hadn't told that to anyone else in the world but his wife, and now Angela was throwing it back at him. He had done what he'd thought was the right thing. If he had pulled the trigger on Sonny Cole that night . . . no, he couldn't have.

"I believe in the system," he said now.

"So do I."

"I thought the system . . ."

"So did I. But Henry isn't the system. It was the *system* that let Cole walk after Henry did his best to put him away. You have to believe that, Steve."

"Why should I?"

"Because we're moving in together."

"Great," he said. "The man who . . ."

"No."

"*Yes!* He *did* screw up, Angela. That's why Sonny Cole is still out there someplace . . ."

. . . his arm going up now, his finger pointing out over the small hill above the park, his finger stabbing at the near distance . . .

". . . maybe killing somebody *else's* father!"

*   *   *

FROM WHERE SONNY LAY on his belly on the grassy knoll overlooking the park below, he thought at first that Carella had spotted him and was pointing at him. He didn't know who the girl with him on the bench was, but all at once both of them were up on their feet and the girl was hugging him and Carella just stood there looking sort of helpless and foolish and then he . . .

There was something so familiar about the gesture.

. . . he brought his hand up and put it on top of the girl's head, just rested it on top of her head. Watching them, Sonny remembered a time long ago when he had a little sister who'd fallen down and skinned her knee and he'd put his big hand on top of her head just the way Carella was doing with the girl down there in the park, gentling her, soothing her, and he knew all at once that this girl was Carella's younger sister, same as Ginny had been his younger sister.

He didn't know why he was all at once trembling.

He got to his feet, and looked once more down the grassy slope. Carella was taking his sister in his arms now, both of them standing there still as stone, crying maybe, Sonny couldn't tell. Crying maybe for the father he'd killed, maybe crying for him.

He ran off down the other side of the grassy slope, away from the scene below, looking for the green Honda where he'd parked it, thinking I got to do this soon, I got to do this fucking thing *soon*.

CARELLA ASKED THE LONG DISTANCE OPERATOR for time and charges before he placed his call to California. This was police business and he was but a poor overworked, underpaid servant of the law who hoped to be reimbursed if he put in a chit. It was eight o'clock here in the East, and they had just finished eating dinner. Out there in San Luis Elizario, it was five P.M.; he hoped convent nuns didn't start their evening meal early. He hoped they weren't still at vespers or something. He hoped Sister Carmelita Diaz, the major superior of the Order of Sisters of Christ's Mercy was well-rested after her long journey from Rome the day before. He hoped God had whispered in her ear the name of the person who had killed Mary Vincent. Or Kate Cochran, as the case might be.

"Hello?" she said. "Detective Carella?"

"Yes, how are you, Sister?"

"Oh, fine," she said. "A bit of jet lag, but otherwise very good."

There was only the faintest trace of Spanish accent in her voice. For some reason, he visualized a large woman. Tall, big-boned, wide of girth. Wearing the traditional black habit of the order, the way Sister Beryl had at the Riverhead convent. He thought he could hear birds chirping out there in California. He imagined a Spanish-style structure, all stucco and tiles, arches and parapets, a cream-colored edifice, a monument to God built on the edge of the sea.

"Am I hearing birds?" he asked.

"Oh, yes, all sorts of birds, you'd think St. Francis was here on a visit."

He dared not ask how old she was. Her voice sounded quite young and robust. Again, he imagined a large woman, perhaps in her early forties.

"Are you by the sea?" he asked.

"The sea? Oh no. Oh dear no. We're in downtown San Luis Elizario, such as it is. The sea? Dear, no, the sea is forty miles away. Tell me what happened, please. We're positively *numb* out here, we all knew poor Katie so well."

He told her she'd been killed, told her that her body had . . .

"How?" she asked at once.

"Strangled," he said.

. . . told her that Kate's body had been found in a big park here in the middle of the city . . .

"Grover," she said.

"Yes. You've been here?"

"Many times."

. . . here in the middle of the city not far from the police station, actually. This was last Friday night, the twenty-first. He told her he'd been talking to many of her friends and associates, sisters in the order, doctors and nurses she worked with, a priest named Father Clemente . . .

"Our Lady of Flowers," she said.

"Yes."

"A wonderful man."

. . . but that so far they hadn't the faintest clue as to why she'd been killed. Unless there was something about her they yet didn't know. Something she may have revealed to Sister Diaz . . .

"Oh, call me Carmelita, please," she said. "I always feel if I have to call myself 'Sister' to let people know I'm a nun, then I'm not getting Christ's message across. They should realize I'm a nun just by taking one look at me."

"Trouble is, I can't see you," Carella said.

"I'm five-five and I weigh a hundred and sixteen pounds. I have short brown hair and brown eyes, and right now I'm smoking a cigarette and sitting in the sunshine in a small garden outside my office. Which is why you're hearing all the bird racket. What makes you think Kate was hiding something?"

"I didn't suggest that."

"But something about her is troubling you. What is it, Detective?"

"Okay," he said. "We think someone may have been trying to blackmail her."

Carmelita burst out laughing.

Her hearty laugh fortified the image of a large woman in a roomy habit. Five-five, he reminded himself.

"That's absurd," she said. "What could anyone hope to extort from a *nun?*"

Echoes of Lieutenant Peter Byrnes, thank you.

"Then was she in debt? She seemed very concerned about money."

"Are you talking about her budget? I'm afraid she was always complaining about the budget. Never had enough to spend.

Always asked me to loosen up a little. Give me a break here, will you, Carmelita? Let me go buy a good pair of shoes every now and then. The problem may have come from being on the outside. Each sister in the order receives a standard diocesan stipend, you see, in our case ten thousand a year. Half of that comes back here to San Luis, to support the mother house and any sisters who are retired or ill. Kate's salary came here, too. As a licensed practical nurse, she earned almost fifty thousand a year. The mother house budgeted her according to her needs, apportioning enough for her to live on. She *did* take vows of poverty, you know. That doesn't mean she had to starve. But neither does it mean she could live extravagantly."

"Then this wasn't a recent thing? Her complaining about money?"

"Hardly. For a while, though, she was used to handling her own finances. And a person develops a sort of independence on the outside."

Carella had missed this the first time around, but this time it registered.

"What do you mean?" he asked. "It was my understanding that she'd been a nun for the past six years. Isn't that so?"

"Oh yes. Entered the convent six years ago, began her training back then. Started as a postulant . . . well, do you know how this works, Detective?"

"I'm not sure I do."

"The training in *our* order . . . there are many orders of Catholic sisters in the world, you see, and they all do things differently. What we all share, of course, is our devotion to Christ. As for the rest . . . oh dear," she said, and he could imagine her rolling her eyes the way Annette Ryan had. "Kate's family objected to her entering the order, you know. I'm sure they'd have taken a fit if they'd seen her going through what I call God's boot camp . . ."

*   *   *

I<small>T IS AS IF</small> V<small>ATICAN</small> II has never happened.

The mistress of postulants is a battle-ax nun who wears her habit like armor. It is she who leads the novitiate Katherine Cochran to the barracks-like building where she will live with eighteen other women in training for the next several years. The room she enters is severe by any standards. The floor is made of wide wooden planks, the walls are a painted white stucco. There is a small window high on one wall, overlooking a garden where now—in this summer six years ago—Kate can hear much the same birds Sister Carmelita is listening to as she relates all this to a detective three thousand miles away. There is a wooden cot in the room, a thin mattress on it, and a slip-covered pillow upon which rests a simple wooden crucifix. There is a chair. There is a hanging curtain that shields a closet with a shelf and a hanging rod. There is a small dresser with a bowl and a pitcher. Throughout the night, Kate wonders if she's done the right thing, is *doing* the right thing. She can hear the gentle snoring of a postulant in the cell next door. She is very far away from home. At last she dozes off. And at last it is morning somehow.

A bell sounds, calling to prayer the postulants and the novices and the seventy-four professed nuns who make their home in the mother house. It is not yet dawn. The sky beyond Kate's small window is pink with morngloam. Before bedtime tonight, she will wash in the communal shower down the hall, but for now she bathes her face, hands, and underarms with a plain white bar of soap, and water she pours from the pitcher into the large white bowl. The water is cold. Although Kate may in the future choose whatever modest clothing she wishes to wear, during this intense period of discernment she dresses in the traditional habit of the order. Her uniform is a three-quarter-length black skirt and a black T-shirt from Gap, black socks, black rubber-soled shoes. On her head, she wears a black cap over which she drapes the white veil. In silence, she follows the others down the white-walled corridor to the chapel, her hands clasped.

The mistress of postulants, whose name is Sister Clare, stands behind the altar and looks out at the young women, their eyes lowered, their heads bent.

"Dear Lord," she says, "open my lips."

Matins is the first morning prayer.

Kate's daily schedule is structured around prayer.

The seven canonical hours.

Prime comes at six A.M. Terce is at nine. Sext is said at noon. Nones is the three P.M. prayer. Vespers is the evening prayer. And compline is said before bedtime.

Structured.

Ritualized.

There are strict rules here.

Although the number of women entering religious life has been dropping steadily—Kate's entering class numbers only eighteen as compared to a hundred and four in 1965—the intensity of OSCM training has not diminished in the slightest. Postulants may not speak to second-year novices or to any of the professed sisters, all of whom are in their fifties or sixties. They may not enter another novice's room. They may not break the code of silence. They may not be tardy for morning prayers. They may not meet privately with another sister. They may not . . .

"Well, it's very *much* like boot camp," Carmelita says, and laughs again. "But they're learning to relinquish the material world and concentrate upon their spiritual selves. They're learning to sacrifice joyously, for those who follow Christ receive in hundredfold."

For Kate, the six-month postulancy seems an eternity.

When at last she is asked by Sister Carmelita if she indeed has a vocation, she answers, "I do, Sister."

"And do you feel ready to enter a year of concentrated spiritual preparation for your first vows?"

"I am, Sister."

"Are you ready to dedicate yourself completely to the work of the apostolate?"

"I am, Sister."

"To give up all to serve our Lord Jesus Christ . . ."

"I am."

". . . for He who clothes the lilies of the field and provides for the little sparrows cares infinitely more for the needs of His brides."

Kate is asked to choose a new name.

She picks "Mary" after Christ's mother and "Vincent," which is her brother's name, but also the name of one of God's saints. When she later becomes a professed nun, she may decide for herself whether she wishes to continue using the name she chose at the beginning of her novitiate. But as she starts her instruction in the Holy Rule, and the obligations of the vows, and the spiritual life, she is Sister Mary Vincent.

A year later, just as she is ready to take her first vows, she tells Sister Carmelita that she wishes to leave the order.

9.1

I'T'S CALLED A QUALIFIED ACT OF EXCLAUS-
TRATION," CARELLA SAID.

"SOUNDS DIRTY," BROWN SAID.

"It's like a leave of absence from the diocese. What it amounted to, Kate wanted to check out for a year."

"The Head Penguin told you this?"

"On the phone last night."

"You can do that, huh? Just say, 'Hey, I think I want to go home for a year, see you later?'"

"It's not that easy. There are complicated church laws regarding all this. From what Carmelita told me, qualified exclaustration isn't a penalty, it's a *grace*. A *favor*. Its purpose is to help the religious person to overcome a vocation crisis. It's granted only when there's a reasonable hope of recovery."

"Meaning they expected to get her back."

"Exactly. Carmelita talked it over with her cabinet, and they tried to figure out the best way they could help Kate. Who was already Mary Vincent by then, don't forget. I wonder why she chose her brother's name?"

"Are they allowed to use men's names?"

"Carmelita says it's okay long as they're saints' names. You think there are any nuns out there named Sister Peter Paul?"

"In a mausoleum colossal," Brown quoted, "the explorers discovered a fossil. They could tell by the bend, and the knob on the end, 'twas the peter of Paul the Apostle."

"You're not a very religious person, are you?" Carella said.

"You suppose? What else did the Top Tux have to say?"

"She said, believe it or not, their conversations with Kate were *not* about getting her to stay. Instead, they were trying to support her, help her make the best possible decision. She told me lots of nuns leave the order for various reasons. They're fed up, they're mixed up, they're in love, they may just want to clear out their heads."

"Why'd *Kate* want to leave all of a sudden?"

"She wanted to be a rock singer."

Brown turned to look at him. The detectives were sitting side by side in proper lightweight business suits, shirts, and ties, on the 9:20 A.M. train to Philadelphia, due to arrive at the 30th Street Station at 10:42. They looked like commuting businessmen, except they didn't have newspapers. Vincent Cochran knew they were coming. Carella had called him early this morning.

"A rock singer," Brown repeated.

"Yes."

"A singing nun."

"That's how she first got interested in the church, remember? The God-given voice?"

"So now she wanted to leave the order . . ."

"Just for a year. To take voice lessons, get a job with a band . . ."

"This must've gone over very big with Carmelita, huh?"

"Actually, she took it pretty calmly. Suggested Kate see a psychiatrist . . ."

"That's taking it calmly, all right."

"Asked her not to be hasty, explained the benefits of exclaustration . . ."

"Still sounds dirty."

". . . and the drawbacks. Told her there'd be documents to sign if she decided to go ahead with this, explained that the order might *not* accept her back if she decided to return after her year away. . . ."

"I thought it was a leave of absence."

"More or less. Carmelita struck me as a very unusual person, Artie. Almost a visionary. She felt that if Kate believed so strongly in what she wanted to do, then maybe it was what *God* wanted for her. A calling of another sort. This new career, this new walk of life. And if that's what God wanted, then Carmelita was there to encourage Kate. Try it, she told her. See what happens. If you're *truly* serious about singing . . ."

"*Rock* singing?"

"I got the feeling she'd have preferred opera. But God works in mysterious ways . . ."

"So they let her go."

"Eventually. It took about four months before she signed off. That was in San Diego. Apparently, you have to end it in your original diocese. Kate went out on her own, started managing her own money . . ."

"Money again," Brown said.

". . . kept in touch with the convent as requested . . ."

"She ever become a rock singer?"

"The last Carmelita heard, she'd signed with a talent agent."

"Which one?"

"She didn't know."

"Here? L.A.?"

"She didn't know."

"Got to be one or the other. Where else are there talent agents?"

"In any case, it didn't work out."

"What do you mean?"

"Knocked on the convent door six months after she'd left. Said she'd had a conversion and seen the light, wanted to be taken back in."

"Big Mama must've been tickled to death."

"She was. This past June, Kate took her final vows."

"And now she's dead."

"Now she's dead," Carella said. "Here's our station."

IT WAS DIFFICULT to draw a family resemblance. They had seen Kate only after she'd been murdered, her face already beginning to look bloated in the summer heat. Vincent Cochran was a tall, thin man with Kate's blue eyes, though hers had been open and staring when first they'd seen her. He had the same blondish hair, too, though hers was disheveled and tangled after the struggle that had left her dead on a park path. Cochran looked as annoyed as he'd sounded on the telephone the *first* time they'd spoken to him, when he'd hung up on them, and the *next* time they'd spoken to him, only this morning, when he'd finally agreed to see them if they came to Philadelphia. The reason he'd acquiesced was the phone bills. Carella showed him those bills now.

"These came from Bell Atlantic this morning," he said. "Kate's bills for the past month."

"So you told me on the phone," Cochran said.

He had the look and the sound of a sniveling spoiled brat. Brown felt like smacking him.

"Your sister called you three times in the past two weeks," he said.

"So?"

"You told us the last time you spoke to her was four years ago."

"I didn't want to get mixed up in her murder."

"Well, now you are," Brown said. "What'd you talk about?"

"The first time, we didn't talk about anything. I simply hung up."

"Bad habit," Carella said.

"Is that a nun joke? Stand-up is *my* turf, Detective."

"What'd you talk about the *next* time?" Carella asked.

"Money."

Money again, Brown thought.

"What about money?" he asked.

"She said she wanted to borrow two thousand dollars."

Blackmail, Carella thought. This *has* to be blackmail.

"Same story as four years ago," Cochran said. "She called me soon as she got out of the convent, said she was here in the East, could she please see me. I asked her was she finished with the fucking nuns, and she told me she was. So she came to Philly and first thing she did was ask me for a loan of *four* thousand dollars. So she could get started, she said. Like a jackass, I gave it to her. Six months later, she's back inside again, doing *penance,* I suppose. Two *weeks* ago, she calls again. Not a word from her in four years, but here she is again. Hello, Vince, darling, may I please borrow two grand this time? Never mind she never paid back the *four* grand! This has got to be the ballsiest nun in the world, am I right?"

"She say why she needed the money?"

"I didn't ask. I hung up."

"But she called back again."

"Yeah. A few days later. Please, Vince, I desperately need the money, I'm in serious trouble, Vince, please, please, please." Cochran sighed heavily. "I told her no. I asked her why the hell she hadn't come to the funeral. Our parents got killed in a car crash, she can't find her way to Pennsylvania?"

"Maybe she didn't know, Mr. Cochran."

"Then God should have sent down a messenger."

"So you refused to give her the money."

"I refused."

"Did she say what kind of trouble she was in?"

"Are you trying to make me feel guilty?"

"No, sir, we're trying to find out who killed her."

"Are you saying she got killed because I wouldn't give her the two thousand?"

"We don't know why she got killed, sir. You just told us she was in serious trouble. If we can learn what *kind* of trouble . . ."

"She sounded . . . I don't know. She kept going on about past and present, the past affecting the present, it all sounded like religious bullshit. She said she would pray for me, and I told her to pray that I get the four thousand back I loaned her four years ago. Then she said . . ." He shook his head. "She said, 'I love you, Vince,' and hung up."

They allowed him the moment, both detectives standing by silently, feeling somewhat foolishly intrusive in what was essentially a private reflection.

"Did she mention having received a letter?" Carella asked.

"No."

"Did she mention any recent decisions she'd made?"

"No. Just said she was in serious trouble and needed two thousand dollars."

"Didn't say for what?"

"No." He shook his head again. "What kind of trouble could a *nun* be in, will you please tell me? The trouble was her being a nun in the *first* place, that was the goddamn trouble."

There was another awkward silence.

"I used to tell a lot of nun jokes in my act," he said. "It was my way of getting back at her for having left. Every night, another nun joke. There has to be a thousand nun jokes out there. Even when she left the convent, I kept doing nun jokes. It was as if I knew she'd go back in one day. I kept hoping she was really out for good, I kept hoping she'd come home again soon, but I guess I knew, I guess I knew she wasn't really finished with it. The day I heard she went back in again, I thought, What's the use? I stopped telling nun jokes that very night. I haven't told a nun joke since. Because, you see, my *sister* was the biggest nun joke of them all."

THAT AFTERNOON, everything broke at once.

First, the rain came.

It had not rained for almost two weeks now, and the storm that broke over the city at a quarter past three seemed determined to make up for lost time. Lightning crashed and thunder bellowed. Raindrops the size of melons—or so some long-time residents claimed—came pouring down from the black sky overhead, drilling the dimmed afternoon, pelting the sidewalks, splashing and plashing and plopping and sloshing until the gutters and drains overflowed like the tub in *The Sorcerer's Apprentice,* poor Mickey overwhelmed. The rain was relentless. It made everyone happy to be indoors, even cops.

Particularly happy on that rainy afternoon were Carella and

Brown, who got back to the squadroom to find a fax from a doctor named George Lowenthal, who said he had indeed performed a surgical procedure on a woman named Katherine Cochran, in the month of April, four years ago.

Equally happy were Meyer and Kling. The address and phone number Marilyn Monroe had given the pawnbroker were—big surprise—non-existent. But now—after also striking out on the six M. Monroes listed in the city's phone directories, none of whom were Marilyns—they came up with the brilliant idea that perhaps the woman who'd visited Manny's pawnshop was either a Munro or a Munroe, the variant spellings of Monroe. In all five directories, there were three listings for M. Munro, and four listings for M. Munroe. There was only one listing for an M. L. Munro, in Calm's Point, over the bridge.

Meyer called the telephone company, who supplied him with the full names of their initialed subscribers. Not surprisingly, four of the *M*'s stood for Mary. Two of them were abbreviations of Margaret, and one of them was short for Michael—odd in that men usually did not list themselves under an initial. There was not a Marilyn among them.

But the M. L. Munro in Calm's Point was a woman named Mary Lynne.

"Son of a *bitch!*" Meyer said.

THIS WAS A CITY OF BRIDGES.

Isola was an island—the very name *meant* "island" in Italian—linked on one flank by bridges to the rest of the city, and on the other flank to the next state. Of all the bridges spanning the city's rivers, the Calm's Point Bridge was the most beautiful. People wrote songs about the Calm's Point Bridge. People wrote about the sheer joys to be found over the Calm's Point Bridge. The sky behind the bridge at four that afternoon was a golden wash, the city clean and new after the sudden storm. They drove with the windows rolled down, breathing in sweet draughts of fresh-

smelling air. The cables still dripped rainwater. The River Dix glis-
tened below in the late afternoon sun. There were sometimes days
like this in the summertime city.

The telephone company had supplied an address for Mary
Lynne Munro, but they did not call ahead because she had hocked
stolen property and perhaps would not be overly delighted to see
them. They didn't know what to expect behind the door to apartment 4C. The Syrian signet ring had not been stolen from the
Cooper apartment where The Cookie Boy—or at least someone
who'd dropped chocolate chip crumbs—had possibly slain a forty-
eight-year-old housewife and a sixteen-year-old delivery boy. But it
had been taken from an apartment where the burglar had left behind, on a bedroom pillow, a small white box of chocolate chip
cookies. So *if* the woman who'd hocked the ring knew the man
who'd stolen the ring, and *if* the man who'd stolen the ring was, in
fact, The Cookie Boy, and *if* The Cookie Boy was, in fact, the person who'd killed two people in yet another apartment he'd burglarized, then there was need for caution here. Admittedly a great
many ifs, but as they approached the door, they drew their pistols
nonetheless, prepared for the worst.

The worst turned out to be the woman Manny Schwartz had
described yesterday, five feet four inches tall, weighing around a
hundred and ten, with brown hair and brown eyes, wearing jeans
and a white T-shirt, no shoes. The detectives were still holding reg-
ulation nines in their hands when she opened the door. They had
announced themselves as policemen, but she wasn't expecting
drawn guns. She almost slammed the door on them.

"That's okay, lady," Meyer said, and glanced swiftly into the
room. The gun was still in his hand. He would not put it away until he made sure she was alone. "Anybody here with you?" he
asked.

"No," she said. "What the hell's the gun for?"

"Okay to come in?" Kling asked.

"Let me see some ID," she said.

Both men were scanning the room. Eyes darting. Searching.

Listening. They saw nothing, heard nothing. Meyer was holding up his shield and his ID card. Mary Lynne was studying it. Both detectives were still standing in the hallway outside the door. This was a garden apartment in Calm's Point, a nice quiet neighborhood. Nobody expected cops in the hallway with guns in their fists.

"Who are you looking for?" she asked.

"Okay to come in?" Kling said again.

"No. Not till you tell me what this is about."

"You hocked a stolen ring, lady," Meyer said. "We want to know where you got it."

"Oh," she said. "That. Come on in, I'm alone."

She stepped aside to let them into the apartment. They fanned out, guns up and ready, no search warrant here, they had to be careful. To the woman this must have looked absurd, two grown men playing cops and robbers as if they were on television. They didn't care how foolish they looked. They cared only about taking two in the head.

"Okay to look around?" Meyer asked.

"Just don't touch anything," she said.

"You Mary Lynne Munro?"

"I am."

Roaming the apartment . . .

"Okay to open this door?"

. . . making sure they were, in fact, alone, and only then holstering their weapons and turning their attention to the woman who'd been in Schwartz's pawnshop.

"That ring was a gift," she said at once. "If that's what's concerning you."

"Who gave it to you?"

"A man I met. Why? Is he some kind of thief?"

"He is some kind of thief, lady," Meyer said. "What's his name?"

"Arthur Dewey."

"Where does he live?"

"I don't know."

"He gave you a ring worth twelve thousand dollars and you don't . . ."

"*Twelve?* That son of a bitch Jew only gave me three!"

This did not endear her to Meyer. When he was a boy growing up, the Irish kids who chased him through the streets used to chant "Meyer Meyer, Jew on fire." Kling didn't much like it, either.

"My partner's Jewish," he said.

"So?" she said.

"So watch your mouth," he said.

"Oh, you mean that son of a bitch in the pawnshop *wasn't* Jewish?"

"Lady, don't press your luck," Meyer said. "How come you don't know where this guy lives?"

"Cause I met him in a bar, that's how come."

"When?"

"Couple of weeks ago."

"Met him in a bar and he gave you a twelve-thousand-dollar ring?"

"Not in the bar."

"Where then?"

"Right here."

"Gave you the ring you hocked the other day?"

"I had no use for it. It was too big for my finger."

"How come he gave it to you?"

"I guess he was stunned by my beauty," she said.

"Oh, was that it?"

"He offered it, I took it."

"What do you do for a living, Miss Munro?"

"I'm presently unemployed."

"When you're not unemployed, what do you do?"

"Various jobs."

"What was your last job?"

"It was a while ago."

"When?"

"Two years or so."

"Doing what?"

"I worked at a Burger King."

"And since then?"

"What is this?"

"We're trying to figure out why a total stranger handed you a ring worth twelve thousand dollars."

"I guess he didn't know it was worth that much. I'll tell you the truth, I was surprised when the Jew offered me three. I thought it was worth tops five hundred, like he said."

"Like who said?"

"Arthur. If that was his name."

"What makes you think it wasn't?"

"I don't know what it was. I don't meet many men who give me their real names."

"You a working girl, Miss Munro?"

"Gee, you blew my cover."

"And he offered you the ring in payment for your services, is that it?"

"Supersleuth," she said.

"Ever been arrested?"

"Never. You arresting me now?"

"Did Arthur—if that was his name—mention the ring was stolen?"

"Would you?"

"I'm asking what *he* did."

"No, he did not."

"Mention how he came into possession of it?"

"Really now."

"Did he?"

"Of course not."

"When you hocked the ring . . ."

"Yeah, I know all about it."

"You told Mr. Schwartz it was an heirloom you had to sell because you'd lost your wallet with all your money and credit cards in it. Is that right?"

"Lost it in a taxi, I told him."

"Why?"

"What was I supposed to tell him? Some guy gave me the ring in exchange for a superior blow job?"

"Is that why he gave it to you?"

"I don't know about superior, though they say I'm pretty good. I told him the price was two hundred. He said he'd give me a gold ring worth five hundred. I looked at it, I thought maybe it was worth three, four. So we traded."

"Ever think it might be stolen?"

"Why would I?"

"Guy carrying an antique ring in his pocket . . ."

"It wasn't in his pocket. It was on his finger."

"Took it off his finger, did he?"

"Before we started."

"Then what?"

"Tipped his hat and left."

"He was wearing a hat?"

"That's just an expression."

"What was he wearing?"

"Who remembers?"

"Notice any scars, tattoos, birthmarks . . . ?"

"What is this? Clinton's cock?"

"Any identifying . . . ?"

"There was a finger missing on his right hand. I noticed it when he took the ring off."

"Which finger?"

"The pinkie. It was almost disgusting."

"Thanks, Miss Munro."

There was a sudden silence. Their brief encounter was finished, there was nothing further to say. It was almost as if she'd entertained a pair of tricks and was now showing them the door.

"Nice after the rain, ain't it?" she said almost wistfully.

*   *   *

Dr. George Lowenthal's waiting room was full of women when Carella and Brown got there at four that afternoon. The office was on Stoner, just off Jefferson Avenue, a high-rent, low-crime neighborhood in the center of the city. The women glanced up curiously; two men were entering a normally females-only preserve. A woman in a green hat kept staring at them. The others went back to reading *Vogue* and *Cosmopolitan*. The detectives told a receptionist who they were. The woman in the green hat kept staring. She was still staring ten minutes later, when they were ushered into Lowenthal's private office.

Lowenthal was a man in his early fifties, Carella supposed, with graying hair and pale eyes. He looked tired. As if he had just come out of a difficult surgery, which he hadn't. The blinds behind him were drawn against the afternoon sun low on the horizon. Kate Cochran's file was open on his desk.

"I remember her well," he said. "There was a waiflike air about her, a sort of otherworldly naiveté. I have to tell you the truth, I don't often try to talk a woman out of breast augmentation. It's her body, after all. I assume if she's uncomfortable with what she has and wants to change it, that's her business, not mine. My job is to serve a patient's needs. But Kate . . ." He tried to find words. "Let me say that her body seemed perfectly suited to her gentle, childlike manner. According to my records, she was twenty-three years old, but she seemed fourteen."

"Did she tell you she was a nun?"

"A nun? No."

"Did she mention the name Mary Vincent?" Brown asked.

"No."

"Sister Mary Vincent?"

"No."

"That's who she was," Brown said.

"On leave when she came to see you."

"I knew nothing of this."

"We're trying to piece together past and present, Dr. Lowenthal. If there's anything you can tell us that might help . . ."

"Like what?"

"Well . . . the ME's Office said this wasn't reconstructive surgery. Is that correct?"

"Yes. It was strictly augmentative. After a mastectomy, we insert the shell behind the chest muscle and in front of the ribs. But Kate's implants were sub*glandular*. That means the shell was placed behind the breast tissue and in front of the pectoral muscle. We make a small incision, usually in the crease under each breast. With saline implants . . . these were saline, the silicone gel was outlawed in 1992."

"So we understand."

"With saline implants, we insert the envelope while it's still empty and fill it when it's in place. This enables us to adjust the size. Kate didn't want outrageous breasts . . . some women do, you know. You have to understand that breast augmentation is the third most common type of cosmetic surgery in the United States. Kate was . . ."

"What are the other two?" Brown asked.

"Liposuction's number one. Eyelid surgery comes next."

"Things women do," Brown said, and shook his head.

"For *us,* usually," Lowenthal said and smiled somewhat ruefully. "Nationwide, we do some fifty thousand saline implants a year. Before the silicone ban, and the attendant cancer scare, we were doing twice as many, maybe *three* times as many silicone gel operations. There's a lot of pressure on American women. They see all the supermodels in the magazines and on television, they think this is what men want. Maybe we do. I don't question it too closely. My job is to serve a patient's needs."

Second time he's said that, Carella thought.

"Kate was doing this for professional reasons, of course. She wanted breasts that looked . . . well . . . rather more like a woman's than a child's."

"How much did this cost her?" Brown asked.

"I don't remember what the manufacturers were charging back then. This was four years ago. I believe Mentor and McGhan were the only ones left in the market after the ax fell. It probably was something like three, four hundred dollars for a set of implants. My fee was the same back then as it is now."

"And what's that, Doctor?"

"Three thousand dollars."

Which is why she needed four grand from her brother, Brown thought.

"I must say she was rather pleased with the results," Lowenthal said. "Kept touching them. Well, most women do that. Smile and touch. It's remarkable." He hesitated a moment, a frown furrowing his brow. "There's something I don't understand."

"Yes?"

"Did she go *back* to the church?"

"Yes. After a very short time."

"That explains it then. She wanted to be a singer, you know. That's why she had the operation done. So she'd look good on a concert stage. Already had a talent agent. In fact, it was Herbie who sent her to me."

"Herbie who?" Carella said at once.

10. H

ERBIE KAPLAN'S OFFICE WAS ON THE TWELFTH FLOOR OF THE KRIMM BUILDING AT 734 STEMMLER Avenue in the Midtown North Precinct. The elevator up was packed with songwriters, musicians, and agents at ten o'clock that Friday morning, all of them speaking an arcane language neither Carella nor Brown understood. Kaplan's office was at the far end of a hallway lined with doors that had wooden lower panels and frosted glass upper panels. All up and down the hallway, there was the sound of pianos playing and voices singing. The cacophony reminded Carella of rehearsals for the sixth-grade production of *Annie,* in which his darling little daughter had played the evil Miss Hannigan, and his handsome son, Mark, had played Daddy Warbucks. Closed classroom doors all along the elementary-school corridor, and behind them, kids bleating "Tomorrow" and "A Hard Knock Life" to the solid accompaniment of the music department's thumping. The lettering on Kaplan's door read HK TALENT. Carella knocked and twisted the doorknob. Brown followed him in.

They were standing in a small entry lined with three sheets of Broadway shows, presumably those utilizing the talents of HK Talent. There were windows to the left, open to Stemmler Avenue and the noisy traffic below. Facing the entrance door, there was a desk with a blonde behind it, a phone to her ear. She glanced up as the detectives entered, and then went back to her conversation. They stood waiting. At last, she hung up and said, "Hi, can I help you?"

"Detectives Carella and Brown," Carella said. "We have an appointment with Mr. Kaplan."

"Oh, sure, just a sec," she said, and picked up the receiver again. She pressed a button in the base of the phone, listened, said, "The cops are here," listened again, and then hung up. "Go right on in," she said, and indicated with a toss of her head a door to the right of her desk. The detectives went to it. Carella opened it. They both went in.

Herbie Kaplan appeared to be about forty-five or so, a short, not unpleasant-looking man with reddish hair and eyebrows, sitting behind his desk in shirtsleeves and a vest. He rose as the detectives came in, said, "Hey, how you doin?" and gestured to a pair of chairs in front of his desk. The detectives sat. There were windows behind Kaplan, facing the side street. On the wall to their left, there was an upright piano with framed pieces of sheet music above it, again presumably the efforts of HK clients.

"I should've called the minute I saw her picture in the paper, I know," Kaplan said. "But I figured a *nun*? How could Katie Cochran end up being a nun? But you got to me, anyway, huh? A week later as it turns out, but you got to me. So it's okay in the long run. Can I get you anything? A cup of coffee? Something to drink?"

"Thanks, no," Carella said.

"Mr. Kaplan," Brown said, "we understand you once referred Kate to a plastic surgeon named George Lowenthal, is that correct?"

"Yeah, I send a lot of my clients to him. Tits and ass, correct? That's the name of the song and the name of the game."

"Tell us how you first met her."

"She walked in off the street. This was, what, four years ago? Cute as could be, she looked thirteen, fourteen, she was twenty-three. Voice like an angel. I had this audition pianist at the time, a guy named Frank DiLuca, he since passed away. She sang two Janis Joplin tunes, are you familiar with 'Cry Baby?' 'Me and Bobby McGee?'"

"Yes," Brown said.

"No," Carella said.

Brown looked at him.

"Knocked down the ceiling," Kaplan said. "I couldn't believe it. This big voice coming out of a kid looks like a war refugee. She told me she wanted to be a rock singer, wanted to know could I hook her up with a good band. She had in mind, like, R.E.M., or Stone Temple Pilots, or Alice in Chains, fat chance. I told her first put on some weight and next buy herself a pair of tits. She asked me how much that would cost, I told her three, four grand, this doctor I knew. Then she asked me . . . can you believe it? . . . she asked me could I advance her the money against the time she was a big rock star. I told her take a walk, kid. She comes back two weeks later with four grand in the kip, wants to know the doctor's name. I sent her to Georgie, him and I went to high school together in Majesta. He does a very nice job. Next time she walks in here, she's wearing a tight cotton sweater, no bra, I tell her *now* you're talking. We changed her name and I started selling her."

"Changed it to what?"

"*Katie* Cochran. Which was better than either Katherine or Kate."

"Did you find a band for her?"

"You have to understand it's rare that a rock group comes along actually *needing* a singer. Very rare. These kids start as a complete entity, they got everybody in place from go, including the lead singer. They write their own music, they make a demo CD, they try to get it played on local stations, they're hoping for a bigtime recording contract. Every now and then, though, somebody's replaced, like Pete Best was by Ringo Starr. But that's rare. Very rare. So it was lucky I represented this group where the girl singer had left to get married cause her boyfriend made her pregnant. A group called The Racketeers."

"The Racketeers?" Brown asked.

He'd never heard of them. Knew every rock group ever cut a record, but not anybody called The Racketeers.

"They later became The Five Chord," Kaplan said.

Brown hadn't heard of *them*, either.

"I get kids in here," Kaplan said, "they call themselves Green Vomit, they think that's cool, Green Vomit. Would *you* like to dance to the music of Green Vomit? The rappers are an altogether different story, they think it's cute to call themselves 4Q2. I sometimes wish I was still in the rag trade, I got to tell you."

"So what happened?" Carella asked.

"What do you mean? Did Katie Cochran become a big rock star? You know she didn't. She ended up a dead nun, didn't she?"

"I meant with The Five Chord."

"Oh. It was a fortuitous happenstance, as they say. Katie was looking for a band, they were looking for a lead singer. Boys, meet Katie Cochran. Katie, here's The Racketeers. Soon to be known as The Five Chord, catchy, no?"

Brown didn't think it was catchy at all.

"So you're saying she joined the band," he said.

"The Five Chord is what that means. *Five* people."

"Then what?"

"I sent them to a booking agent."

"And?"

"He booked them."

"Who was he?"

"The booking agent? Guy named Hymie Rogers, no relation to Richard Rodgers. Or even to Buck Rogers. He's dead now."

"Do you remember the names of anybody in the band?"

"Sure, all of them. Addresses and phone numbers, forget it. For that, you have to go to the musicians' union."

THE WOMAN WHO ANSWERED THE PHONE at the number the musicians' union had given them identified herself as Alan's mother, Adelaide Figgs, and when Carella asked if he could speak to her son, please, there was a long silence on the line.

"Alan is dead," the woman said.

The words were chilling, not only because the woman's voice

was so sepulchral, but also because they conjured up the instant horror of someone methodically knocking off members of The Five Chord. What Carella definitely did not need at the moment was a serial killer. Let all those other detectives out there occupy themselves with serial killers. He himself could count on the fingers of one hand all the serial killers he'd encountered in all his years on the force.

"I'm sorry to hear that," he said.

"He died last month," the woman said.

This enforced the notion of someone out there stalking The Five Chord. Please don't tell me he was strangled, Carella thought. He waited. The silence on the line lengthened. For a moment, he thought he'd been cut off.

"Ma'am?" he said.

"Yes?"

"How did he die, ma'am?"

"AIDS," she said.

Gay, he thought.

"He was gay," she said, echoing his surmise, the short sentence laden with such bitterness that he dared not pursue it further.

"Sorry to have bothered you," he said.

"No bother," she said, and hung up.

SAL ROSELLI WAS WATERING HIS LAWN when they found him.

A short, wiry man with curly black hair and brown eyes, barefoot and in shorts and a tank-top shirt, he stood happily spraying his grass. "I could turn on the sprinkler," he said, "but I enjoy handling the hose. I'm sure that's Freudian."

The lawn was at the back of a development house on Sand's Spit, near the airport. It had taken Carella and Brown half an hour to drive here in light traffic, and it was now a little before noon. The heat was beginning to build again. The water splashing from the hose made them think of yesterday's rain, made them long for rain again today.

"You got my number from the musicians' union, huh?" he said.

"Yes."

"They probably thought it was for a job."

"No, they knew we were policemen."

"So Katie's dead, huh?"

"You didn't know that?"

"No. First I heard was when you told me on the phone. Something, huh? Do the others know?"

"We haven't talked to the others yet," Brown said.

"Last time I saw them was at Alan's funeral. He died last month, did you know that?"

"Yes."

"AIDS," Roselli said. "Well, I'm not surprised. I always thought he had tendencies. Anyway, we were all there. Not Katie, of course, God only knew where *she* was. Now she turns up here. Dead. A nun. It's difficult to believe."

"When's the last time you saw her?"

"When the band broke up. Four years ago? Right after we finished the tour. She told us she was quitting. We had a little farewell dinner, and off she went."

"Did you know she was returning to the order?"

"Didn't know she'd ever been *in* an order. I figured she might be going back to Philadelphia. I knew she had a brother there, inherited a lot of money when their parents died in a car crash."

"So that's the last time you saw her."

"Yes. Around four years ago."

"And the other guys in the band last month sometime."

"Yes. It was really sad. Made me realize how much I miss The Five Chord. What the band was—well, first off, we had no leader. Like The Beatles, you know? We all had equal billing. There was Davey on drums, and me on keyboard, and then Alan on lead guitar, and Tote on bass. Davey Farnes, Alan Figgs, and Tote Hollister. Everybody but me sounded Dickensian. Tote was short for Totobi, though, which didn't exactly come from *Great Expectations,* either. Tote's black, I guess you already know that . . ."

"No."

"He is. Which caused a bit of difficulty in the South, but that's another story. His real name is Thomas. Thomas Hollister. The Totobi was his stab at finding roots. I'll tell you the truth, the band was just a run-of-the-mill, all-American garage band—until Katie came along."

You think of The Supremes, you think of Diana Ross. You think of The Mamas and the Papas, you think of Mama Cass. You think of Big Brother and the Holding Company, you think of Janis Joplin. Mention The Five Chord, and after the wild applause and uncontrollable hysteria die down, you think of Katie Cochran. Well, you know the trite scene, don't you? Singer starts her song, everybody stops sweeping. Mouths fall open, jaws hang agape, even the gods are awestricken. Struck? Whatever.

That's what happened the first time she walked into the Oriental, where we were rehearsing. You know the Oriental rehearsal studios off Langley? She looked sixteen, she could've been anybody's kid sister. Herbie Kaplan had sent her down, he was representing us at the time, we were still calling ourselves The Racketeers. She did "Satisfaction" for us, giving the old Stones tune a spin old Mick never dreamt of in his universe, and promptly knocked our socks off. Here's a kid who looks like she needs permission from her mother to attend the senior prom, and she's got a wisdom and maturity in her voice and in her eyes that signal Sign me, Sign me, Sign me— though at the time The Racketeers didn't have contracts to sign, not even on napkins.

We got The Racketeers from Davey's father, by the way. He came in one day while we were rehearsing in Davey's living room, and remarked in his Deliberately Dense Parent mode, "This racket you're making . . . is it supposed to be music?" Hence The Racketeers, imminently to become The Five Chord the moment Davey's father came up with yet another name for the band. This was after Katie had joined us, there were now *five* of us in the band. This time Davey's father was in his Learned Elder mode, explaining that rock bands play mostly in the key of G, and the five chord in the key of G is the D triad. That's D, F sharp, and A, if you'd like

to try it on your accordion. So what Mr. Farnes—that's Davey's father's name, Anthony Farnes, *he* sounds Dickensian, too, I just realized. *Looked* sort of Dickensian, for that matter. Anyway, what he
was trying to do was convey the fact that this was a rock band, and
there were *five* of us in it. The *five* chord, dig? And the five chord in
the key of G, which is the key favored . . .

"Forget it," Roselli said. "I guess you had to be there." He
turned the nozzle of the hose, began spraying another section of
lawn. "A nun, huh?" he said. "Who'd have expected it?"

"The Sisters of Christ's Mercy," Carella said.

"I mean . . . it wasn't that she was *wild* or anything, quite the
contrary. But a *nun?* I mean, come on. Katie?"

She may have *looked* like your kid sister, but this was the girl
who wrote songs you could fry eggs on. Five-seven, weighed about
a hundred and ten pounds, skinny as a wren, but nice breasts. She
was wearing her hair in a ponytail that first time she sang for us,
you never expected this sexy voice to come out of her mouth.
Turned out she knew all the R&B repertoire, could do all the later
rock stuff, too—well, *everything*, for that matter. Pop, Broadway
show tunes, you name it, Katie could sing it. I guess we all four of us
fell in love with her that very first day. Summertime was just around
the corner, this must've been April when we auditioned her.

I remember the booking agent Herbie sent us to wanted to
know if the name of the band was supposed to be *plural.* Hymie
Rogers, his name was, a short, fat guy with a cigar he kept chomping. "Is it The Five *Chords?*" he wanted to know.

"No, it's The Five *Chord,*" Davey said, sounding a little pissed
off that the guy hadn't understood the reference, a booking agent
for *rock* bands, for Christ's sake! At the time, I felt this was a mistake on Davey's part, getting so agitated, I mean. I mean, we
weren't Pink *Floyd*, we were a garage band with a girl singer whose
voice could shatter concrete. Which, of course, the agent recognized the minute Katie opened her mouth.

Make a long story short, he booked us for "a summer tour of
Dixie," as he called it, which meant we'd be following a club circuit

that ran through Virginia and the Carolinas, and then swung through Tennessee, Alabama, and Georgia before heading into Florida, where we'd play Tampa and St. Pete, and a town near the Everglades, and then back north again to end the tour in Calusa. Every rock band's dream tour, right?

This was three years ago.

Well, let me see, I was twenty-five at the time. So that makes it . . . well, wait a minute, it was *four* years ago. That means I was only twenty-four. Jesus. We all had beards back then, all the guys on the band. Davey was exactly my age, give or take a few weeks. Tote was a little older. You ought to talk to him. I mean, he'd probably give you a different slant. He knew Katie better than any of us.

Anyway, we left the city here on the last day of June, for the beginning of the tour, a Fourth-of-July-weekend gig in Richmond, Virginia. The way we traveled was in a sports utility wagon, a used Jeep actually that Davey had picked up cheap from a bass player leaving for a gig in London. There was plenty of room for the five of us plus the instruments, speakers, amps, all of it, inside the car. Every night, we carried *everything* into whichever cheap motel we were staying at. Some of these towns we played, you wouldn't leave a stick of *chewing* gum in the car, no less instruments and equipment worth thousands of dollars.

A favorite joke of ours was "Are you *sure* the Beatles got started this way?" That was whenever anything went wrong. Like when we pulled up in front of a club called The Roadside *Palace* or some such and it turned out to be this ramshackle dive on the edge of a cliff. Or when we plugged in one night—this was in Georgia someplace—and blew out every light in the club. The owner took a fit till we advised him to put candles on all the tables and find us some acoustic guitars and an upright piano, which for Georgia worked remarkably well, Katie singing all kinds of bluesy shit and all of us playing sort of hushed and reverential behind her, a kind of *intime* evening, if you dig. Then there was the time . . .

On and on, Roselli went, reminiscing about that summer tour four years ago, painting it in glowing terms while the sultry afternoon waned and the detectives worried about hitting heavy traffic going back into the city. Finally, he turned off the recitation and the hose.

"I hope I've been helpful," he said.

He hadn't.

HE WAS AFRAID he might never do another burglary.

Burglary was his entire life. He truly enjoyed what he did, but now he was fearful that he might never derive pleasure from it again. He'd really been frightened that day, he admitted it to himself now. And because he'd been so frightened, he hadn't done another job since. Nor had he baked any cookies. The one enjoyment was linked to the other, and all because of a clumsy accident he'd been deprived of both pleasures. All he could think was that the police would knock on his door at any moment.

They had to know he was the one who'd been in that apartment. He didn't know how they'd found out, but he knew they knew. Otherwise, why had all the television stories stopped? How come there was nothing more about The Cookie Boy? No cute little stories about the burglar who left behind chocolate chip cookies. He was sure the police were behind that. They'd been told to throw a blanket over any news release about him. Probably some trick to keep him complacent while they closed in. Any minute now, they'd knock on his door. Probably were questioning everyone in the neighborhood right this minute. Know anybody who bakes cookies? Tightening the net. See anybody who looks like this man? Did they have a composite drawing of him? Had someone seen him going in or coming out of the building that day?

He tried to think of any mistakes he'd made in the apartment. Had he wiped everything clean? He couldn't remember. He usually did that because he knew his fingerprints were on file from his days in the army, but now he couldn't remember. That's because he'd been so frightened. Such a stupid encounter. He sometimes thought he should go to the police, tell them he hadn't killed any-

body in that apartment, it was the *woman* who'd done all the goddamn shooting, it was the *woman* who had the weapon! Had he
somehow left fingerprints on it? No, his hands were over hers, she
was the one with her finger on the trigger, she was the one who'd
first shot the boy and then shot herself. Maybe he *should* go to the
police. Sure, how are you, they'd say, nice you stopped by. That's
two counts of felony murder, so long, fella, see you in a hundred
years.

If only . . .

Well, look, there was no sense second-guessing this. What
happened happened. He should have been more careful, he
should have listened more intently, he shouldn't have taken a step
into that goddamn apartment until he was dead certain nobody
was in it.

Had he left something behind?

He didn't think so.

But had they been able to trace him somehow? Were they this
very instant climbing the steps to the fourth floor here, ready to
knock on the door, you are under arrest, you have the right to remain silent, you have the right to . . .

The ring.

The one he'd given that hooker.

Could they link him to that?

Well, even if they did . . .

Marilyn Monroe, was that what she'd told him her name was?
Jesus, why hadn't he gotten her real name? Jesus, how could he
have been so stupid?

But even if they did . . .

Wait a minute here.

Suppose somehow they got to the hooker, and suppose, somehow, she told them how she'd got the ring, and suppose, somehow, they knew this was a ring he'd stolen from an apartment
three weeks *before* that dumb fucking woman shot herself and that
stupid little boy, suppose *all* that. Okay, how could they possibly
link the murders to the ring?

They couldn't.

But suppose they could?

Suppose somehow . . .

He'd given the woman a phony name, same as she'd given him, he couldn't even *remember* what name he'd given her. So there was no danger there.

But suppose she'd identified him?

Look, it was *impossible* that they'd been able to track down a cheap whore he'd met in a shitty little bar. But suppose they had, and suppose they'd shown her the ring, and suppose she told them yes this man gave me the ring, this man whatever his name was, whatever name I gave her, traded the ring for my services. And this man was missing the pinkie on his right hand, suppose she'd mentioned *that*? Suppose she'd been as revulsed by that missing pinkie as most women seemed to be? Suppose she'd remembered that *one* thing about him, never mind anything else, never mind people telling him he looked a little like a young John Travolta, just remember the fucking missing *pinkie!*

Well, so what?

He didn't have a criminal record, so no one was going to be able to tap into a computer and call up all the burglars in the world who had a pinkie missing on the right hand. So fuck you, lady, you remembered the missing pinkie, so who cares?

The only thing they could possibly trace were his fingerprints if he'd left any in that apartment. Go back to his army records, hello, fella, come right along.

He wished he could remember whether or not he'd wiped that apartment clean before he'd left it.

He must have.

He always did.

THE CALL FROM THE MOBILE CRIME LAB came at six-thirty that night, just as Meyer was taking his nine-millimeter service pistol from his locked desk drawer in preparation for heading home.

The technician calling was a man named Harold Fowles who, to-gether with his partner had dusted and vacuumed and otherwise scrutinized the Cooper apartment for hairs, latent prints, semen stains, and the like.

"I'm the one found the cookie crumbles, remember?" he asked.

"Yes, I do," Meyer said. "How are you, Harold?"

"Fine, thanks. Well, a little hot, but otherwise fine."

"So what've you got for me?"

"Well, we went over the latents, and all of them match prints of either the woman or her husband or the kid was banging her, and other members of the family, too, we had a lot of cooperation here, and the maid, and the super who was in there a few weeks ago to unclog the toilet. All people who had legitimate access to the apartment. No wild prints is what I'm saying. Nothing that didn't belong there, so to speak. Okay."

Meyer waited.

"We know the guy went in through the dining room window just off the fire escape," Fowles said. "There were wipe marks out-side and inside the window, and imprints of his feet in the carpet where he dropped to the floor and then walked across the room. He left the window open behind him. We also know he went *out* of the apartment by way of the front door. It was unlocked and there were wipe marks on both the inside and the outside knobs. Okay. Something occurred to me."

Meyer waited.

"If he went to all the trouble of wiping everything clean, then he wasn't wearing gloves. Maybe he was afraid someone would spot him with gloves on in this heat, who knows, I'm not a crimi-nal. But if he *wasn't* wearing gloves, and if he didn't go *out* the same way he went *in*, which I'm positive is the case, then there was one thing he couldn't have wiped."

"What was that?" Meyer asked.

"The ladder."

"What ladder?"

"The fire-escape ladder. The one he had to jump up for. I went back there this afternoon. I recovered some nice latents from the bottom rung where he pulled the ladder down and also some good ones from the rungs above it, which he left when he was climbing to the first-floor landing. I'm running them through the system now. If the guy's got any kind of record, criminal or military, maybe we've got something. It may take a while, but . . ."

"I'll give you my home number," Meyer said.

SONNY FINALLY CAUGHT UP with him at ten that night in a private club called Siesta, all the way uptown in a section of the city called Hightown. Here in the shadow of the bridge connecting Isola to the state next door, you had more damn drug dealers than you could find in the entire nation, all of them Dominican, all of them linked to the Colombian cartel. This was dangerous turf, man. Worth your life to look cockeyed at a man standing on a street corner here, lest he believe you were invading his turf. Sonny couldn't understand what Juju was doing all the way up here where Spanish was the language and a person's sensitivity could easily turn into a challenge. He was glad he had the Eagle tucked in his belt. He drove around the block three times, looking for a space, and finally parked in front of the club in a zone clearly marked NO PARKING. Fuck it, he thought, and went inside.

The owner of the club was a man named Rigoberto Mendez. Sonny introduced himself and told him he was looking for his good friend Juju Judell. A CD player was oozing dreamy close-dancin music when Sonny stepped into the place. The sweet scent of marijuana floated on air thick with smoke, and skinny girls in clingy, tight summer dresses swayed in the arms of dudes black and tan. Juju sat at a table in the corner chatting up a tall black girl with bleached blonde frizzy hair and earrings long as fingers hanging from her ears, low-cut dress about to pop with righteous fruit within. He had an eye for the women, Juju did.

"Well now looka here," he said as Sonny approached, and rose from the table, extending his hand, shaking it warmly, "Sonny Cole, meet Tirana . . . I didn't catch the last name, honey."

"Hobbs," she said, a little disdainfully, it seemed to Sonny, as if she was looking down her nose at him, for what reason he couldn't fathom.

"Tirana Hobbs," he said, "how you doin, honey?" and extended his hand, which she didn't take, so he figured he'd be taking her to bed tonight, Juju notwithstanding. He pulled up a chair. Tirana was sitting across from him at the small round table, Juju on his right. All their knees almost touched under the table.

"Choo drinkin, man?" Juju asked, and signaled to a man wearing jeans and a white T-shirt with an NFL logo on it. "They got ever'thin, juss name it."

"What's that you're drinkin there, Tirana?" Sonny asked, trying to be friendly, trying to let her know she was gonna end up in bed with him, so let's cut the thaw, honey, no sense playin games here.

"Gee," she said, "what can it possibly be comes in a brown bottle and pours out yellow with foam on it?" To demonstrate, she poured more beer into her mug. Sonny grinned.

"I'll have a beer, too," he said. He wanted to keep a clear head for what was coming later. Started drinking anything harder, he'd liable to fuck up. "So how you been, Juje?" he said.

"What's that stand for, anyway?" Tirana asked.

She had yellow eyes, Sonny noticed, sort of glassy now, as if she'd been smoking before he got here. Maybe that's why she sounded so harsh. Grass sometimes did that to people. They either got mellow or they got mean. He didn't mind a mean girl, long as she understood who had the cock.

"Juju stands for Julian Judell," he said.

"That's a nice name," Tirana said. "Why'd you shorten it to Juju?"

"Didn't do it myself, honey. Kids started sayin it and it stuck."

"Tirana's a nice name, too," Sonny lied. He thought it was one of those bullshit names lots of black mothers picked outta some

African baby-name book. "Where'd you get such a pretty name?"

"It was supposed to be Tawana."

"Oh? Yeah? Tawana?"

"My mother didn't know how to spell it. She thought what they were sayin on the TV was *Tirana*. You remember Tawana Brawley, the one got raped by all those white guys smeared her with shit later?"

"She was full of shit, anyway," Juju said.

"I don't think so," Tirana said.

"I think she was tellin the truth," Sonny said.

Tirana smiled.

"How'd you get the name Sonny?" she asked.

"I don't know how. My real name is Samson."

"Ooooh," Tirana said. "Strong."

"Still got all my hair, too," Sonny said, and smiled charmingly.

"I'll bet," Tirana said.

If Juju was noticing any of this, he wasn't showing it. In any case, Sonny wasn't about to let pussy intrude on what was the real order of business here tonight. He suddenly wondered if Tirana bleached herself down there, too, be interesting to find out. But Juju came first. What had to be done with Juju came first. Then they'd tend to other matters. If there was to be any other matters.

Juju said, "So how come you knew where I was at?"

"I asked around," Sonny said.

"Why was it you wanted to see me?"

Sonny tried to calculate was he suspicious. He decided no.

"Couple things we should talk about," he said, "you have a minute."

"Want to take a walk?" Juju asked.

"You mind, Tirana? Just take a few minutes."

"Time and tide wait for no man," Tirana said.

"Be the tide's loss," Sonny said, and shoved back his chair.

Tirana looked up at him. Same mean smile on her face like when he first came over to the table. He knew for sure now she'd be waiting for him when he got done with Juju.

Outside, the night was cool.

They strolled through streets full of people jabbering in Spanish. He wondered all at once if Juju was of Spanish descent. Julian could be Spanish, he guessed. But Judell? He doubted it. Still, what the hell was he doing all the way up here in Hightown? Lots of laughter, too, on the summer air. People hanging out of windows, looking down into the street. People drinking. Some of them dancing. Like some kind of carnival atmosphere, you'd think it was still early in the evening, number of people in the street.

"So what is it?" Juju asked.

"I been having trouble finding a piece," Sonny said.

Juju looked surprised.

"You can get any kind of weapon you wish, this city," he said. "Where you been looking?"

"Well, I had to be discreet."

"Naturally. But where you been looking?"

"I been asking around."

"Who you been askin?"

"Point is, Juju, I was wondering you could help me."

"You want to link me to a gun you goan use in a murder?"

"Who's talking about any murder?"

"Oh, scuse me, I thought you were planning to do some police officer."

Juju had been drinking. Otherwise he wouldn't be talking so loose now. People in the street here were all speaking Spanish, but they understood English fine, and Juju's voice was too loud. Mention the words "police officer" in this neighborhood, ears went up.

"I don't know where you got that idea," Sonny said.

"Maybe from *me*," Juju said, and burst out laughing.

Sonny laughed with him, faking it along. They were walking north toward the bridge. The crowd was beginning to thin, except for teenyboppers ambling down toward the water for their hand jobs. Behind him, Sonny could hear the laughter trailing, the crowd noises fading. It was a cool, clear, beautiful night.

"Sure, I'll help you find a piece," Juju said.

"That's kind of you, Juje."

"What I'll do, I'll make the initial inquiry, set you up. Then you go do the deal yourself. That way, I'm out of it."

"Sounds good to me."

A pair of thirteen-year-olds were standing close together on the rocks down by the water, the girl's blouse open, the boy's fly open, too. They saw two big black guys approaching, they zipped up and buttoned up mighty fast, got the hell out of there in a hurry. The men sat on the rocks the kids had vacated. Juju offered Sonny a joint. Sonny shook his head no. Had to stay clear. Had to be cool. Juju lit up. The cloying smell of grass wafted out over the water.

"I've been thinkin what you advised me that night in jail," Sonny said.

He was scoping the area now, making sure there wasn't anybody else lingering. Two more teenagers were climbing down the bank now. He didn't have to wave them off. They saw Sonny and Juju sitting there on the rocks, they made an abrupt about-face, moved right on out again. Black power, Sonny thought, and smiled.

"What's funny?" Juju said, and sucked on the joint. The tip glowed hot in the dark.

"What you said. In jail that night."

"What'd I say?"

"You said to do it clean, man."

"Thass right. Why is that funny?"

"Clean piece . . ."

"We'll get one for you, don't worry."

". . . no partners. In, out, been nice to know you."

"That was good advice, man," Juju said, and took another hit off the joint.

"But what I realized just recently," Sonny said, "is I already *got* a partner."

Juju turned to look at him.

"*You*," Sonny said. "You the partner. You the only one knows what I'm goan do, man."

Juju was all at once looking into the barrel of a Desert Eagle.

"Thought you couldn't find a piece," he said dryly.

"I found one," Sonny said.

"Ain't no need to do this, man," Juju said. "I'm the one advised you."

"That's right."

"So come on, put away . . ."

"I'm just *takin* your advice," Sonny said, and fired two shots into his face.

In this neighborhood, the sound of gunfire was as common as the sound of salsa. Four teenagers, laughing as they came down the bank, heard the shots and immediately turned back. Sonny dragged Juju to the edge of the river.

"Been nice to know you," he said, and rolled him off the rock wall and into the water.

THERE WAS A PARKING TICKET under Sonny's windshield wiper when he got back to the club. He read the ticket and then tore it up and threw the pieces down the sewer. Rigoberto Mendez was watching him from the doorway, his arms folded across his chest. He told Sonny that Tirana and her bleached blonde hair had gone off with a Dominican who looked very white.

"Where's Juju?" he asked.

"Last I seen him, he was with some hot babe we met on the street."

"That's Juje, all right," Mendez said.

"That's him," Sonny said.

11.

THE MORNING STARTED OUT GOOD. SATURDAY, THE TWENTY-NINTH DAY OF AUGUST.

Not too hot, not too muggy. Looked like it was going to be a great day for the beach. Looked like there wouldn't be too much traffic on the highways leading to the mountains or the beaches; most people who had the wherewithal had got out of the city yesterday afternoon. All in all, it looked good, A distinct change from the night before. Well, the start of the weekend. You had to expect things.

Last night, for example, some kid in a Calm's Point mall had shot up seven or eight innocent bystanders while trying to target a fifteen-year-old girl who'd had the temerity to quit a violent street gang. The shooter missed her entirely. He also got away. Last night, too, because this was a big city and it was the summertime, and tempers flared during the summer, a man threw another man's pigeon coop off the roof in an area of the city called Cascabel, which was the Hispanic section of Diamondback. For good measure, he also threw the owner of the pigeon coop off the roof. Nobody knew what had caused the argument between them.

In another part of the city last night, a kid trying to light a crack pipe had accidentally set fire to his T-shirt, and had ripped off the shirt and tossed it into a corner that unfortunately happened to have a pile of newspapers stacked in it. The papers had caught fire and caused a consuming blaze in the Riverhead apartment where the kid's three-month-old sister was asleep in her crib.

The little girl suffered third-degree burns all over her body. The kids' parents had been out dancing.

Also last night, a body came floating in downstream of the Hamilton Bridge on the River Harb, and it was identified as that of a small-time drug dealer and part-time pimp known as Julian "Juju" Judell, who had been arrested for illegal possession only a week earlier, and was out on bail awaiting trial when someone shot him and tossed him in the river. Half his face had been blown away with a high-caliber weapon. The other half had been gnawed away by river rats before the body was discovered under the pilings off Hector Street.

None of this happened in the Eighty-seventh Precinct.

It was a big city.

But on Saturday morning at eight o'clock sharp, because both cops and lab technicians get to work early, Harold Fowles called the Eight-Seven and asked to speak to Detective Meyer Meyer, who had got in some twenty minutes earlier and was drinking a cup of coffee at his desk. Fowles reported that they'd come up roses on the felony-murder suspect, and he gave Meyer a name for the man whose fingerprints he'd lifted from the fire escape. He also gave him an address that was three years old and probably no longer valid.

The good day was starting to go bad.

WHAT SONNY WAS STARTING TO REALIZE was that except when he was home with the wife and kiddies, Carella was joined at the hip to his partner, the big black cop whose name Sonny didn't even know. So unless he wanted to shoot up the whole fuckin police department and Carella's family besides, he had to catch him either going in the house or coming out of it. Alone. Had to catch the man by his lonesome or a lot of innocent people would suffer. Sonny had no desire to hurt any innocent person.

It never once occurred to him that Carella's father had been an innocent person who'd been gunned down minding his own business during a holdup. It never occurred to him that Juju Judell had been an innocent person merely imparting wisdom about the ways cops carried grudges over the years. It never occurred to him that Carella—the target of all this surveillance and scrutiny—was himself an innocent person who had, in fact, not blown Sonny away when he'd had the opportunity to do so. None of this occurred to him.

His focus now was in getting the job *done*.

Because, you see, it was beginning to trouble him, the glimpses he had of this man kissing his wife goodbye when he left the house in the morning, the glimpses he had of this man laughing and joking with his partner, the glimpses he had of this man leaving the station house at night, his brow furrowed, his face troubled, like he was deep in thought. This man was beginning to seem like someone he *knew,* someone he might have hung with, the way he felt certain his black partner hung with him when they weren't out chasing people like Sonny. If circumstances had been a little different he wouldn't have shot this man's father—he couldn't even remember now the series of events leading to the shooting—and wouldn't now have to take out Carella himself because he represented a lifelong threat.

That was the whole damn thing of it.

The man had to go because Juju was right, Sonny'd never be able to breathe easy while he was still alive. At the same time, if circumstances were just a little different—

Fuck that noise, circumstances were *not* a little different! Circumstances were what they *were.* Circumstances were what they'd been for Sonny from the day a doctor smacked his black ass and brought him into this fucking white world. The thing had to be done. And it had to be done fast. Before Sonny went all pussy. Before it started going bad.

He didn't know that it had already started going bad up there in Hightown, where the owner of a social club named Siesta had told a detective from the Eighty-eighth Precinct that the last person they'd seen Juju with was a man named Sonny Cole.

*   *   *

THE FINGERPRINTS BELONGED TO A MAN named Leslie Blyden.

He was twenty-seven years old, and had served with a mechanized cavalry division during the Gulf War. He'd got his right hand caught between a drive wheel and a crawler track, crushing the pinkie and necessitating amputation. He'd earned a Purple Heart, a medical discharge, and a plane ride back home. His last known address was on Beasley Boulevard in Majesta, but the super there said no one by that name was living there now. The super himself was new, so he couldn't tell them when Mr. Blyden had moved away.

Blyden was not a common name. Only six of them in the Isola directory, none of them Leslies. Four in Riverhead, ditto. Another half dozen in Calm's Point, only two in Majesta. None of them were Leslies. But one of the three Blydens listed in the *Bethtown* directory was a person named Leslie. Male or female, they couldn't tell, but they guessed a woman would have used the letter *L* instead of her full name. They dared not call ahead to find out. If Leslie Blyden was their man, he had killed two people. Besides, it was a good day for a ferry ride.

It would start turning bad for them in about forty minutes.

THOMAS HOLLISTER, the man who'd played bass guitar for The Five Chord nee The Racketeers, had stopped calling himself Totobi Hollister the moment he recognized that if you deliberately chose a name that branded you as an African-American, you were limiting your job possibilities. Tote Hollister was fine for a bass guitarist in a rock band, but it was not so fine for a lawyer. The minute the band broke up, Hollister had gone back to school, getting his law degree last year from Ramsey University, right here in the city. He'd been working for the firm of Gideon, Weinberg and Katzman since last July, more than a year now.

"When did the band break up?" Brown asked.

"Minute we finished the tour that summer. Katie decided she'd had enough, told us so long, boys. Without Katie, we were just another garage band."

The men were sitting in a small pocket park across the street from Hollister's office. He had come in on a Saturday to finish some work in preparation for the start of a Monday morning trial. A slight, slender man, he was wearing designer sunglasses and a tan tropical suit that complemented his coconut-shell color. He was lighter than Brown. Hell, Brown's wife said every brother in the city was lighter than he was. Brown took this as a compliment. He enjoyed looking mean and tough. He enjoyed the hell out of being a big black cop.

"Why'd she decide to quit, do you know?" Carella asked.

"Well . . . I'm not sure I know why," Hollister said.

"Did you ever talk about it?"

"Never."

"We understand you were close to her," Carella said.

"I think we were. You know how it is," he said to Brown. "There are limitations."

Brown nodded.

"Be nice if there weren't, but there are," Hollister said. "As it was, we were very good friends. Which in itself was a miracle. Poor black kid from the ghetto, upper-middle-class white girl from Philadelphia? Her father a college professor, her mother a psychiatrist? Hell, *my* mother packs groceries in a supermarket. My father drives a bus. It probably wouldn't have gone farther, anyway. At least we ended up good friends."

"Would you have liked it to go farther?" Carella asked.

"Yes. Sure. In fact, I think I might have been in love with Katie. In fact, I think she might have loved me, too. It's funny, you know. There are no color lines in the music business. You make good music, it doesn't matter who or what you are. If there's any prejudice at all, it's the other way around. Black musicians, white musicians, there's always a sort of rivalry as to who's better. Like *you* invented harmony, man, but *we* invented rhythm. Look, I'm not saying anything would have developed between Katie and me if we hadn't been traveling through Dixie. It just made it more difficult. It pointed up our differences instead of our samenesses, do you see what I mean? We were both damn good musicians. *That* should have been the point."

Behind them, a wall of water flowed down a high wall, creating an artificial waterfall that seemed to cool the day and possibly might have. The air stirred. Mist touched their faces. They did not want Hollister to go into the same sort of reverie Roselli had indulged in yesterday. At the same time, they wanted to know what had happened down South that had caused Katie Cochran to leave the band when the tour was over.

"The South isn't what it used to be, you know," Hollister said. "You go into any expensive restaurant in Georgia, you'll see more blacks in it than you will in a similar restaurant up here. Integration is a *fact* down south. Up here, it's a myth. Up here, there isn't even a pretense of races mingling. In the South, you don't have to sit in the back of the bus anymore and you don't have to drink at separate water fountains, but at the same time you don't see any pepper-and-salt couples, at least I didn't. I do a lot of business in San Francisco, I see more mixed couples there than I do either here or in the South, mostly Asian-white, but mixed anyway. The prejudices linger, man, they linger."

Brown nodded again.

"There's integration in the South," Hollister said, "but there isn't *oneness*, do you follow me? They don't *say* nigger anymore, but they still *think* nigger. Same as up here. The *N* word is forbidden, but that doesn't stop the white man from thinking it. The only reason he doesn't say it out loud is he knows it can get him killed. Excuse me, Detective, that's prejudice in itself, isn't it?"

"But maybe you're right," Carella said.

Brown looked at him.

"I remember one thing that really disturbed me one night," Hollister said. "In fact, it still bothers me . . ."

This was in Alabama, we were maybe a third of the way into the tour. There was this crowd of young college professors at the place we were playing, drinking a lot, laughing it up, really digging the music. A very hip, white clique. Some single guys, some guys with their wives, all of them educated, all of them color-blind, right? So one of the professors asked us to come back to his house when we quit for the night, he and his wife wanted to extend the evening, this was one o'clock on a Saturday night, what the hell, they could all sleep late tomorrow morning. This was the *New* South, nobody had to stand up for my rights. It was understood that if the band went to this party, then Tote went *with* the band. There was no quarrel there, not even a murmur of dissent. We packed our axes and off we went.

Well . . .

One of the single guys, a professor who taught anthropology or archeology or whatever thought it might make me feel more comfortable if he invited a black girl to join us. This was already condescension, can you dig? I was *already* perfectly comfortable. I was a college graduate, and a skilled musician besides, here with my friends and fellow musicians who had just made superb music in a roadside joint that frankly didn't deserve us. But the professor decided to make me feel more comfortable by asking one of the waitresses at the club to come on along to the party.

The girl wasn't a college girl putting herself through school, she wasn't an aspiring model or actress or anything but a very dumb eighteen-year-old black girl who spoke largely black English and drank too much bourbon and made a complete fool of herself while the professor stood by waiting to get in her pants. That was the whole point of the exercise. He no more wanted this mud-eating nigger at that party—yes, *nigger*—than he wanted me there. All he wanted to do was humiliate her and fuck her. And by doing so, he was humiliating me as well. He was raping us both.

"I'll never forget that night," Hollister said. "I told Katie how I felt afterward. The others had all gone to sleep, we were sitting on the porch outside this motel we were staying at, one of these old run-down Southern motels surrounded by trees hung with moss."

For a moment, he was silent, lost in the memory.

"She kissed me that night," he said. "Just before we went to our separate rooms. Kissed me and said goodnight. That was the one and only time we ever kissed. I'll remember that night as long as I live. Kissing Katie Cochran on the porch of that old Southern motel. Two months later, she quit the band."

"WHAT'D YOU MEAN BACK THERE?" Brown asked.

"When?" Carella asked.

"When you told him maybe he was right. About the white man *thinking* nigger. *You* don't think nigger, do you?"

"No."

"So why'd you say maybe he was right?"

"Because lots of white people do."

"Let me tell you my own band story," Brown said. "I used to play clarinet in the high school marching band, this was a long time ago. Some guys . . ."

"I didn't know you played clarinet."

"Yeah. B-flat tenor, too, later on. But at the time, all I played was clarinet. And these guys I knew in high school, they were all of them white, were starting a band and they asked would I like to join them. This was kind of weird instrumentation for a rock group, it wasn't your usual rhythm and guitars. We also had a trumpet in there. Actually, we got a good sound. Five of us in the group. Lead guitar, bass, drums, clarinet, and trumpet. We only played weekends, we were still in high school, you know.

"Anyway, we go to this wedding job up in Riverhead one Saturday night, and the bride's father takes one look at me and he pulls the leader aside—a kid named Freddy Stein, I'll never forget his name—and he tells him either the black guy goes or we can forget about the job. I think back then it was *colored* guy. Either the colored guy goes or there's no job for you here. So the band took a vote. And Freddy went to the father of the bride, and told him either the colored guy stays or your daughter has no music for her wedding. He reconsidered. We played the job and everybody went home happy."

"Nice story," Carella said.

"True story," Brown said. "It was an Italian wedding."

"Figures."

"You think that guy *still* thinks nigger?"

"I'm sure," Carella said.

"That's the pity of it," Brown said. "We made damn good music that night."

FOUR OF THEM WENT IN WITH KEVLAR VESTS because maybe this was a murderer inside the apartment. There was Meyer on point and Kling directly behind him, with Parker and Willis flanking the door and ready to charge in as backups. It was about to go bad in the next three minutes, but none of them knew that yet. They were prepared for anything, jacketed and unholstered, and ready to go the minute Meyer kicked in the door. They were equipped with a No-Knock warrant. This was maybe a murderer inside there.

In a minute, it would start going bad.

Meyer listened at the wood.

Not a sound in there.

He shrugged, turned to the others, shook his head, signaled nothing in there.

In thirty seconds, it would go bad.

He listened again.

Turned to the others again.

Nodded and backed off the door, knee coming up, arms spread like a punter going for the extra point, sole and heel of his shoe smashing into the lock, splintering the wood and breaking the screws loose. "Police!" he yelled and behind him Kling yelled "Police!" and all four of them rushed into the room.

In ten seconds . . .

A man wearing gold-rimmed eyeglasses was standing in his undershorts at the kitchen counter, a bread knife in his right hand, his left hand cupped over a loaf of Italian bread on the counter.

"Leslie Blyden?" Meyer shouted.

"Don't move!" Kling shouted.

Five seconds . . .

Behind them, Willis and Parker had fanned into the room.

In three seconds . . .

"Leslie Blyden?" Meyer shouted again.

And it went bad.

The man turned on them with the bread knife in his hand. He must have seen that they were all wearing vests because he went directly for Meyer, raising the knife high over his head like Anthony Perkins in *Psycho*, coming at him with the same purposeful stiff-legged stride.

There was an instant . . .

There is always an instant.

. . . when Meyer hesitated, but only for an instant because the blade of the knife was rushing toward his chest with seemingly blinding speed, the man's downward thrust fierce and decisive, he was going to plunge the knife into Meyer's chest. His eyes said that, the grim set of his mouth said that, but most of all the plunging knife said that.

Meyer shot him.

So did the other three cops in the room.

The man's chest exploded like the villain's chest in a Sylvester Stallone movie, holes appearing everywhere, fountains of blood erupting. He was dead even before the knife fell from his hand and he collapsed to the floor.

"Jesus," Parker whispered.

Trouble was, the guy laying dead on the floor there had all five fingers on both of his hands.

FAT OLLIE WEEKS CALLED THE SQUADROOM at twelve-fifteen that Saturday afternoon and asked to talk to his good old buddy Steve Carella. Sergeant Murchison, sitting the muster desk, told him

Carella and Brown were in the field just now, was there anything *he* could do to help?

"I hear you guys are getting very trigger-happy, hm?" Ollie said.

He was sitting at his own desk in the Eight-Eight squadroom farther uptown, looking out the window and eating a ham sandwich on a buttered roll with mustard. Half the sandwich was on his tie. It was rumored that Ollie was the only man in the world who could eat and fart at the same time. Actually, he managed this alternately, taking a bite of the sandwich, swallowing, drinking chocolate milk shake from a cardboard container, passing wind, biting again, chewing, farting, drinking, occasionally belching, a virtual perpetual digestion machine. "First you shoot a guy with a sling-blade knife in your own squadroom, and next you shoot *another* guy with a bread knife in his own kitchen. You trying to rid the world of knifers, is that it?"

Murchison didn't know what he meant about the guy with a bread knife because Meyer and the others were still downtown at Headquarters, trying to explain why they'd thought it necessary to kill the man who'd rushed them, and Murchison didn't yet know there'd been a hassle. Not to appear stupid, he said, "Must be something like that," and grinned into the mouthpiece. He liked the idea of shooting guys who wielded knives. To Murchison, knives and razors were the most frightening weapons in the world. That was one of the reasons he was very careful shaving every morning.

"I also hear Steve caught a dead nun," Ollie said.

"Where do you hear all these things?" Murchison asked.

"Eyes and ears of the world, m'boy, ah yes," Ollie said, doing his world-famous W. C. Fields imitation. "I got a nun joke for him. Too bad he ain't there."

"Tell me instead," Murchison said.

"You sure you're old enough?"

"Sure, go ahead."

He was already smiling in anticipation.

"This nun is driving along in a car . . ."

"Is this Parker's pisspot story?"

"Parker's what?"

"His chamber pot story."

"No, no, this is about the flat tire. Do you know it?"

"Tell it," Murchison said, his grin widening.

"This nun is driving along in a car and she gets a flat tire, do you know it?"

"No, let me hear it."

"So she gets out to change it, but she doesn't know how to do it cause she's a nun, what the fuck do they know about changing flat tires? So she's fiddlin around with the jack, trying to dope out how it works, when this truck comes along, and it stops, and the driver gets out and offers to change the tire for her, did you hear this one?"

"No, go ahead."

"So he puts the jack under the car and starts jacking it up and the car slips off the jack and he yells, 'Son of a bitch!' Well, the nun is shocked. She says, 'Please don't swear like that, it isn't nice,' and the truck driver says, 'Sorry, Sister,' and he starts jacking up the car again, and again it slips off the jack, and again he yells, 'Son of a bitch!' Well, this time the nun gets angry. 'You mustn't use that kind of language,' she says. 'If you can't control yourself, I'll change the tire myself.' The truck driver apologizes all over the place, and the nun says, 'If you find yourself about to swear, just say "Sweet Jesus, help me." It'll calm you.' So he starts jacking up the car again . . . you sure you didn't hear this?"

"I'm positive. Go ahead."

"He starts jacking up the car again, and it slips off the jack again, and he's about to say 'Son of a bitch!' when he remembers what the nun advised him, and instead he says, 'Sweet Jesus, help me!' And lo and behold, right there in front of their eyes, the car starts lifting off the ground and into the air all by itself. The nun is astonished. 'Son of a *bitch!*' she says."

Ollie burst out laughing. Then, because he was eating and

laughing and belching and farting and drinking all at the same time, he also started choking. It took him a moment or two to realize that Murchison wasn't laughing with him.

"What's the matter?" he asked. "Didn't you think it was funny?"

"It's just I heard it before," Murchison said.

"So whyn't you say so in the beginning?"

"I didn't recognize it."

"What took you so long to recognize a joke about a nun with a flat tire?"

"I thought it was Parker's pisspot joke."

"I told you it wasn't."

"The chamber pot joke."

"You let me go through a whole long fuckin joke you already heard?"

"Yeah, but I didn't know I heard it."

"I almost choked here."

"Yeah, I'm sorry."

"Tell Steve I called," Ollie said angrily, and hung up.

And forgot to tell him that last night he'd caught a floater named Juju Judell under the docks off Hector Street, and it now looked like he was last seen alive with the guy who'd killed Carella's old man.

THE NAME OF THE RESTAURANT WAS DAVEY'S, and the owner was Davey Farnes, who'd been the drummer in the band his father had first named The Racketeers and later The Five Chord. His father had also bought him the restaurant, which was a steak-and-potatoes joint in the financial district downtown, as still as a tomb on this Saturday at one P.M.

"This is not the case on weekdays," Farnes was quick to point out. "We do a very brisk lunch business Monday to Friday. But Saturdays are Tombstone, Arizona."

This was the old city, first settled by the Dutch, and still traversed by narrow streets and tight little cobblestoned alleys. Here

was where the mercantile world collided with the judicial and the
municipal, the high-rise stone-and-glass towers of finance nesting
cheek by jowl with the splendid colonnaded temples of the law
and the undistinguished gray structures of state and city government. The areas spilled over from one to the other, all equally deserted on weekends, when the stock market was closed, and
citizens of the city could seek neither magisterial nor civic re-
dress—nor even a good steak, if Davey's was any example.

Davey Farnes himself was a tall, thin man in his late twenties,
broad-shouldered and narrow-hipped, wearing on this hot afternoon a ponytail with a blue-rag tie, a red tank-top shirt, and sawed-
off blue jeans. His hair was a reddish brown, his eyes blue. When
the detectives arrived, he was supervising the unloading of a pro-
duce delivery at the back of the restaurant, ticking off cardboard
cartons of fruit and vegetables on a clipboard with an order form
attached to it.

"You know," he said, "I *thought* that might be Katie when I saw
the nun's picture on television, but I wondered how that could be.
Katie? A nun? Not the Katie I knew."

Two restaurant employees were carrying crates of cauliflower,
spinach, broccoli, and strawberries from the loading platform into
the restaurant kitchen. The driver of the truck kept moving crates
onto the platform. On the river drive several blocks south, there
was the occasional sound of automobile traffic. This was a hot
summer Saturday, and people were at the beach or sitting on fire
escapes catching air from electric fans. There was the occasional
rumble of distant thunder, but it seemed as if any rain would by-
pass the city entirely, worse luck.

"Mr. Hollister was telling us about a party in Alabama. Do you
remember that party?" Brown asked.

"Well, there were parties everywhere we went," Farnes said.
"Did he mean the one where the girl got drunk?"

"Black girl one of the professors invited," Brown said.

"Yeah, that's the one. What about it?"

"Seemed to bother Mr. Hollister," Brown said.

"Bothered all of us. The band was color-blind. We didn't dig that kind of shit."

"How much did it bother *Katie*?"

"I didn't discuss it with her."

"What we're trying to find out," Carella said, "is why she quit the band and went back into the order. Did anything happen that might have occasioned . . . ?"

"Nothing I can think of," Farnes said. "Hold it, let me see that," he said, and motioned for a short Hispanic man to put down the carton of melons he was carrying into the restaurant. Farnes knelt beside the carton, opened it, and looked into it. "These were supposed to be honeydews," he said to the driver.

"That's what they are," the driver said.

"No, they're cantaloupes," Farnes said. "It says so right on the carton. Cantaloupes. And that's what they are." He picked up one of the melons. "This is a cantaloupe," he said. "Honeydews are green."

"You don't want it, I'll give you credit and put it back on the truck," the driver said.

"Haven't you got any honeydews on the truck?"

"These are all the melons I've got. There's no problem. You don't want them, they go back on the truck."

"Yeah, but why should I accept cantaloupes when I ordered honeydews?"

"You don't *have* to accept them. I'll put 'em right back on the truck."

Just put 'em back on the damn truck, Brown thought.

And remembered that it was Davey Farnes who'd got all agitated when the booking agent thought the name of the band was The Five *Chords* instead of The Five *Chord*.

The thing went on for another five minutes, Farnes complaining that this was the third time in a month he'd ordered one thing and another thing was shipped, the driver explaining that all he did was make deliveries, he was just the messenger here, so don't chop off his head, okay? Finally, Farnes accepted the cantaloupes and signed for the entire order, and the truck driver moved out into the city.

It was very still again.

"Come on inside," Farnes said, "have a glass of beer."

The detectives opted for iced tea instead. They still didn't know that four of the squad were at this moment in the Chief of Detectives' office, trying to justify their earlier actions, but they were still on duty, and you never knew who was going to make a phone call saying two cops were sipping beer at one, one-thirty in the afternoon. The restaurant inside was furnished like a true steak joint, all mahogany and brass and green leather booths and hanging pewter tankards. If the food tasted as good as the place looked, Davey's was indeed a find, albeit far from the beaten track. Carella was tempted to ask for a menu he could take home.

"The band had no leader, right?" Carella asked.

"Right. We made all our decisions by vote. We were very close, you know. It's a shame what happened."

"What do you mean?"

"Well, Katie quitting, first of all. And then the band breaking up, and Alan dying last month. And, of course, Sal."

"What about Sal?"

"Well . . . I really shouldn't tell you this, I guess . . ."

Carella nodded. Not in agreement, but in encouragement.

"But at the funeral last month, he was doing cocaine."

"Crack cocaine?" Brown said.

"No, he was snorting the white stuff."

"You saw this?"

"Oh yes. I shouldn't have been surprised. Even back then, he was smoking pot."

"Back then?"

"On tour. Four years ago."

"That's normal, though, isn't it?" Carella asked. "Musicians doing a little pot?"

"This wasn't a *little* pot. It was day and night. I just never thought it would escalate."

"Katie Cochran do any dope when she was singing with you?" Brown asked.

"No, sir. She came from a good family in Philadelphia. Her father taught political science at Temple. Her mother was a psychiatrist. From what she told us, they were very well off. I never saw her go near anything."

"How about you?"

"Pot, sure. But that's all."

"Who'd she go to?" Carella asked. "When she decided to quit the band."

"I think she told *all* of us. If I remember correctly, we were discussing our plans for the fall when she said she was quitting."

"Did she give you any reason?"

"She just said she didn't think this was the life for her."

"Did she say she was going back to the order?"

"We didn't know there *was* an order to go back to. She never once mentioned she'd been a nun."

"So she just said this wasn't the life for her."

"Maybe not in those words. But that was the essence."

"Did she say what she didn't like about the life?"

"No. Up till then, I thought she was pretty happy."

"When was this, Mr. Farnes? That she told you?"

"Right after Labor Day. We'd ended the tour, we were back here in the city. The last of the tour was really terrific, especially down in the Everglades. We played a little town called Boyle's Landing, just south of Chokoloskee. Man named Charlie Custer ran a roadhouse there. Called it The Last Stand because of his name and also because it was the last watering hole before you jumped off into the glades. He did a lot of business. We played to packed houses every night we were there. Which wasn't easy on the edge of the wilderness . . ."

Boyle's Landing is on the northernmost rim of the national park. The greater part of the town is situated on the Gulf of Mexico. The rest sprawls haphazardly toward an inland marsh teeming with wildlife, a precursor of the wilder glades themselves. Custer has built his roadhouse with its back to the swamp, its entrance on Route 29, a secondary road running from Ochopee through Everglades City and Chokoloskee, dead-ending at Boyle's Landing. On any given night, the sound of the band competes with noises from the "swamp critters," as Charlie Custer calls them, the birds, frogs, and insects that make their home in the river and the marsh. There are great white herons here and short-tailed hawks and flamingos. And alligators.

The alligators make no sound.

But you know they are in the water behind the roadhouse. If you stand on the waterside dock and run a flashlight over the bank, you can see their yellow eyes in the dark. Charlie tells Sal that they've already taken two of his dogs, one of them a German shepherd the size of a panther. Sal shivers when he hears this, and the notion that he's managed to frighten him tickles Charlie no end. "There's panthers here, too," he tells him, chuckling. "You better watch your ass, Piano Boy."

They are booked to play a full week at The Last Stand, arriving on a Friday morning, and playing through the weekend and most of the next week, departing on the following Friday for a Labor Day weekend stand in Calusa, some hundred and thirty miles to the north. The Calusa gig will be the end of the tour. Calusa is supposed to be the Athens of southwest Florida, and Hymie Rogers has booked them into a club called Hopwood's, one of the younger places in town, on Whisper Key.

Here in Boyle's Landing, they play to capacity crowds on Friday, Saturday, and Sunday nights, and then to almost full houses on Monday and Tuesday. Charlie is absolutely delighted with the band's spectacular success. He has hired an unknown rock group and they are pulling in teenagers not only from neighboring towns like Copeland and Jerome, directly to the north, and Monroe Station and Paolita, to the east, but also more distant places like Naples, to the northwest, on the Gulf of Mexico.

On Wednesday morning, in newspapers as far north as Fort Myers, the first of Charlie's ads appears. They announce that tonight and tomorrow night will mark the final appearances of The Five Chord in "the Wildlands of Southern Florida," as he calls them. That night, to accommodate overflow crowds, he has to set up tables on the deck overlooking the river where the alligators silently watch. On Thursday night, following a repeat of the ad, there are cars backed up all along Routes 41 and 29. He is compelled to do three shows that night, one at eight, another at ten, and the last at midnight. He has never done better business in his life. The irony, of course . . .

"Well, I guess the others told you about it," Farnes said.

"What's that?" Brown asked.

"The drowning," Farnes said.

On TELEVISION THAT NIGHT, the Chief of Detectives said there was no way his officers could have known beforehand that the man in that apartment was not the Leslie Blyden they were looking for. They could not understand why the man in the apartment had come at them with a knife. The man had no reason to behave so irrationally. They had announced themselves as police. He knew they were police. They had asked him to identify himself. What had got into the fellow?

"My four detectives all acted within the guidelines," he told the estimated four million people watching the eleven o'clock news. "They had a No-Knock warrant backed by probable cause. They had good reason to believe a burglar who had murdered two people was in that apartment. They went in with service pistols drawn because there was the distinct possibility that the man who'd already shot two people might be armed and dangerous on this occasion as well. They opened fire because the suspect had come at one of the detectives with a knife in his hand, was in fact ready to plunge that knife into the officer's chest if they hadn't taken preventive action when they did."

The Chief of Detectives told the anchorman that in spite of all this there would be a thorough investigation.

Meanwhile, The Cookie Boy was still out there.

12. The girl's name was Tirana Hobbs and she told Ollie Weeks she'd never seen this

Sonny character before Friday night, hadn't seen him since, and didn't care to see him ever again, thanks. So what was this all about?

"Owner of the Siesta says you were sitting with Sonny Cole, is his full name, and a person named Julian Judell on Friday night, must've been around ten, ten-thirty, is that correct?"

"I just told you that's the first and onliest time I ever seed the man."

They were in the Diamondback apartment the girl shared with her mother and her two younger brothers. The brothers were still asleep in one of the rooms at the rear. Mama was in church. The girl was wearing a red robe over cotton pajamas. No makeup. Frizzed blonde hair looking like straw that had got hit by lightning. They were sitting at an enamel-topped table in a window open to the backyard. It was a bright hot sunny Sunday, and church bells were calling to the faithful and anyone else who cared to enjoy their mellifluent clamor.

"How about Judell? He goes by Juju. What was your relationship with him?"

"*Relationship?* What kind of *relationship?* I met him ten minutes before I met the other guy. What'd the two of them do, anyway?"

"One of them got himself killed," Ollie said, trying to look sorrowful, the way television newscasters do when they're reporting a tragedy they don't give a damn about. Ah yes, the bullshit of it all, he thought in his best W. C. Fields mode. "I was wondering did him and Sonny say where they might be going when they left the club?"

"For a walk."

"A walk where?"

"Couldn't be far cause they said they'd be back in a few minutes."

"Way I understand it," Ollie said, "Sonny came back about twenty minutes later, looking for you."

"I don't know nothing about that."

"Owner told him you were gone."

"Then I guess I must've been."

"What time did they leave for their little walk, would you remember?"

"I got no idea."

"Ten-thirty? Around then?"

"I didn't look at my watch."

"Did Juju mention some hot babe he was going to meet?"

"No, all Juju did was put the moves on me."

"So you didn't get the impression they were leaving there to meet some woman."

"No, Sonny said there were a few things him and Juju should talk about if he had a minute. That's what prompted him to say they should take a walk."

"Sonny?"

"No, was Juju who suggested it. Sonny was the one said it wouldn't take but a few minutes."

"Okay, thanks a lot, miss," Ollie said.

For nothing, he thought.

THIS COULD HAVE BEEN SANTO DOMINGO on any given day of the week. The women dressed in their church finery, the men looking slender and sleek and clean-shaven, the people out for a Sunday morning stroll, the sun shining brightly overhead. Almost made you forget for a minute that this was one of the shittiest parts of the city, rife with drugs and teeming with people itching to get the hell out of here the minute they made enough money to go back home and start a little business—or so Ollie conjectured. He'd probably have been surprised to learn that as many immigrants from Ireland went back home as did immigrants from the Dominican Republic. The Irish simply *looked* more American. But to Ollie, looks were ninety percent of the argument.

He figured the only route Sonny and Juju could have taken on Friday night was straight down to the river. Two black guys might've been mistaken for spics in this neighborhood, but only if they kept their mouths shut. Miracle was that they'd been in a Dominican club to begin with, but that's where the ass was, Ollie supposed. He automatically figured Tirana Hobbs was a bleached-blonde black hooker peddling her wares to any spic came along. He didn't know she was a manicurist, and he wouldn't have believed her if she'd told him so. The nice thing about Ollie's beliefs was that they were unshakable.

So he guessed the two black gents out for a friendly little walk wouldn't have stopped in any local bar to sample the beer or the broads because Friday night could turn suddenly mean and dangerous in this neighborhood unless you were in a social club like the Siesta, where apparently Juju was well-known, according to the owner. Who'd also volunteered that he suspected Juju had connections with the drug people here in Hightown, though he didn't suggest *which* drug people, of whom there were only thousands. Ollie figured he was sucking up because he had a brother in jail or a sister in rehab. Around here, nobody offered information unless they were plea-bargaining. The man did not, however, mention that Juju was also a pimp who probably ran girls out of his little old Club Siesta here. Kept *that* bit of information strictly to himself, lest a padlock appear on his front door one fine night.

So if Sonny and Juju were walking to a quiet place where they could talk, why *not* down to the river? Have a seat on the rocks in the shadow of the bridge, discuss this pressing matter that was on

Sonny's mind. Not a bad surmise, ah yes, considering the fact that Juju's body with his face all gone had been found nudging the pilings under the dock on Hector Street, not too terribly far downriver.

Ollie took a stroll down to the river himself, not expecting to find anything there, and not disappointed when he didn't. His thinking, of course, was good riddance to bad rubbish, a black dope-dealer pimp, who gave a shit? But it irked him that Sonny Cole was out there thinking the cops couldn't reach him. Bothered him further when he remembered that this was the guy Blue Wisdom said had put away Carella's father, which made it nice if Ollie could run into him in a dark alley some night and repay the favor.

Thing was, first he had to find him.

SAL ROSELLI ALL AT ONCE REMEMBERED that the guy who ran The Last Stand had fallen into the water dead drunk the very night they ended their engagement there.

"We didn't learn that until we were already up in Calusa," he said.

"That he'd fallen into the river behind the club . . ."

"Yeah."

"And drowned."

"Yeah."

"Is what Davey Farnes told us," Brown said.

"We were long gone when it happened," Roselli said. "We didn't find out about it till the next day. Calusa cops came around, wanted to know if we'd seen anything, heard anything, you know how cops are."

They were sitting not far from a small inflatable plastic pool behind Roselli's development house on Sand's Spit. His two little girls were in the water, splashing around. Brown was wondering why there had to be kids making noise every time they talked to somebody. Roselli's wife, a somewhat overweight brunette wearing

wedgies and a brown maillot, had gone into the house to mix
some lemonade.

Roselli was wearing one of those skimpy swimsuits that made it
look like all he had on was a shiny black jockstrap. Brown wondered how he had the balls, so to speak, to wear such a suit in front
of his two little girls, couldn't have been older than two or three.
Roselli seemed oblivious. Black hair curling on his narrow chest,
sweat beaded on his forehead under matching curly hair, he re-
clined in a lawn chair, smiling at the day. Brown wondered if he'd
done a few lines just before they arrived. He had the look of a man
serenely oblivious.

"How come you didn't mention it when we were here?" he
asked.

"I didn't think it was important," Roselli said, and shrugged.

"Man drowns, you didn't think it was important?"

"It had nothing to do with us. We were transients. Play the music, take the money, go our merry way."

"How many places you been where a man drowned?" Brown
asked.

"Not very many. Not any, in fact."

"But you didn't think it was important enough to mention?"

"I'm sorry. I just didn't think of it."

"Did the drowning have anything to do with Katie's decision?"
Carella asked.

There was a slight edge to his voice; *he* didn't like Roselli's
choice of swimwear, either.

"What decision was that?"

"To leave the band."

"To call it quits."

"To go back to the order."

"I have no idea what prompted her decision," Roselli said.
"Josie!" he called. "No splashing, honey."

His wife was coming out of the house, carrying a tray with a
pitcher and several glasses on it. The screen door slammed shut
behind her. She put the tray down on the table, said, "Help your-

selves, please," and then went to sit in a plastic folding chair near the pool where her daughters splashed and squealed. Occasionally, she glanced back to where the detectives and her husband were sitting, a concerned look on her face. They figured their presence here a second time was making her nervous. The daughters seemed a little skittish, too. Altogether, Brown and Carella sensed an almost palpable air of tension around the pool.

But four years ago a man had drowned.

And a week ago Friday a nun had been strangled in the park.

"You said you were long gone when it happened," Carella prompted. "Can you tell us . . . ?"

"I'll try to remember the sequence," Roselli said.

Odd choice of language, Carella thought. Sequence.

"We played three shows that Thursday night," Roselli said. "That was because Charlie ran some ads. And also because we were damn good, he said modestly, but we *were,* truly. After that tour, if Katie hadn't left the band . . . but that's another story. What's done is done, what's gone is gone."

He lifted the pitcher, poured lemonade for all of them. From the pool, Mrs. Roselli and the little girls watched. Brown felt the way he had in Dr. Lowenthal's office, when the woman in the green hat kept staring at them.

"The last show ended at two in the morning. We'd planned to drive up to Calusa the following day, sometime in the afternoon, set up when we got there. This was the Friday before Labor Day, we were scheduled to play that whole long weekend in Calusa, and then head north again. But we were all so high none of us could sleep," Roselli said. "Well, except for Tote, he could sleep through World War III. He went back to his cabin, but the rest of us couldn't stop jabbering. Have you ever felt that way? Where everything was so exciting, you just couldn't calm down afterward?"

Like after a shoot-out in a bank, Brown thought. You answer a 10-30, and there are six guys in masks holding Uzis on the tellers, and all hell breaks loose. Like after that. When you're drinking saloon beer with the other guys and you can't go home, you can't even think of going home, this is where it is, this is what you shared. Like that.

"It was Davey who suggested that we pick up our pay, pack the van, and drive up to Calusa right then. Two-thirty, three in the morning, drive the hundred and fifty miles, whatever it was, go straight to sleep when we got there. We all thought it was a terrific idea. So Alan and I started packing the van . . . he's dead now, you know. Died last month. Of AIDS. We all went to the funeral. Not Katie, of course, who the hell knew where *she* was? Disappeared from the face of the earth. Well, sure, a nun. Sister Mary Vincent. But who knew that?"

"So you and Alan were packing the van," Brown said.

"Yeah. Carrying the instruments out while Davey and Katie went to get our pay. What a lot of these club owners did, they paid the musicians in cash. We'd been there a full week, there was a sizable amount of money due. This was now close to three in the morning, the parking lot was empty, you could hear the night insects racketing down by the water . . ."

From where he and Alan are loading the instruments into the van, Sal can see Davey and Katie going into Charlie Custer's office. The air here in the Everglades is always laden with moisture; the two musicians are sweating heavily as they carry gear from the bandstand to the van. Down here in Florida, they've been performing in blue slacks and identical T-shirts with alternating blue and white stripes. Katie wears a blue mini and the T-shirt without a bra, the better to demonstrate her singing prowess. They are wearing the uniforms now, the trousers wrinkled, the T-shirts stained with perspiration as they pack for the trip north.

Over the past several months, they have learned how to pack the van most efficiently, fitting in the drums, the speakers, the amps, the guitar cases, and the keyboard like pieces in a Chinese box. Davey's drums are the biggest problem, of course. They take up the most room. Besides, he is enormously fussy about how they are handled and usually insists that he himself be the one to pack them. Back and forth the pair of them go, Alan and Sal, from bandstand to van, Sal and Alan, to the rooms for the suitcases, Alan and Sal knocking on Tote's door to wake him up, and lastly going to the kitchen to make sandwiches for the long drive north. Out on the water, they can hear the splash of an alligator.

It takes them perhaps half an hour to finish all they have to do. Alan gets behind the wheel and honks the horn. In the stillness of the night, it sounds like the cry of one of Charlie Custer's swamp critters. Tote comes running out of his cabin and tosses his suitcase into the back of the van. A moment later, Davey and Katie come out of Custer's office. Alan starts the car. Climbing onto the back seat, Davey says, "Got the bread, let's go." Katie sits beside him and pulls her T-shirt away from her body, encouraging the cool flow from the air conditioner.

"We made it to Calusa in an hour and forty minutes," Roselli tells them now. "That afternoon, we found out Charlie had fallen in the river and drowned. And got eaten by alligators."

THEY DID NOT REACH DAVEY FARNES again until nine o'clock on Monday morning. He explained that he'd been at the beach all day yesterday, and had gone directly to dinner afterward—

"I like to check on the competition," he said. "Didn't get home till around ten. Were you trying to reach me?"

"On and off," Carella said. "I wonder if we can stop by now."

"Oh?" Farnes said. "Something come up?"

"Just a few questions we'd like to ask."

"I have to leave for the restaurant at ten-thirty. Will that give you enough time?"

"Sure," Carella said. "See you in half an hour."

They got to Farnes's building at a quarter to ten. He lived in a part of the city not far from his restaurant, an area undergoing intensive urban renewal. Where once there'd been shabby tenements housing illegal aliens, there were now four- and five-story elevator buildings, many of them with doormen. Farnes's apartment was on the fifth floor of a building renovated a year or so ago. There was no doorman, so they announced themselves via the intercom over the downstairs buzzer, and then took the elevator up.

Farnes led them into a living room modestly furnished with a teakwood sofa and two matching easy chairs upholstered in bleached linen. There was a teak coffee table in front of the sofa. A pair of standing floor lamps with glass shades, one blue, one orange, flanked the sofa. An open door led to a small kitchen. A closed second door led to what they supposed was the bedroom. Another closed door beside it probably opened onto a bathroom. The apartment was pleasantly air-conditioned, the windows closed to the noise of the traffic below and the incessant rise and fall of police and ambulance sirens.

"Something to drink?" he asked.

"Thanks, no," Carella said. "We're sorry to bother you again, Mr. Farnes . . ."

"Hey, no problem."

". . . but I wonder if you can tell us again what happened on that last night in Boyle's Landing."

"The night Charlie drowned, you mean."

"Yes."

"You don't think that had anything to do with Katie's murder, do you?"

"No, but we were wondering if it influenced her decision."

"To quit the band, you mean?"

"Yes. You told us on Saturday that she broke the news right after Labor Day. That would've been immediately after the tour ended. So it's possible . . ."

"Yeah, I see where you're going. Well, I guess it *might* have been upsetting to her. The thing is, we didn't find *out* about it until the next day. It wasn't as if we *witnessed* the drowning, or anything. I mean, we didn't actually see any alligators tearing him apart. So . . . I don't know. I just don't know."

"Maybe we can try reconstructing what happened that night."

"Well . . . sure."

"You finished playing at two, is that right?"

"Two A.M., correct. We did three shows that night."

"Tote went to sleep . . ."

"Man would sleep around the clock if you let him."

"The rest of you were up talking . . ."

"Talking, drinking."

"You, Alan, Katie, and Sal, is that right?"

"Charlie joined us a little bit later."

"When was that?"

"Before he paid us. I was the one who suggested we pick up our pay, pack the van, and drive up to Calusa right then, instead of waiting till tomorrow. Well, it already *was* tomorrow, this was two-thirty, three in the morning. I suggested that we drive the hundred and fifty miles or so, go straight to sleep when we got there. They all thought it was a terrific idea. So Alan and I started packing the van . . ."

"Wait a minute," Brown said. "It was Alan and *Sal* who packed the van, wasn't it?"

"Not the way I remember it. Who told you that?"

"Sal did. That's the way he remembers it."

"No, he's mistaken. I wouldn't let anyone touch my drums."

"So the way *you* remember it, it was Alan and you who packed the van, is that right?"

"That's absolutely right."

"Packed the van and you all drove off."

"Yes. Around three-thirty, something like that."

"And the Calusa cops came around the next day."

"Yes."

"Asked you did you know anything about what happened the night before."

"That's right."

"But nobody could tell them anything."

"Nobody."

"Cause none of you were there when Charlie Custer drowned."

"None of us were there."

"Well, thanks a lot, Mr. Farnes," Carella said. "We appreciate your time."

"And got eaten by alligators," Brown added.

"None of us," Farnes repeated.

IT WAS ALMOST TWELVE NOON in Calusa, Florida, when Cynthia Huellen buzzed Matthew Hope and told him that a detective named Steve Carella was on line five.

"Hey," Matthew said, surprised. "How are you?"

"Fine. How's the weather down there?"

"Hot."

"Here, too. What are you doing these days? You still out of the crime business?"

"Planning a trip to the Czech Republic, in fact," Matthew said.

"Why there?"

"Prague's there."

"When are you leaving?"

"Got to find a woman first."

"Plenty of women there, I'll bet," Carella said.

"Can't chance it. I'm getting old, Steve."

"So am I. I'll be forty in October."

"Now *that's* old, man."

"Tell me about it."

They chatted on for another five minutes or so, two old friends who had never met, one a lawyer in the sleepy Florida town of Calusa, the other a detective in a noisy northern city, strangers when first they'd met on the telephone, strangers still, perhaps, though each felt a kinship they could not explain.

"So what occasions this call?" Matthew asked at last.

"Well, if you're *really* out of the crime business . . ."

"I am."

"Then you can't tell me what the Calusa police learned from four musicians and a girl singer who were down there around this time four years ago."

"Why were the Calusa cops interested in them?" Matthew asked.

"Because a man named Charlie Custer drowned and got eaten by alligators."

"Piece of cake," Matthew said.

THE MAN MURCHISON put through to the squadroom told Meyer that he knew the Leslie Blyden they were looking for.

"I saw the Chief of Detectives on television Saturday night," he said, "talking about a Leslie Blyden. I said to myself, What? Then yesterday's papers said he had a pinkie missing, the Blyden you're looking for. I said to myself, That has to be the Les I knew in the Gulf. What I want to know now . . ."

"Yes, sir?"

"Is there a reward?"

"No, sir, there is not."

"Then thanks a lot," the man said and hung up.

Meyer guessed he didn't know that police departments had Caller ID capability and that his name was already displayed on Meyer's desktop LED panel. FRANK GIRARDI was what it read, with a telephone number directly above it.

Meyer didn't think they'd be calling ahead.

"SO WHAT WE'VE GOT," Brown said, "is a piano player and a drummer who each say they were packing instruments in a van with a person who's now dead of AIDS. And we've got the piano player saying he saw the drummer, together with a lady who later got strangled in the park, go in the office of a man who later got eaten by alligators. And we've got the drummer saying the same thing about the piano player."

"That's what we've got," Carella said.

"So one of them's got to be lying."

"Not necessarily. Four years was a long time ago. They may not be remembering clearly."

"They remembered every *other* detail about that night, though, didn't they?" Brown said. "Drummers lie a lot, Steve. So do piano players. In fact, been my experience most musicians do. Specially when there's nobody alive can contradict them."

"You'll get letters."

"I hope not," Brown said, and turned to look over his shoulder. "Am I dreaming," he asked, "or has that Honda been with us the past half hour?"

"What are you talking about?"

"Behind us. Little green Accord."

Carella looked in the rearview mirror.

"I hadn't noticed," he said.

"Black man at the wheel."

"Makes him a wanted desperado, right?" Carella said.

"It's the next left," Brown said.

"I know."

He made the turn at the next corner. Brown's apartment building was three doors in. He pulled up in front of it. The little green Accord drove right on by. Brown gave it a hard look, and then got out of the car.

"See you tomorrow," Carella said.

"Want to come up for a drink?"

"Got to go pick up the dope money from Riverhead."

"Tell them to mail mine."

"The protection we give, they should messenger it."

"No respect anymore," Brown said, and grinned, and closed the door on his side. Carella returned the grin and drove off.

FRANK GIRARDI HAD LOST BOTH LEGS in George Bush's television war, which featured surgical strikes and hardly any deaths on either side, to hear the generals and the politicians tell it. Girardi had been wounded in the First Cavalry Division feint up the Wadi al Batin, and now he worked at a computer in his small Calm's Point apartment, addressing envelopes for any firm that was willing to pay him for this onerous task.

"Reason you get so many letters with handwritten addresses on them is because a lot of people don't know how to do the envelopes on their computers. I make address files for these various companies, and then I run off the envelopes on my printer and send them back by messenger. I get ten cents an envelope. It's not bad work."

Girardi looked to be in his late twenties. Each of the detectives had a good ten years on him. They were each suddenly aware of their legs, the fact that they had legs and Girardi didn't. They were here to pry Leslie Blyden's address from him, but it was a little difficult to put the muscle on a man who was sitting in a wheelchair.

"Reason I asked if there was a reward," Girardi said, "is I figure I got one coming, don't you? I get all shot up in what was basically an *oil* war, I think my country owes me something, don't you?"

Meyer did not think it appropriate to inform Girardi that the city's police department was not his country. They had come here prepared to offer what they would have given any police informer, a sum ranging from a hundred to a thousand, depending on the value of the information. They took this money from a squadroom slush fund, the origins of which were obscure, but in police work petty detail often fell between the cracks and the point was to get the job done. Just before he and Kling left the squadroom, Meyer signed out a thousand dollars in hundred-dollar bills. If this money had originally belonged to a dope dealer and it was now being used to buy information that would lead to a killer, that was justification enough not to ask questions.

The trouble here, though, was that Girardi wasn't a sleazy two-bit informer who'd sell his ax-murderer brother for a cup of coffee and a donut. Girardi was a war hero. A man with both the Purple Heart and the Medal of Honor. You couldn't offer a war hero a dope dealer's dirty money in exchange for information. You couldn't pressure him, either. You couldn't say, Okay, Frank, you want us to take another look at the open file on that grocery store holdup? You couldn't bargain. You couldn't say, So long, Frank, this shit isn't worth more than a hundred. The man was a war hero.

"Look," Meyer said, "we don't want to insult you . . ."

"I've been insulted by experts," Girardi said.

"As I told you on the phone, there's no reward on this thing. But we're prepared to give you money out of our own pockets . . ."

"Bullshit," Girardi said.

"Whatever. It embarrasses me, believe me. A man who did so much for his country, I wish I could offer more. But all we can go is a thousand."

"I'll take it," Girardi said.

13.

THE PROBLEM WAS ALL THE BACK-GROUND.

BLYDEN'S LANDLADY HAD TOLD them that she'd seen him leaving the building at around six-thirty P.M. What he usually did, she told them, was walk up to the McDonald's on the next block, catch himself a bite there. Did it every night, far as she could tell. A creature of habit was Mr. Leslie Blyden.

The sign out front was claiming billions and billions of hamburgers sold, but Meyer figured that was an underestimate. The place at a quarter to seven that Monday night was packed with diners inside and cars outside. They had no clear picture of what Blyden looked like because the Feebs hadn't yet sent along his army ID photo. All they had was the description of him from when he'd entered the service nine years ago. They also knew he'd lost the pinkie on his right hand since then.

This same information hadn't helped them much when they killed the Leslie Blyden who now turned out to be a man named Lester Blier, who was wanted in the state of Arizona for mail fraud, and who'd been living here in the city under a touch-close alias for nearly two years—which perhaps explained his panicky reaction on Saturday. The new data somewhat lessened the public hue and cry over four armed and armored police detectives nailing an innocent man in his own kitchen. But only somewhat. Mail fraud was perceived in the public imagination as some sort of gentlemanly crime, far distant from armed robbery or rape. You didn't go gunning down a man who had a mail fraud warrant chasing him from Wee Mesa, Arizona. This was a sophisticated city, man, and it did not expect its police officers to behave like barbaric goons.

There was a good possibility that public misapprehension might escalate on this muggy Monday evening. The cars lined up at the drive-thru window, the crowd inside waiting on line to place orders or sitting at tables happily munching away, constituted what was known in the trade as "background." In this city, the presence of background was one of the conditions that defined when a police officer might draw or fire his weapon. If Leslie Blyden, aka The Cookie Boy, was indeed inside this fast-food joint enjoying his usual evening repast, and if indeed he had killed two people, then it could not unreasonably be assumed that he was certainly dangerous and possibly armed. Two guideline conditions already satisfied. He was also a fugitive. Chalk off a third condition. Going in was another matter.

The presence of background severely limited their choice of engagement. This was not a matter of the English and French deciding like proper gentlemen to settle their ancient dispute on the level though muddy field of Agincourt. The guidelines clearly stated that if you anticipated shooting, then you made your arrest where there wasn't no background, kiddies. The Gang of Four, as the media had immediately dubbed Meyer, Kling, Parker, and Willis, congregated on the sidewalk outside, working out a game plan.

They decided that two of them would go in to scout the joint, see if they could spot a guy with the pinkie missing on his right hand. Even though Willis and Parker had caught the murder of the lady and her teenybopper lover boy, Meyer and Kling had caught the initial Cookie-Boy burglary. The cases were now irrevocably joined at the hip, but the doctrine of First Man Up prevailed, and Meyer and Kling caught the brass ring.

Parker was delighted. All that background in there made him very nervous. Suppose The Cookie Boy spotted fuzz on the premises and decided to shoot his way out? Guidelines applied only to law-enforcement officers. The rest of the population could fire at will. So Parker took up a position in the parking lot outside the side door, and Willis planted himself outside the front doors, and Meyer and Kling went in looking for a man some six feet tall, with black hair and blue eyes, weighing around two hundred pounds, and missing the pinkie finger on his right hand.

The air conditioning provided a welcome oasis of relief after the soggy atmosphere outside. Meyer and Kling fanned out, one heading for the service counter on the right, the other moving toward the seating area on the left. Each cop looked like any of the other customers in the place. Not many men here were wearing jackets, but Meyer and Kling were wearing them only to hide the hardware, and their clothing was wrinkled and limp from the weather outside. No one in the place gave them a second look.

Meyer got on the line closest to the door, scoping the crowd, alternately glancing at the menu on the wall above the counter and the customers waiting to place orders. Kling was doing the same thing on the other side of the room, peering around like a guy looking for his wife and three little kids. First came height, weight, color of hair and eyes. They were easier to check at a glance. Searching for a missing pinkie demanded a scrutiny of hands. Nobody ever looked at another person's hands unless he was some kind of pervert. The missing pinkie came only after all the other criteria were met.

Kling was the one who spotted him.

He was sitting silhouetted in a western window, drinking a cup of coffee, the sun dipping lower on the horizon behind him. He looked a lot like John Travolta, but what would John Travolta be doing in a McDonald's in Calm's Point? For a moment, Kling felt like going over to the table and asking him if he was John Travolta, but then he noticed the missing pinkie on the hand holding the coffee cup, and any thought of getting an autograph went straight out of his mind. He walked swiftly toward the utensil counter, turned sideways so he could keep an eye on Blyden while at the same time shielding the walkie-talkie that came out of his pocket and up to his mouth.

"Got him," he said. "Third table on the western wall. Sitting alone, looks like he's finished his meal and is ready to go."

There was a silence.

Then Meyer's voice said, "I see him."

"What do we do?" Parker asked.

"Let him jump," Kling said.

From the corner of his eye, he saw Meyer moving off the line and heading toward the dining room. In that same instant, Blyden put down his coffee cup, wiped his mouth with a paper napkin, picked up his tray, and started for where Kling was standing. Kling moved away at once. Blyden went to the trash container at the end of the counter, scraped his tray clean, stacked it, and again moved toward where Kling was now standing near the side exit door.

"Moving out," Meyer said. "Side exit."

"I'm here," Parker said.

Willis, hearing this out front, began moving toward the parking lot.

Blyden walked past Kling without looking at him. He shoved open the exit door, walked past Parker without looking at him. Meyer and Kling came out immediately behind him. Parker fell in on Blyden's left. Willis, spotting their approach, took up position ahead of him. The classic three points of a moving-target triangle. If he'd come here in a car, they'd have to close in before he entered it. Either that, or lose him. Plenty of background out here, too, but not as closely packed as it was inside. No one dared use a walkie-talkie again, not just yet. One false move and he'd bolt.

Somebody made that false move.

They would later debate who it might have been.

Maybe the entire setup was the false move, the short guy in a jacket moving some ten feet ahead of Blyden, the guy needing a shave and also wearing a jacket moving parallel to Blyden some twelve feet on his left, the two guys in jackets behind Blyden, maybe all at once there were too many guys in jackets on a hot summer night, and maybe all at once Blyden smelled cop.

Whatever it was, he suddenly darted to his right, the open side of the surveillance triangle, and began racing up the avenue. Willis was closest to him when he made the break. He started after him at once, and shouted the initial warning mandated by the guidelines, "Police! Stop!" but Blyden kept running because he knew he was looking at a positive burglary and two possible felony murders. "Police! Stop!" The second warning. But a different voice this time. Parker's voice. Coming up fast on Willis's left, his legs longer than Willis's, pounding past him and closing on Blyden, who would have thought it? Andy Parker?

None of the detectives dared open fire. There was simply too damn much background on this hot August night with everybody out for a walk, the sky purple now as Blyden fled westward into it. Moreover, they were literally gun shy, having been lambasted in the press and on television, having been severely chastised by a publicly defensive but privately furious Chief of Detectives. So they followed Blyden down the avenue into the setting sun, four of them in a Keystone Kops opera, echoing one after the other, "Police! Stop!," the choruses overlapping, the crowds parting, but not one of them firing the weapon that would have decisively stopped Blyden in his tracks.

It was Parker . . .

Andy Parker?

. . . who finally took a headlong dive at Blyden, throwing himself in the air like a football hero, which he'd never been, grabbing for Blyden's churning legs and pounding feet, making a tackle he'd never before made in his lifetime, and bringing Blyden and himself crashing to the sidewalk in a sprawling tangle of arms and legs. The other detectives came thundering up, nobody yelling "Stop" anymore because Parker . . .

Andy Parker?

. . . had finally stopped Blyden.

So all there was to say now was "Police."

Which Meyer said.

And breathlessly added, "You're under arrest."

And began reciting the Miranda rigmarole.

"You have the right to remain silent, you have the right . . ."

And so on.

This was America.

NELLIE BRAND WONDERED why it was that every time she was on homicide call there was a murder in the Eighty-seventh Precinct. Her home phone rang at seven-thirty P.M. She and her husband were just about to leave the apartment. She was wearing a pretty white summer frock with a yoke neck and pale blue French-heeled pumps. Simple silver and turquoise pendant on a peach-colored silk cord. Sand-colored hair swept back and caught in a ponytail. Jeff Callard was the cop calling from the D.A.'s Office downtown.

"Hello, Jeff," she said.

"Nellie," he said, "they caught The Cookie Boy."

Nellie didn't know who The Cookie Boy was. She figured he was a sex offender who lured kiddies into his car. Callard told her who he was. She said she was all dressed up to go out to dinner with her husband. Callard said he was sorry, but this was August, and half the world was on vacation. She told him her husband would divorce her.

"That's okay," Callard said, "*I'll* marry you." She went into the bedroom to change her clothes.

When she got uptown at eight-fifteen, she was wearing simple tailored slacks, a tailored shirt, and a fawn-colored linen jacket. Her hair was still in a ponytail. She was expecting Carella, but the desk sergeant told her he'd already gone home. He told her The Gang of Four had made the arrest here. She didn't know who The Gang of Four was, either. Working for the District Attorney's Office did not leave much time for watching television. She liked Carella, and was a little disappointed that he hadn't been the arresting officer.

The Gang of Four was waiting upstairs. Meyer and Kling, she knew. Kling introduced her to the other two detectives, Willis and Parker, and then told her Blyden's lawyer hadn't yet arrived, so they had a little time to talk here. Blyden was The Cookie Boy. Full name was Leslie Talbot Blyden. Gulf War veteran, lost his pinkie in an accident overseas. Admitted to the burglary, but said he had nothing to do with killing two people.

"We're looking at a Burg Two and two counts of felony murder," Meyer said.

"He looks like John Travolta," Parker said.

"Does anyone know Marilyn Monroe's real name?" Kling asked.

"Is this a game show?" Nellie said.

"Who's in charge here?" a voice asked. They turned to see a rather corpulent man in a pinstriped suit standing just outside the slatted wooden railing that divided the squadroom from the second-floor corridor. "Attorney Marvin Meltzman," he said, "representing Leslie Blyden. Where's my client?"

"Assistant District Attorney Nellie Brand," Nellie said, and walked to the railing and extended her hand. Meltzman took it. "Sorry I'm late," he said.

"Just got here myself," she said. "Where's the suspect?" she asked Meyer.

"Interrogation Room down the hall," he said, and then to Meltzman, "I'll take you there, counselor."

The two of them walked off.

"Who questioned him?" Nellie asked Kling.

"Me and Meyer."

"And you say he admitted the burglary?"

"Said *maybe* he did the burglary, but not the murders."

"Only maybe, huh?"

"Better than no."

"Who'd he say did the murders?"

"The woman. Shot the kid and then herself. Accidentally."

"Any prints on the weapon?"

"Only hers."

"So maybe he's telling the truth."

"Maybe I'm Robert Redford."

"You kind of look like him."

"I know, it's a curse. You kind of look like Meg Ryan."

"Let's go talk to Travolta. Maybe we can all make a movie to-gether."

They didn't actually get started until a little past nine o'clock that night. That was when Blyden and Meltzman finished their private conversation. By that time, the detectives had also given Nellie everything they had on the crimes. The Q and A started in the Interrogation Room at 9:07 P.M. Meyer and Kling were present, as were Willis and Parker, and Lieutenant Byrnes, and the D.A.'s Office technician who was videotaping the session. Nellie read Blyden his rights again, got his lawyer's consent to proceed, elicited Blyden's name, address, and pedigree, and then got down to brass tacks.

"Mr. Blyden," she said, "I want you to tell me everything you remember about the afternoon of August twenty-fifth."

His resemblance to John Travolta was a little unnerving. He did not seem to possess Travolta's cool, however. Instead, he seemed shy, almost timid, not unlikely traits for a burglar. Nellie suddenly wondered if she really did look like Meg Ryan. All at once, the video camera made her feel self-conscious, even though it was trained on Blyden.

Q: Mr. Blyden?

A: Yes, I'm thinking.

Q: This would've been a Tuesday.

A: Yes.

Q: Do you remember where you were that afternoon? This would've been around three-thirty, four o'clock, can you recall?

Blyden seemed to be having a little difficulty here. He had already told the arresting detectives that maybe he'd committed the burglary, but not the murders. His lawyer had probably asked him—without advising him to lie, of course—to think about whether he hadn't been someplace else *entirely* on the day of the burglary.

"Mr. Blyden?" she said. "Would you answer the question, please?"

"I was home baking cookies," Blyden said.

Okay, he was opting to lie. Though in a singularly stupid way. If the cops thought you were The Cookie Boy, why admit to baking cookies? Listen, Nellie would take whatever she could get.

"Anyone with you, Mr. Blyden?"

"I was alone."

"Anyone *see* you baking these cookies?"

"The window was open. Maybe somebody saw me."

"But you can't say for certain that anyone saw you."

"No, I can't."

"What kind of cookies were you baking, Mr. Blyden?"

He hesitated. Admit to baking chocolate chip cookies and he was reaching out for The Cookie Boy's hand.

"I forget," he said. "I bake all kinds of cookies."

"Like to bake, do you?"

"Oh, yes."

"Ever bake chocolate chip cookies?"

"Sometimes."

"Were you baking chocolate chip cookies on August twenty-fifth?"

A: I don't remember.

Q: Have you *ever* baked chocolate chip cookies?

A: I don't particularly care for them.

Q: But have you ever . . . ?

A: Chocolate chip cookies.

Q: I understand. But have you ever baked them?

A: I don't think so.

Q: Never baked chocolate chip cookies in your life?

A: I don't think so.

Q: Yes or no, Mr. Blyden?

"He's already answered the question," Meltzman said.

"Not to my satisfaction."

"You'll be satisfied only when he says Yes, he *has* baked chocolate chip cookies."

"No, I'll be satisfied when he gives me a straight yes or no answer."

Q: Mr. Blyden, have you ever baked chocolate chip cookies in your life?

A: Yes. Maybe. Once or twice.

It was not uncommon for a person being interrogated to reverse direction, especially when he wasn't under oath. Blyden was probably thinking they knew somehow that he baked chocolate chip cookies. Maybe one of the neighbors could tell by the smell that they were chocolate chip cookies. Or maybe they'd entered his apartment since they'd arrested him, and found his recipe. Or maybe they could later confiscate his pots and pans, do tests on them, find out he'd baked chocolate chip cookies in them. So it was better to admit he'd baked them once or twice.

Q: How about August twenty-fifth? Did you bake chocolate chip cookies that day?

A: No.

Q: What did you bake? What kind of cookies?

A: I don't remember.

Q: Well, that was only six days ago. Don't you remember what kind of cookies you baked six days ago?

A: No, I don't.

Q: Then how do you know they weren't chocolate chip cookies?

A: I rarely bake chocolate chip cookies.

"Excuse me, counselor," Meltzman said. "Where's this going?"

"Excuse *me*, counselor," Nellie said, "but this isn't a courtroom, and I really must ask you to refrain from interjecting."

"I realize . . ."

"This is a simple Q and A, Mr. Meltzman. No objections, no rules of evidence, nothing to constrain me from getting at the truth."

"Just which truth are you seeking?"

"You *do* know that your client is thought to be a burglar the media has nicknamed The Cookie Boy, don't you?"

"That is the allegation, yes."

"You know, too, that The Cookie Boy leaves chocolate chip cookies at the scene of all his burglaries."

"A singular idiosyncrasy, to be sure. But, Miss Brand . . ."

"Mrs. Brand."

"Forgive me. We're dealing here, Mrs. Brand, with a specific burglary and a specific pair of murders committed during this burglary. My client has no prior criminal record of any kind, and he has just told you that he's only baked chocolate chip cookies on one or two occasions in his lifetime. Why he was arrested at all is beyond my comprehension. Are you planning to *charge* him with these murders?"

"We are."

"Then why don't you do so?"

"I'd like a few questions answered first," Nellie said.

"I think you've asked enough questions for now," Meltzman said. "If you're going to charge him, do it. If not, we're out of here."

"Is that your client's decision?"

"Mr. Blyden?" Meltzman said, turning to him. "Do you wish to answer any further questions?"

"I do not wish to answer any further questions," Blyden said.

"Can we put it any more plainly?"

"That's it then," Nellie said, and signaled to the video guy. "Have a seat, counselor. I'd like to discuss this with the officers here."

"Five minutes," Meltzman said, and looked at his watch.

Together, she and the detectives went down the hall to Byrnes's office.

"This makes it tough," she said. "We were weak going in. Now that he won't tell us anything, what've we got? Nothing that'll stick."

"We've got blood in the apartment," Parker said.

"If it's his. We won't know that without a DNA test. And we can't take a sample without a court order."

"So let's get one," Byrnes said.

"I'm sure we can. We've got probable cause coming out of our ears. But meanwhile, he'll run to China."

"Not if we charge him with the burg," Meyer said. "That'd give us six days to chase the murders."

"Get our court order and our blood sample in that time," Willis said.

"He just *recanted* the burglary," Nellie said.

"So what?" Kling said. "We've got cookie crumbs found at the scene. Chocolate chip."

"That only means someone in the apartment was eating chocolate chip cookies and left a mess. It didn't have to be Blyden."

"The lab's running tests right this minute," Byrnes said. "If the crumbs match the other cookies he left behind . . ."

"Then *maybe* we've got him in the apartment," Nellie said, "but only maybe. Anyway, defense'll bring in ten thousand different chocolate chip cookies that all tested basically the same."

"Tasted?"

"*Tested.* Tasted, too, I'll bet."

"We've also got his prints on the ladder going up," Meyer said.

"Places him behind the building, but not necessarily in the apartment. And not necessarily on the day of the murders. Have we got his prints in the apartment?"

"No."

"What else have we got?"

Nobody answered.

"*Have* we got anything else?" she asked.

They were all looking at her now.

"It's weak," she said.

"You've got no idea the flak on this one," Byrnes said.

"You're saying hit him with the burg, anyway," Nellie said, "take our chances. Okay, I'm saying there's a huge risk of flight here. The judge sees a weak burg, he's liable to order low bail or no bail, Blyden's on his way."

For a moment, she wished this *was* a movie. Wished she really *was* Meg Ryan in a movie. In a movie, everything always worked out all right. In real life, killers sometimes walked.

"So what do you want to do, Nell?" Byrnes asked, and sighed heavily.

"What else *can* we do?" she said. "I'll tell Meltzman we're charging his man with Burg Two, and asking for a court order to draw blood for a DNA test. At tomorrow morning's arraignment, it's the judge's call."

"Too bad chocolate chip cookies ain't DNA," Parker said.

"Too bad," Nellie agreed.

"Don't worry about any of this," Meltzman said. "You'll be out on bail tomorrow, I promise you. It'll take weeks before they get the DNA results. But even *if* they get a match . . ."

"They *will,*" Blyden said. "My blood was all over the place. I had a nosebleed."

"Don't worry about it," Meltzman said.

"But I *am* worried about it."

"Don't be."

"Because I didn't kill them," Blyden said.

"Of course you didn't."

"I mean, *really*. I didn't kill them. I really *am* innocent."

"Don't worry about it," Meltzman said.

Matthew Hope called Carella at home that Monday night, just as he was about to turn on the ten o'clock news. Carella's routine was more or less fixed whenever he was working the day shift. He got home at around four-thirty, five o'clock, depending on traffic, spent some time relaxing and reading the paper, had dinner with Teddy and the kids around six-thirty, read again after dinner—his taste ran to nonfiction—watched the news on television, and was in bed by eleven for a six A.M. alarm-clock wakeup. He usually left the house by seven and drove down to the station house, getting there at seven-thirty, seven-forty, again depending on traffic. During the winter months, he allowed himself more time. Now, in August, with the city relatively quiet, he could even leave the house at seven-fifteen and still be in the squadroom by a quarter to eight.

Matthew called at five to ten.

"It's not too late, is it?" he asked at once.

"Not at all," Carella said. "Let me take this in the other room."

The other room was a spare room they had fitted out as an office for whoever in the family chose to use it. The kids' computer was in there, as was Teddy's and Carella's. There were bookshelves and a battered desk they had picked up in a consignment shop. Two lamps from the same shop. Their housekeeper, Fanny, called the room The Junk Shop. Maybe it was.

"Still there?" Carella asked.

"Still here. How are you?"

"Good. You?"

"Good. I'm enjoying this. Practicing law again instead of running around after bad guys."

"I'm still running around after bad guys," Carella said.

"So I see. I've got that information for you, if you've got a pencil. I can fax the newspaper stuff later if you like . . . have you got a fax there?"

"Yes, I have."

"Good. But I also spoke to Morrie Bloom, and he sent me his report. He's a detective on the Calusa P.D., he was the one who talked to the kids the day after the accident."

"Is that what they called it? An accident?"

"Yeah. The police down there in Boyle's Landing figured Custer was drunk when he fell in the water. Blood tests were inconclusive—the alligators did a good job—but the kids told Bloom he was drinking heavily before they went up to get paid."

"Was their word the only evidence the police had?"

"That he was drunk? No, there were also half a dozen empty beer bottles in his office. So apparently he'd been drinking hard liquor with the kids, and then continued drinking beer after they were gone."

"That could do it."

"It could. Railing on the deck behind his office was about four feet high. Police figure he fell over into the river and the alligators got him right away. They're fast. Have you ever seen an alligator run? Man, watch out."

"Who went up to the office with him?"

"To get paid? I don't know. Let me take another look here."

Carella could hear Matthew turning pages on the other end. Either looking at a photocopy of the newspaper story or else a copy of Bloom's D.D. report.

"Newspaper says they were the last ones to see him alive."

"Who?"

"Mentions all the band members by name."

"Which two went up to the office?"

"How do you know it was two?" Matthew asked.

Good question, Carella thought.

"I'm getting conflicting stories up here," he said.

"I'm looking," Matthew said.

"What's the date on Bloom's report?" Carella asked.

"Let me see."

Carella waited.

"Here it is. September second. That would've been the Friday before Labor Day."

"And the newspaper story?"

"Next day."

"Bloom give it to them?"

"'Reliable police sources,' it says. There's another story on Sunday, a review of the band."

"Good? Bad?"

"'Derivative rock,' it says. But apparently the kids drew a big crowd on Saturday night. Because of all the publicity."

"Say anything about who went up for the money?"

"I'm still looking. There's nothing in the paper, I'm checking

Bloom's report. I'll FedEx this to you, if you like. It's too long to fax."

Carella waited.

"Kid named Totobi Hollister was asleep while they packed the van," Matthew said.

"He tell this to Bloom?"

"Yes."

"Who was packing the van?"

"Nothing here about it."

"Who went up to the office?"

Bloom *had* to have asked that question. Because the last persons to see Custer alive were the ones who'd gone up to get paid.

"Here we go," Matthew said. "Here's the girl's story. Q and A format, shall I read it to you?"

"Please."

"The Q is Bloom, the A is Katherine Cochran."

"I'm listening."

Q: You understand, Miss Cochran, we're following up on this as a courtesy to the Boyle's Landing police.

A: Yes, I do.

Q: Because, from interviews they had with employees of the club, the band was still there when everyone else left. Which means the five of you were the last ones to see Mr. Custer alive.

A: That's true.

Q: One of the waiters told the police he said goodnight to all of you when he left. He said Mr. Custer and the band were sitting near the bar drinking. Is that true?

A: Not all of us. Tote had already gone to bed.

Q: Tote?

A: Tote Hollister. Totobi Hollister. Our bass guitarist. We woke him up later. After the van was packed and we were ready to go.

Q: So the four of you . . . let me consult this a moment, please. That would've been you, and David Farnes, and Alan Figgs, and Salvatore Roselli, is that correct?

A: Yes. The four of us.

Q: Were sitting and drinking with Mr. Custer.

A: Yes, that's right.

Q: How much did he drink?

A: Charlie? I think he had two or three drinks.

Q: Which? Would you remember?

A: Three, I think.

Q: Do you remember what he was drinking?

A: Scotch, I believe. He had a bottle of beer later.

Q: Later?

A: In his office. He opened a bottle of beer and was drinking it when he went to the safe for our money.

Q: So, in your presence, then, he drank three scotches and a bottle of beer.

A: Yes, that's right.

Q: Did he go out onto the deck while you were up there in the office?

A: No, sir, he didn't. He paid us our money, said he enjoyed our being there, and hoped we'd come back real soon. We were a big hit, you know. People came from all over.

Q: You left after he paid you?

A: Yes, we did.

Q: What time was that, would you remember?

A: Around three, three-thirty.

Q: And what did you do then?

A: In the morning, that is. Three-thirty in the morning.

Q: Yes, I understand. What did you do then?

A: We went to the van and drove off. We were coming up here to Calusa, you see. We had a long drive ahead.

Q: Was Mr. Custer still alive when you left the club?

A: I would hope so. He was certainly alive when we left his office.

Q: And you say you drove off immediately after leaving the office?

A: Well, within minutes. The van was running, it was already cool when I climbed inside. So, yes, we were on our way maybe five minutes after we said goodbye to Charlie.

Q: He didn't come out of his office to say goodbye or anything, did he?

A: No. He told us he was going to have another beer and then go to bed. There were lots of empty beer bottles around. He drank a lot of beer.

Q: So he'd finished the first beer already? The one he'd opened?

A: He was just finishing it.

Q: And he opened another bottle?

A: I didn't see him opening it.

Q: But he said . . .

A: Not while I was there.

Q: He said he was going to have another beer . . .

A: Yes.

Q: . . . and then go to bed?

A: Yes.

Q: And you went out to the van . . .

A: Yes.

Q: . . . and left.

A: Yes. The others were already in the van. They were all set to leave when we came down to join them.

Q: What you say the *others* . . .

A: In the van.

Q: There were three of them in the van, is that correct?

A: Yes. Waiting for us to come down with our money.

Q: So it was just *two* of you who went up to the office, is that right?

A: Yes. Just two of us.

Q: You, of course . . .

A: Yes.

Q: . . . and who else? Who went with you to Mr. Custer's office?

A: Sal Roselli.

14.

THE ONLY TIME THE MAN WAS ALONE WAS WHEN HE WAS COMING OUT HIS HOUSE EARLY IN THE morning, walking over to his garage, getting in his car to drive to work. That was the time to do it. Cause any other time he was with either family or other cops and Sonny had no quarrel with anyone cept him.

Fact of the matter, he had no quarrel with *him,* either. Man hadn't done nothin to him. What this was, it was insurance plain and simple. You got the man today so he wun't haunt you the rest of your life, that's what this was all about. Nobody ast the man's father to start a ruckus in his shop, causin Sonny to shoot in self-defense. Life was that way, man. Shit happened.

So what this was going to be tomorrow morning was a clearing of the books. Like consolidating your debts when you had too much on too many credit cards. You borrowed from one source, you wiped out all the other debts. You had just one *single* debt then, you didn't have to worry all the time about the collector comin round. Carella was the collector. You either worried about the collector or you set your worries aside. Tomorrow morning, Sonny'd be able to breathe free again, no more collector on his ass all the time.

He'd driven past the house three times today alone. This was his fourth and final pass. Last time around, some red-haired lady wearing eyeglasses came out carrying something over to the garage. On the path between the house and the garage was where Sonny planned to do it. Lay in wait for the man, surprise him.

Redhead had glanced at the Honda as he drove on by, not the kind of hard look the big black cop had give him yesterday. Just a curious glance, but it was enough to make Sonny think maybe she'd spotted the car doin its dry runs and it was time to quit. This time he drove past slow but not too conspicuous. Man went to work at the crack of dawn, half the neighborhood was still asleep at that hour. Sound of the Desert Eagle be like a cannon goin off in the stillness, this was one powerful pistol he had here. Man comes out his house, starts walkin to his car, gets shot in the face. *In, out, been nice to know you.*

The house looked like the one in that movie *Psycho,* where the guy was runnin aroun in drag stabbin people. Hard to believe a cop livin in a place looked like it was from olden times. Once, drivin by at night when he was still thinkin maybe the best time to do it was after dark, he could see inside to where a floor lamp was standin, looked like the shade was all different-colored jewels. Touched his heart cause he seemed to recall a similar lamp when he was comin along, maybe in his grandma's house, though he couldn't imagine her possessing anything looked like it was jewels. Took him back, though. To someplace he couldn't hardly remember. Touched him.

Do it in broad daylight, shoot the man in the face and run off to where he'd have parked the car. What he planned on doin was giving the Honda back to Coral tonight, thank her proper in bed with a yard and a half. Then go out around midnight, boost a car on the street, use the stolen vehicle for the thing tomorrow. He planned to wake up at five in the morning, drive up here to Riverhead, be in position by six-thirty latest, case the man decided to get to work even earlier than any human being had cause to.

Red-haired lady coming out of the house again, busy, busy, busy. Carrying garbage to the bins on the side of the house this time. Figured her to be in her sixties, maybe she was a maid, did cops have maids? In which case, how come she wun't black, huh? Or maybe a nanny. Did he have small kids? Woman hesitated on her way, gave the Honda another look as it went by. Sonny didn't speed up, didn't do nothin to indicate he was in any way troubled by the redhead's scrutiny. She was lookin at a car'd be ancient history by sundown tonight. Wearin glasses, probly squintin through 'em, tryin'a catch the numbers on the license plate. So long, lady, been nice to know you.

Tomorrow mornin, Carella be history, too.

SAL ROSELLI WAS GIVING a piano lesson when they arrived at his house that Tuesday morning. His wife said he'd be finished at eleven o'clock, would they like to wait inside for him, where it was cool? They elected to sit out back in the sun. From inside the house, they could hear some kid murdering something that used to be classical before he got his hands on it. Or she. From the pounding, Carella automatically assumed it was a boy in there venting his fury. Except for the cacophony, the neighborhood was still. Roselli's two little girls were in the pool, their mother watching them from the kitchen window. The detectives almost dozed.

Roselli was wearing black jeans, loafers without socks, and a white, long-sleeved shirt with the cuffs rolled up when he joined them at a few minutes past the hour. He appeared sleepy-eyed, though it was already late in the morning. He explained to the detectives that he'd been out jamming late the night before, sitting in with a bunch of guys he knew who had a steady gig down in The Quarter.

"It's tough to find steady work these days," he said. "I give lessons to supplement my income, got to pay the mortgage, hm? There's only one piano player in a band, you know. In a marching band, you can have seventy-six trombones, and a hundred and twelve cornets, but no piano at *all*. A rock group? Sometimes a keyboard, but just as often not. A symphony orchestra? *One* piano, but only sometimes."

"I used to play clarinet when I was a kid," Brown said.

Roselli gave him the disinterested nod of a professional who didn't give a damn about the music lessons amateurs took when they were kids.

"So what brings you out here again?" he asked, and took a seat facing them. The detectives were looking into the sun. They shifted their chairs.

"Boyle's Landing," Carella said.

"September first, four years ago," Brown said.

"Payday."

"Charlie Custer's office."

"What happened in there, Sal?"

First-name basis now, no more polite bullshit. You lied to us, Sal, so you're not Mr. Roselli anymore. You are Sal, and we are cops, Sal.

"In where?" Roselli said.

"Custer's office."

"When you and Katie went up there."

"It was Davey who went up there," Roselli said.

"Not according to him."

"Then he's lying."

"Not according to Katie, either."

Roselli looked at them.

"Katie's dead," he said.

"She wasn't dead when she gave her statement to Detective Morris Bloom in Calusa, Florida, four years ago."

"How'd you . . . ?" Roselli started, and then closed his mouth.

"Sal?"

He looked away.

"Want to tell us what happened that night, Sal?"

He turned back sharply.

"What happened was Custer got drunk and fell in the river," he said. "*That's* what happened. Just what I told you before."

"Only after a second visit, Sal."

"You neglected to mention the drowning the first time around."

"You said you didn't think it was important."

"How do you feel about being in Custer's office?"

"Alone with him and Katie?"

"How do you feel about that?"

"Do you think *that's* important?"

"All right, look, I didn't want to get involved."

"Involved?"

"You were here investigating Katie's murder, I didn't want to get involved, that's all."

"We're still investigating her murder, Sal."

"And I *still* don't want to get involved."

"Why'd you lie to us, Sal?"

"Because I had nothing to do with it."

"With what?"

"Charlie drowning."

"But he drowned after you left, didn't he?"

Silence.

"Sal?"

"He drowned after the band was long gone, isn't that what you told us?"

"Yes."

"So how could you have had anything to do with it?"

"I didn't."

"Then why'd you lie to us about being in his office?"

Silence.

"Sal?"

"Why'd you . . . ?"

"Okay, I was trying to protect Katie, okay?"

"But Katie's dead."

"You told me she was a nun."

"Yes?"

"Okay, I didn't want it to reflect upon her."

"Didn't want *what* to reflect upon her?"

"Didn't want it to tarnish her memory."

"What do you mean?"

"Charlie drowning."

"Would somehow tarnish her memory?"

"If it got out."

"If what got out?"

"If I told you."

"Told us what?"

"What happened."

"What *did* happen, Sal?"

Silence.

"Sal?"

"Tell us, Sal."

"What happened, Sal?"

"She shoved him over the railing," Roselli said.

"I CAN'T TELL YOU what a great job I think you kids did," Charlie says. He's been drinking too much and his speech is slurred. A bottle of beer in one hand, he staggers as he walks to the safe, catches his balance, says, "Oops," gives a gurgly little giggle and then grins in broad apology and winks at Katie. He raises the bottle in a belated toast. "Here's to next time," he says, and tilts the bottle to his mouth and drinks again. Sal is hoping he won't pass out before he opens the safe and pays them.

Charlie is wearing a wrinkled white linen suit, he looks as if he's auditioning for the role of Big Daddy in *Sweet Bird*. Chomping on a cigar, belching around it, he takes it out of his mouth only to swig more beer. He finally sets the bottle down on top of the safe. This is a big old Mosler that sits on the floor, he has some difficulty kneeling down in front of it, first because he's so fat, and next because he's so drunk. Sal is really beginning to worry now that they'll have to wait till morning to get paid. How's Charlie even going to remember the combination, much less see the numbers on the dial?

It is unbearably hot here in the office. The window air conditioner is functioning, but only minimally, and Charlie has thrown open the French doors to the deck, hoping to catch a stray breeze.

Outside, there is the sound of insects and wilder things, the cries of animals in the deep dark. Only the alligators are silent.

Katie is slumped in one of the big black leather chairs, exhausted and sweaty, her hair hanging limp, her T-shirt clinging to her. She has her legs stretched out, the mini riding high on her thighs, she looks sort of like a thirteen-year-old who's just come home from the junior high hop. Charlie is kneeling in front of the safe, having difficulty with his balance, reciting the combination out loud as if there's no one in the room with him, three to the right, stop on twenty. Two to the left, past twenty, stop on seven. One to the right, stop on thirty-four—but the safe won't open. So he goes through the same routine once again, and then another time after that until he finally hits the right numbers, and boldly yanks down the handle, and flamboyantly flings open the safe door. All grand movements. Everything big and baroque. Like drunken Charlie himself.

The night's proceeds are in there. Charlie's crowd is composed largely of teenagers, and they pay in cash. He starts counting out the bills, has to count *them* three times, too, before he gets it right. He puts the rest of the money back in the safe, hurls the door shut, gives the dial a dramatic twist. He's now holding a wad of hundred-dollar bills in his left hand. With his right hand, he braces himself against the safe and pushes himself to his feet.

He turns to Katie where she's sprawled half-asleep in the black leather chair.

"Now, young missy," he says, and staggers over to her. "You want this money?"

Katie opens her eyes.

"Would you like to get paid?" he says.

"That's why we're here, boss," Sal says, smiling, and moves to where Charlie's standing in front of the chair.

"You want this money?" Charlie asks again, and shakes the bills in Katie's face.

"Stop doing that," she says sleepily, and flaps her hands on the air in front of her, trying to wave the money away.

"Sweet missy, you want this money, here's what you got to do," he says, and shoves the wad of bills into the right-hand pocket of his jacket. They bulge there like a sudden tumor. He unzips his fly. And all at once he's holding himself in his hand.

"Come on, Charlie, put that away," Sal says. For some reason, he is still smiling. He cannot imagine why he is still smiling, unless it's because the situation is so absurd.

"Whut you want me to put away, boy?" Charlie says. "The money or my pecker?"

"Come on, Charlie."

Sal is no longer smiling.

"You want me to put this money back in the safe? Or you want me to put my pecker in Katie's mouth?"

"Come on, Charlie."

"Which?" Charlie says. "Cause that's the way it's gonna be, boy. Either the little girl sucks my dick, or you don't get paid."

Sal doesn't know how to deal with this. He's a city boy unused to the ways of wildland crackers. He thinks for a moment he'll run outside and get the others, all for one and one for all, and all that. But Charlie has grabbed Katie's chin in his hand now, and he is moving in on her with a drunk's bullheaded determination, waving his bulging purple cock at her the way he waved the wad of money only minutes ago. There is a look of such unutterable horror on Katie's face that Sal knows this is going to be resolved in the very next instant without any help from the rest of the band, without any help from him, either, for that matter. City-boy coward that he is, he stands frozen to the spot, watching, incapable of movement, unable to do anything but repeat, "Come on, Charlie."

Katie comes out of the chair like a lioness.

She shoves at Charlie's chest, and he staggers backward toward the open French doors.

"Hey," he says, "I was only . . ."

But she is on him again, shoving out at him again, a hundred and ten pounds of sweaty blind fury pushing the fat drunken fool out onto the deck, and then lunging at him one last time, her fingers widespread on his chest, a hiss escaping her lips as she pushes him over the railing. There is a splash when he hits the water, and then, instantly, a terrible thrashing that tells them the alligators are getting to him even before he surfaces.

Katie is breathing very hard. The sweaty T-shirt clings to her, Sal can see her nipples puckering it in excitement, she has just killed a man.

"The money," Katie says.

"Katie, you killed him."

"The money. It was in his pocket."

"Fuck the money," Sal says.

"Do you remember the combination?"

"No. Let's get out of here. Jesus, Katie, you *killed* him."

"The combination. Do you remember it?"

On the river below, there is an appalling stillness.

Three to the right, stop on twenty, two to the left, past twenty, stop on seven. One to the right, stop on thirty-four.

He recites the numbers aloud to her as she slowly turns the dial to the right, and to the left, and then to the right again. She opens the door. From the wad of money in the safe, she peels off the money due them, and returns the rest to the safe, and closes the door, and twists the dial to lock it again. Sal watches as she wipes the dial and the handle clean. She looks around one last time, and then they leave the office.

In the van, Sal says, "Got the bread, let's go," and Katie pulls her T-shirt away from her body, encouraging the cool flow from the air conditioner.

RIGOBERTO MENDEZ WAS SETTING UP his bar at the Siesta when Ollie Weeks caught up with him at one o'clock that afternoon. Weeks ordered himself a beer, for which he did not offer to pay. Sitting at the bar, Ollie slurped noisily and happily from the Heineken bottle, watching Mendez as he polished glasses and checked whiskey levels.

"So tell me," Ollie said, "where does this guy Sonny Cole live?"

"I got no idea," Mendez said.

He was one of these Dominicans who thought he was handsome as hell, black hair slicked back, little toothbrush mustache under his nose, wearing a tank-top shirt bulging with muscles he probably got lifting weights in the slammer.

"Man comes in your club . . ."

"First time I ever saw him."

"He killed a cop's father, you know that?" Ollie said.

"No, I didn't know that."

"That makes it very serious," Ollie said. "He maybe killed Juju, too, which is no great loss, but justice must be served, hm? I'm eager to talk to him. Find out where the two of them went when they left here. Find out what they talked about. Find out did Sonny shoot him in the head, what do you think?"

"About what?"

"About did Sonny shoot him?"

"I don't know what Sonny did. He never came back here since that Friday night. I don't know where he lives, or what he does for a living. You're pissing up the wrong tree."

"Maybe so. Can I have another beer? This is very nice beer."

Mendez opened another Heineken for him.

"You think he lives in the neighborhood?" he asked.

"I'm pretty sure he don't."

"How you suppose he got here?"

"He came looking for Juju."

"I didn't say *why*, I said *how*."

"I don't follow you."

"Transportation," Ollie said.

Mendez looked at him.

"Everybody has to have a means of transportation. He comes all the way up here to Hightown, how did he get here? Did he walk? Did he take the subway? Did he ride a bus? Did he come in a tax . . ."

"He drove here," Mendez said.

Ollie put down the beer bottle.

"How do you know that?"

"I saw his car."

"What kind of car?"

"A Honda."

"What color?"

"Green."

"You didn't happen to see the license plate number, did you?"

"No. Why would I look at the license plate?"

"Anything peculiar about the car? Dented fender? Broken tail-light, anything that might identify it?"

"Not that I saw."

"When was this?"

"That I saw the car?"

"Yeah."

"Friday night. When he came back to the club lookin for Tirana."

"The hooker, yeah."

"She's a manicurist."

"I'm sure she does great nails. That's when you saw the car, huh?"

"Yeah. There was a parking ticket on the windshield. He tore it up and drove off."

Bingo, Ollie thought.

BACK AT THE PRECINCT, Ollie called the One-Oh-Seven and asked for a kick-up on parking tickets written Friday night, August 28, targeting a green Honda parked in front of the Club Siesta. One of the sergeants there didn't get back to him until three o'clock. He informed Ollie that the green Honda was an Accord registered to a woman named Coralee Hilbert, who lived at 1114 Clarendon Avenue, in a better section of Diamondback, such as it was. Ollie took a cab uptown. He didn't like to drive because the steering wheel and his belly were always in contention. Besides, when he took a cab, he charged it to squadroom petty cash, and if anybody questioned this, he told him where to go. There was another benefit to taking taxis. It enabled him to enter into lively discussion with Pakistani drivers.

The first thing Ollie always did with a Pakistani cabdriver—or for that matter, any cabdriver who looked like a fuckin foreigner, which was only every other cabdriver in the city—was show his shield. This was so there'd be no heated arguments later on; some of these fuckin camel jockeys were very sensitive.

"Police officer," he said at once, flashing the tin. "I'm going to 1114 Clarendon Avenue."

The driver said nothing.

"If you heard me, blink," Ollie said.

"I heard you, sir."

"Good. Do you know where Clarendon Avenue is?"

"I know where it is, sir."

"Terrific, we're already ahead of the game. I'm in kind of a hurry, Abdul, but I wouldn't want you to speed."

The driver's name was Munsaf Azhar, displayed on a red card to the left of the yellow cab license, but Ollie called every Paki cabdriver Abdul. Not only did it make life much simpler, it also provided the enjoyment of watching the slow burn when the cabbie realized he couldn't get pissed off at a cop.

"I see you got the bomb these days," Ollie said pleasantly.

"Yes, sir," the cabbie said.

"Does that mean you'll be declaring war on America soon?"

"America is our friend," the cabbie said.

"Bullshit," Ollie said.

"Truly, sir."

"Even though we ain't sending you no more money?"

"I suppose we'll have to get by somehow," the cabbie said.

Had Ollie detected a slight touch of sarcasm there? One thing he hated—among everything else he hated—was baggy-pantsed foreigners trying to be clever.

"How you gonna get the bomb to the launching pad?" he asked. "Carry it on a donkey cart?"

The cabbie said nothing.

"Pack it on a camel?"

"We have means of transportation, sir."

"Oh, I'm sure you do. Must be yellow cabs all over the country, same as here. Big industrialized nation got the bomb now, can blow everybody to bits."

"We live in a bad neighborhood, sir."

"Bullshit," Ollie said. "*Everybody* lives in a bad neighborhood. *This* is a bad neighborhood right here. You see any nuclear bombs in this neighborhood?"

"We have powerful enemies, sir."

"Ah, yes, m'boy, I'm certain you do, and what a pity it is. Are you in a hurry to get home now that your country's got the bomb? Go defend your nation against all these powerful enemies?"

"I am in no hurry, sir."

"I'll bet you're not. What'd you live in there, a fuckin mud hut?"

"I had a proper apartment, sir."

"I'll bet you made a fortune there, driving a yellow cab all over the place."

"We are a poor country, sir, that is true."

"But rich enough to build a fuckin bomb, huh?"

"We are only trying to protect ourselves, sir. America has the bomb, too, you know."

"Oh, do we? But in America we don't marry off our six-year-old daughters, do we?"

"You're thinking of India, sir."

"Gee, is that India? Where they marry off their six-year-old daughters to their eight-year-old cousins? I thought it was Pakistan. Pakistan must be the place where you wipe your ass with your left hand, is that Pakistan? The unclean hand?"

"We are a proud nation, sir. And we are proud to have built the bomb, yes, sir."

"Now all you got to do is use it, right? That should make you real proud. Two big industrialized nations in a hurry to blow up the world. It's just ahead there, Abdul. Clarendon Avenue."

"I know the street, sir."

"Oh, I'm sure you do. I'll bet you could even get a job driving a cab in London, you know the streets so good."

The cabbie pulled to the curb in front of 1114. The fare was six dollars and ten cents. Ollie gave him ten dollars and told him to take seven and give him a receipt. The cabbie gave him a receipt and three dollars in change. Ollie opened the door. There was not a word from the driver.

"What language do you speak in Pakistan?" Ollie asked.

"Urdu or Hindi," the cabbie said. "Why do you ask, sir?"

"Is there a word for 'Thanks' in those languages?"

"Sir?"

"Because it's the custom with big nuclear powers to say thanks when somebody gives you a fuckin dollar tip on a six-dollar ride. Or are you too busy buildin bombs?"

"I *said* thank you, sir."

"Bullshit," Ollie said, and got out, and left the door on the curb side open so the driver would have to get out of the cab to come around and close it.

1114 Clarendon was a six-story brick in a row of similar buildings. Ollie checked the mailboxes in the entry, and found one for an L. Hilbert in apartment 2A. He hit all the bell buttons under the mailboxes, heard a chorus of answering buzzers and pushed open the inside door. This was a nice quiet building, no cooking smells, no smells of piss in the hallway. He climbed to the second floor, found 2A at the top of the stairs, looked for a bell button, found none, and knocked on the door.

"Yes?" a woman's voice called.

"Police," he said.

"What?"

"Police, ma'am, would you open the door, please?"

"Police?" the woman said.

"Yes, ma'am."

He waited. He knocked again. The door opened almost at once. A girl who couldn't have been older than twenty, twenty-one, was standing there in jeans and a cotton T-shirt.

"Coralee Hilbert?" he said.

"Coral," she said.

"Okay to come in, Coral?"

"Why?" she said.

"You own a green Honda Accord with the license plate WU 3200?"

"I do."

"Like to talk to you about a violation, ma'am. Is it okay to come in?"

"Let me see your badge," she said.

"Shield," he corrected.

"What?" she said.

"Never mind," he said, and took out the leather fob and showed her his gold and blue-enameled shield with the word DE-TECTIVE in an arc over the city's seal.

"A detective?" she said, surprised. "What kind of violation *is* this?"

"Just a parking ticket, miss," he said, "nothing to worry about," and closed the door behind him. "You know anybody named Sonny Cole?"

They were standing in a small kitchen in a neat apartment, living room beyond, doors leading off to what he supposed were two bedrooms. Windows facing south. Afternoon sunlight streaming in. The place hummed with air-conditioning. It was cool and clean and pleasant. He wondered if the girl was a hooker.

"What about him?" she asked.

"Was he driving your car this past Friday night?"

"He's been driving my car for almost two weeks now."

"How come?"

"I lent it to him."

"What's your relationship with him, miss?"

"We're friends."

"How long have you known him?"

"About three months."

"And you loaned him your car?"

"He's a good driver."

"Must be. Parked in a no-parking zone, must be an excellent driver."

"So what's the big deal? A parking ticket? They send out detectives on parking tickets?"

"You know anyone named Juju Judell?"

"No."

"Sonny ever mention him to you?"

"No."

"When's the last time you saw Sonny?"

"He stops by every now and then."

"When's the last time he stopped by?"

"Coupla days ago."

"Did he happen to stop by on Friday night?"

"No."

"This past Friday night. Didn't stop by then?"

"No."

"When did he stop by?"

"Sunday?"

"Well, was it or wasn't it?"

"I just told you."

"You made it sound like a question."

"No, it was Sunday. We went to the street fair on Culver."

"He isn't living here, is he?"

"No, I live here with my mother."

"What do you do for a living, miss?"

"I'm a student."

"You're not a manicurist?"

"A manicurist? What?"

"Do you know where Sonny lives?"

"No, I don't."

"Never been to his apartment?"

"Never."

"He just stops by here, is that it?"

"Yes."

"Gets his nails done, right?"

"What?"

"Where do you go to school, miss?"

"Ramsey U."

"Studying what?"

"Communications."

"Learning to communicate, huh?"

"Learning television broadcasting."

"Why'd you lend him your car?"

"He's trying to collect money he lent his cousin's husband."

"His *what?*"

"His cousin had an operation and Sonny lent her husband thousands of dollars to pay for it."

"His cousin's husband, huh?"

"Yes. His first cousin. Well, they're separated now. Which is why Sonny needed a car. So he could follow him and maybe he'd lead him to his cousin."

"Where'd you get this story, miss?"

"It isn't a story. Sonny needs to find his cousin, the one who had the kidney operation . . ."

"A kidney operation, I see."

"So he can ask her to plead his case, tell her former husband to pay him back the money."

"So he's trailing this guy around."

"Yes."

"In your car."

"Yes. He's a cop, you may even know him."

"Who's a cop?"

"The guy who owes him the money."

"Sonny Cole is trailing a *cop?*" Ollie said.

"That's what he told me."

Oh, Jesus, Ollie thought.

15.

E CALLED THE EIGHT-SEVEN THE MINUTE HE FOUND A PAY PHONE. THIS WAS NOW AROUND THREE-thirty. Parker answered the phone and told him Carella was in with the lieutenant just then.

"Tell him the guy who killed his old man is trailing him," Ollie said. "In a green Honda."

"No kidding?" Parker said.

"Sonny Cole. Tell him. The license plate number is WU 3200. Did Murchison tell you my nun joke?"

"No."

"Forget it, I got a better one."

"Let me hear it," Parker said.

"These two nuns are riding back to the convent on their bicycles, and they take a wrong turn?"

"Yeah?"

"They're bouncing along the road, and one of the nuns realizes they're lost so she asks the other nun, 'Have you ever come this way before?' And the other nun says, 'No. It must be the cobblestones.'"

"I don't get it," Parker said.

"Discuss it with Murchison," Ollie said. "And don't forget to tell Carella. Sonny Cole. A green Honda. WU 3200."

"Yeah, yeah."

"Write it down."

"Yeah, don't worry."

"Put it on his desk."

"Yeah, fine. Is it that she realizes they're lost because of the cobblestones?" Parker asked.

"Yeah, you got it, pal," Ollie said, and hung up.

"So WHAT ROSELLI'S SAYING IS she killed the man, is that it?" Byrnes asked.

"That's what he's saying," Brown said.

"Who's to contradict him? A dead woman?"

"Is what he's counting on."

"Have you got a theory?"

"Well . . . let's say Roselli's telling the truth. She *did* kill Charlie Custer. In which case, she quit the band and went back to the order so she could hide."

"From who? The police down there already closed it out, didn't they? Who's she hiding from?"

"Roselli."

"The only witness to the crime. Okay, that makes sense."

"On the other hand, if she *didn't* kill him . . ."

"Then Roselli did."

"Right. And she *still* went back to the order so she could hide from him."

"Because *she* witnessed *his* crime."

"So she disappears completely, becomes Sister Mary Vincent again."

"None of these guys knew she'd once been a nun, is that right?"

"Came as a total surprise to them."

"So running back to the convent was actually a good idea."

"Perfect way to vanish."

"So what happened? He found her?"

"That's what *he's* got to tell us, Pete."

"Why should he?"

The office went silent.

"You think he's the one who wrote that letter to her?"

"Could be."

"But we haven't got the letter."

"That's right."

"So we don't know what it said."

"If he's the one who ransacked her apartment, that's what he was looking for."

"And if he found it, he burned it a minute later."

"So we're back to zero."

"He's a user, Pete."

"How do you know?"

"Farnes told us. Four years ago he was doing pot . . ."

"Everybody does pot when he's a kid."

"Not such a kid, Pete. He was twenty-four."

"Even *I* did pot when I was twenty-four," Byrnes said.

"He graduated. At Figgs's funeral, he was sniffing coke."

"Still according to Farnes?"

"Yes."

"Reliable?"

"Who knows?"

"Okay, let's say he's a user. What are you looking for?"

"Guy's on cocaine, he needs money. He told us he's having a hard time finding work, been giving piano lessons to make ends meet. Okay, let's say he tracked Katie down, tried to blackmail her. Told her he'd blow the whistle on the murder unless she paid him two grand. So she . . ."

"That's assuming she did it. You can't blackmail a person who's . . ."

"No, it's assuming he'll *say* she did it."

"He's already got his story, Pete. The same one he told us. Katie killed Custer."

"All he has to do is tell it again."

"Or *threaten* to tell it."

"That's blackmail, Pete."

"Give me two grand or I go to the police."

"Where'd you get that figure?"

"That's how much she asked her brother for."

"But he turned her down," Brown said.

"Okay, so she goes to the park empty," Byrnes said. "What then?"

"He kills her."

"Why?"

The office went silent again.

"Find something," Byrnes said.

IT WAS ALMOST FOUR-THIRTY when they came out of Byrnes's office. Andy Parker had already left for the day. As always, he'd been in a hurry to get out of there. Maybe this was why he'd neglected to leave a note about Sonny Cole and the green Honda. Or maybe he simply didn't think it was important.

In the Chevy sedan, on their way home, Carella and Brown tried to dope out their next move. They concluded it would be fruitless to ask for a search warrant for the letter stolen from Katie's apartment—if indeed a letter *had* been stolen and if, further, the letter had been stolen by the person who'd murdered her. Byrnes was right. If the letter was that important, it would have been burned a minute after the thief left her apartment.

They couldn't search Roselli's house for a murder weapon, either, because the weapon had been the killer's hands. Nor could they go to a judge and say they wanted to look through the house for cocaine because they couldn't for the life of them see how they could show probable cause and they knew a judge would tell them to go home and be nice boys.

They could arrest Roselli and put him in the box, of course, in the hope that he'd fall all to pieces without a fix and tell them all about how it was he himself who'd shoved Custer over that railing and not little Katie Cochran. But that was for the movies. If Roselli had, in fact, killed Katie he'd simply refuse to answer any questions. Only this time there wasn't a handy burglary they could charge him with. Earlier today, the judge at Leslie Blyden's arraignment had set a very low bail of one thousand dollars, which The Cookie Boy had easily met. Whether he now left town was entirely up to him. They didn't want a repeat performance from Roselli.

It was a little past six P.M. Brown was driving Carella home first, and they had almost reached his house in Riverhead.

"I keep wondering if she'd still be alive," Brown said.

"How do you mean?"

"If the brother had only lent her some of that money he inherited."

The car went silent.

And then, both detectives started speaking at the same time.

"Didn't Roselli say . . . ?"

"How'd he know . . . ?"

And all of a sudden, everything fell into place.

On the phone, Roselli's wife told them he'd already left for a job in the city.

"Where in the city?" Carella asked.

"What is this?" she said. "You're beginning to upset me and the children, bothering us all the time."

"Sorry, Mrs. Roselli," Carella said. "We just have a few more questions."

"He's playing in the bandshell at the Seventh Street Seaport. I wish you'd leave us alone. Really," she said, and hung up.

The seaport was a reconstructed area on the River Dix. Two blocks of souvenir shops and food stands lined a boardwalk that ran into an oval-shaped dance floor with a bandshell behind it. Pennants flapped on a hasty river wind. Music wafted on the soft evening summer air. Roselli was part of a four-piece rock group playing all the golden oldies Carella knew by heart. Hearing the music that had been so vital to him when he was growing up, seeing all the pretty young girls in the arms of handsome young boys, he remembered again that he would soon be forty. On the river, a cruise boat drifted past. Carella could hear the guide over the loudspeaker, telling the passengers they were passing the Seventh Street Seaport. Everything suddenly seemed so poignant to him, as if it were in imminent danger of becoming lost forever. It was seven-forty P.M. and the sky was already melting into the river.

"There he is," Brown said.

The tune ended. The teenagers on the floor applauded. The band played a little signature riff, and came down off the platform. Carella could not shake the feeling of impending loss.

"Hey," Roselli said, "what are *you* guys doing here?"

"Mr. Roselli," Brown said, "how'd you know Katie's parents were dead?"

"She told me," he said.

"When?"

"While we were on tour. She was very upset about it."

"Told you they'd been in a car accident?"

"Yes."

"Told you this four years ago?"

"Sometime on the tour, I don't know if it was exactly four years ago."

"Explained that her rich brother who'd inherited all that money didn't want to have anything to do with her, is that right?"

"Yes."

"Did she happen to mention *when* the car accident took place?"

"No."

"Last July, Sal."

"Not four years ago, Sal."

"The Fourth of July, Sal. Last year."

He looked at them. He wasn't doing any arithmetic because he knew it was too late for arithmetic. He knew exactly what they knew. He knew Katie couldn't have told him about her parents unless he'd seen her since last July. He knew he'd made a mistake, and the mistake was a bad one, and he couldn't see any way of correcting it. Across the river, lights were beginning to show in apartment buildings. When night came in this city, it came with heart-stopping suddenness.

He put his head in his hands and began weeping.

"I CAN'T TELL YOU what a great job I think you kids did," Charlie says. He's been drinking too much and his speech is slurred. A bottle of beer in one hand, he staggers as he walks to the safe, catches his balance, says, "Oops," gives a gurgly little giggle and then grins in broad apology and winks at Katie. He raises the bottle in a belated toast. "Here's to next time," he says, and tilts the bottle to his mouth and drinks again. Sal is hoping he won't pass out before he opens the safe and pays them. He himself has been smoking pot all night long, and is a bit dazzled, so to speak. He certainly hopes Katie isn't too tired to count the money.

Charlie is wearing a wrinkled white linen suit, he looks as if he's auditioning for the role of Big Daddy in *Sweet Bird*. Chomping on a cigar, belching around it, he takes it out of his mouth only to swig more beer. Finally, he sets the bottle down on top of the safe. This is a big old Mosler that sits on the floor, he has some difficulty kneeling down in front of it, first because he's so fat, and next because he's so drunk. Sal is really beginning to worry now that they'll have to wait till morning to get paid. How's Charlie even going to remember the combination, much less see the numbers on the dial? And how is he himself, Salvatore Roselli, going to know the difference between a single and a hundred-dollar bill, so absolutely wonderfully stoned is he.

It is unbearably hot here in the office. The window air conditioner is functioning, but only minimally, and Charlie has thrown open the French doors to the deck, hoping to catch a stray breeze. Outside, there is the sound of insects and wilder things, the cries of animals in the deep dark. Only the alligators are silent.

Sal is slumped in one of the big black leather chairs, T-shirt all sweaty, legs stretched out, beginning to doze. Charlie is kneeling in front of the safe, having difficulty with his balance, reciting the combination out loud as if there's no one in the room with him, three to the right, stop on twenty. Two to the left, past twenty, stop on seven. One to the right, stop on thirty-four—but the safe won't open. So he goes through the same routine once again, and then another time after that until he finally hits the right numbers, and boldly yanks down the handle, and flamboyantly flings open the safe door. All grand movements. Everything big and baroque. Like drunken Charlie himself.

The night's proceeds are in there. Charlie's crowd is composed largely of teenagers, and they pay in cash. He starts counting out the bills, has to count *them* three times, too, before he gets it right. He puts the rest of the money back in the safe, hurls the door shut, gives the dial a dramatic twist. He's now holding a wad of hundred-dollar bills in his left hand. With his right hand, he braces himself against the safe and pushes himself to his feet.

He turns to Sal where he's sprawled half-asleep in the black leather chair.

"Hey, Piano Boy," he says, and staggers over to him. "You want this money?"

Sal opens his eyes.

"Would you like to get paid?" he says.

"That's why we're here, boss," Katie says.

"You want this money?" Charlie asks again, and shakes the bills in Sal's face.

"Stop doing that," Sal says, and flaps his hands on the air in front of him, trying to wave the money away.

"Sweet Buns, you want this money, here's what you got to do," he says, and shoves the wad of bills into the right-hand pocket of the jacket. They bulge there like a sudden tumor. He unzips his fly. And all at once he's holding himself in his hand.

"Come on, Charlie, put that away," Katie says.

"Whut you want me to put away, girl?" Charlie says. "The money or my pecker?"

"Come on, Charlie."

"You want me to put this money back in the safe? Or you want me to put my pecker in little Sally's mouth here?"

"Come on, Charlie."

"Which?" Charlie says. "Cause that's the way it's gonna be, Katie. Either the boy here sucks my dick, or you don't get paid."

Sal doesn't know how to deal with this. He's a city boy unused to the ways of wildland crackers. He thinks for a moment he'll run outside and get the others, all for one and one for all, and all that. But Charlie has grabbed Sal's chin in his hand now, and he is squeezing hard and moving in on him with a drunk's bullheaded determination, waving his bulging purple cock at him the way he waved the wad of money only minutes ago. City-boy coward that he is, Sal sits frozen in Charlie's grip, incapable of movement.

It is Katie who says, yet another time, "Come on, Charlie," and hits him from behind with the beer bottle he left on the safe. Beer flies in a fine spray as she swings the bottle at his head. The man staggers, but he is not essentially wounded, Katie's blow is ineffectual at best. But Sal is instantly on his feet, shoving out at Charlie's chest, pushing the fat drunken fool through the open French doors and out onto the deck, and then lunging at him one last time, his fingers widespread on Charlie's chest, a hiss escaping his lips as he pushes him over the railing. There is a splash when he hits the water, and then, instantly, a terrible thrashing that tells them the alligators are getting to him even before he surfaces.

Sal is breathing very hard. He has just killed a man.

"The money," he says.

"You killed him," Katie says.

"The money. It was in his pocket."

"Never mind the money."

"Do you remember the combination?"

"Sweet mother of God, you *killed* him!"

"The combination. Do you remember it?"

On the river below, there is an appalling stillness.

Three to the right, stop on twenty, two to the left, past twenty, stop on seven. One to the right, stop on thirty-four.

Katie recites the numbers aloud to him as he slowly turns the dial to the right, and to the left, and then to the right again. He opens the door. From the wad of money in the safe, he peels off the money due them, and returns the rest to the safe, and closes the door, and twists the dial to lock it again. Katie watches as he wipes the dial and the handle clean. She is moving from foot to foot, like a little girl who has to pee. He wipes the beer bottle, too, and puts it back on the safe top where Charlie had earlier left it. He looks around one last time, and then they leave the office.

In the van, he says, "Got the bread, let's go," and Katie pulls her T-shirt away from her body, encouraging the cool flow from the air conditioner.

THEY WERE AFRAID HE MIGHT SPOOK. They had read him his rights and taken him back to the precinct, and now they were fearful he might not say another word. He was still in tears. They didn't want him to collapse entirely, so they decided to let Carella handle it alone, less threatening that way. They were in the Interrogation Room now. The other detectives were behind the one-way mirror in the room next door, watching, listening, scarcely daring to breathe. Carella turned on the video camera, and read Roselli his rights again.

Sometimes they spooked when they heard the Miranda recitation for the second time. It made everything seem irrevocable beyond that point. Made them think Hey, maybe I *should* ask for a lawyer. With professionals, there was never any question. They *always* asked for a lawyer first thing. With the amateurs, like Roselli, they either figured they could outsmart the police, or else they were so guilt-ridden they wanted to spill it all. Carella waited. Roselli nodded. Yes, he understood his rights and was willing to answer questions without a lawyer present. Carella needed it in words.

"Okay to go on then, Mr. Roselli?"

"Yes."

No more Sal. Now they were equals. Mr. Roselli and Mr. Carella, two old friends sipping cappuccino and discussing politics at a round outdoor table in the sunshine. But the light was fluorescent, and the table was long and cigarette-scarred, and the coffee was made down the hall in the Clerical Office and served in cardboard containers, and the subject was murder.

"Want to tell me what happened, Mr. Roselli?"

Roselli sat there, looking at his hands.

"Mr. Roselli?"

"Yes."

"Can you tell me?"

"Yes."

Carella waited.

"I spotted her by accident."

"Katie?"

"Yes."

"Katie Cochran?"

"Yes. I hadn't seen her in four years, she'd changed a lot."

He fell silent, remembering.

"She used to look like a teenager," he said. "Now she looked . . . I don't know. Mature?"

Carella waited.

"She seemed so . . . *serious,*" Roselli said. "I didn't know she was a nun, of course. Not just then. Not when I first saw her."

He began weeping again.

Carella moved a box of tissues closer to where Roselli was sitting. The tears kept streaming down his face. Carella waited. The room was still except for the sound of Roselli's sobbing and the faint whirring of the video camera. Carella wondered if he should risk a prod. He waited another moment.

"Where'd you run into her?" he asked.

Gently. Softly. Casually. Two gents sipping their coffees. Sunshine gleaming on white linen.

"Mr. Roselli?"

"At St. Margaret's."

He took another tissue from the box, blew his nose. Dried his eyes.

"The hospital," he said, and blew his nose again. He sighed

heavily. Carella was hoping he wasn't about to quit. Call it off. That's it. No more questions. He kept waiting.

"I thought a friend of mine had OD'd, I rushed him to the emergency room," Roselli said. "It turned out he was okay, but Jesus, his face had turned blue! Katie just walked through, I couldn't believe it. I was busy with my friend, I thought he was going to die. I see this woman who looks like Katie, but doesn't look like Katie. I mean, you had to know Katie back then. When she was singing? A million kilowatts, I swear. This woman looked so . . . I don't know . . . serene? Walking into the emergency room. Straight out of the past. Composed. She stopped to say a few words to one of the nurses, and then *whoosh*, she was out the door and gone. I asked the nurse who she was. She said That's Sister Mary Vincent. I said *What?* Sister Mary Vincent, she said again. She's a nun. Works upstairs in Extensive Care. Sister Mary Vincent? I thought. A nun? I figured I'd made a mistake."

He shook his head, remembering, remembering.

Carella glanced up at the video camera. The red light was still on. The tape was still rolling. Don't quit on me now, he thought. Keep talking, Sal.

"I went back. I had to make sure this wasn't Katie. Because if it *was* her, I wanted to ask her about that night four years ago. The way you want to ask your mother things about when you were a kid, do you know? I wanted to ask Katie about what had happened that night. Wanted to make sure that night *had* really happened. That night with Charlie Custer. When we killed him."

It occurred to Carella that the only one who'd killed Custer was Roselli himself. He was the one who'd pushed him over that railing to his death. Yes, technically, they'd acted in concert, Katie hitting him with the bottle, Roselli shoving him over to the alligators. And technically, yes, a prosecutor could make a case against both of them. Katie's intent hadn't been to kill, though, and Roselli had been acting in self-defense. A defense attorney could make a case for that as well. There were times when Carella was grateful he was merely a cop.

"I waited outside the emergency room door," Roselli said, "in the parking lot there, where the ambulances come in. This was two or three days later. Nurses were walking in and out. It was Katie, no question about it. I didn't approach her because I wasn't sure what she might do. She'd quit the band and disappeared. She'd become a nun and taken a new name. Had she run because she was afraid of the law? Or afraid of *me?* Had she become a nun because she was hiding? From the law? Or from *me?*"

He nodded again, remembering. Kept nodding. Trying to understand. Hands folded on the tabletop. Fingers working. Kneading his hands on the tabletop.

"I looked her up in all the phone books, but there were no listings for anyone named Mary Vincent. So I followed her home one day," he said. "She lived in a walk-up on Yarrow. I checked the mailboxes and found one for Mary Vincent. So now I knew how to reach her if I wanted to. But why would I want to?"

And now Roselli seemed to drift, his voice lowering almost to a whisper, confiding to Carella as if indeed the two of them were basking alone in the sun somewhere. Unaware of the camera now, he turned his gaze inward, and words spilled from his heart like shattered glass.

Carella listened, pained.

I KNEW A NUN wouldn't have a pot to piss in, but she came from a well-to-do family, you know. In Pennsylvania someplace. On the road, she was always talking about them. Her father was a university professor, her mother was a psychiatrist. That was money there. What would a couple of thousand mean to a family like that? I didn't know her parents were dead, of course. I learned that later. That night in the park. I didn't know her brother had inherited all their goddamn money. I just thought . . . you know . . . if I asked her for a little money, just to tide me over, just until I could square myself with the man, get a steady gig someplace, then maybe she could get it from her parents, you know? I know if one of *my* daughters was a nun, I'd give her the world. The world. I love those little girls. I'd give them the world. So maybe Katie's parents would help *her* out. Was what I thought.

I couldn't phone her, she wasn't listed, but I didn't want to walk up to her on the street, either. Hey, Katie, remember me? Remember the night you and I killed Charlie Custer? Remember the alligators eating him? A laugh riot, remember? Do you remember all of it, Katie, the way *I* remember all of it except when I'm lost in Dopeland? Do you remember, Katie?

I wrote her a letter.

It was dated Monday, August tenth. I know because I read it again after I broke into her apartment to get it back. I tore it up the minute I got home. Flushed the bits and pieces down the toilet. The letter said Hi, Katie, it's good knowing you're still alive and well. I don't want to bother you, Katie, I know you have a new life now, but I'm in a little trouble, and maybe you can help me out. This is what it is. I need a couple of thousand dollars to square a debt. I was hoping you could ask your parents for a loan until I get on my feet again. Do you think that would be possible? I would appreciate your help. Please call me, Katie. I'm living out on Sand's Spit just now, in a small development house. The number there is 803-7256. I mean you no harm. I just need money. Considering our past together, I feel certain you'll help. Please call.

She never called.

I figured she must have got the letter sometime that week. Even if she got it *late* in the week, say Thursday or Friday, she should have called. But she didn't.

So I wrote her a second letter. This one was dated Saturday, August fifteenth. *It* went down the toilet, too, right after I found it in her apartment. What it said was I really had to have the money right away because the man I owed it to was making serious threats. I told her I knew her parents were wealthy, so please ask them for it, can you? All I need is two thousand. I asked her to meet me the following Friday in Grover Park. August twenty-first.

Six-thirty P.M., I said. Come in on Larson Street. Go to the third bench on the right. I'll be sitting there waiting for you. Please bring the money. I won't harm you, Katie. I promise. Please meet me, Katie. We are old friends. Don't you remember, Katie? Please help me.

I was waiting there for her at six-thirty that night.

She didn't arrive until seven. I was just about to leave. She told me she'd been walking through the park. She told me she'd been praying. Affirming that God still approved of the decision she'd made. That was the word she used. Affirming.

So here we are, she said.

Smiling. Looking serene and placid and . . . well . . . almost beatific.

She told me I was looking very good, which was a lie, and I told her I was happy she'd decided to meet me. I told her I was so surprised to learn she was a nun, had she given up singing altogether? You were such a good singer, I said.

I sing on the ward sometimes, she said. To my patients.

She told me she dealt mostly with terminally ill patients. I said I found that so hard to imagine. Katie Cochran a nun on a hospital ward? Singing to terminally ill patients? Come on, I said.

"Come on, Charlie."

I told her I was married now and had two little girls, Josie and Jenny. My wife's a lovely girl, Katie, I'd like you to meet her one day.

I'd love to meet her, Katie said.

I told her I was sorry I had to bother her this way but I really was in a bind.

I really need the money, I said. Really, Katie.

Katie, I'm a drug addict, I said.

I'm sorry to hear that, she said.

My wife is clean, though, totally sober. Well, she's what you might call a recreational user, she does it just to keep me company every now and then. I told her I was in serious trouble. I told her because of the cocaine I owed close to three thousand dollars to my dealer. If I could pay him two now, he'd let the rest slide till I could get a steady gig someplace.

So did you bring the money? I asked.

Your letters sounded so threatening, she said.

No, no. I meant you no harm.

Yes, those words especially. "I mean you no harm." Why *would* you want to harm me?

I don't.

But your words. "Considering our past together." And in the second letter, "Don't you remember, Katie?" Such threatening words.

No, no, I didn't mean them that way.

They frightened me, Sal. Your words. I prayed that God would forgive your words. It was odd, receiving your letters when I did. After I'd already made my decision.

Katie, did you bring the money?

I tried to get it, she said.

Tried?

I called my brother in Philadelphia. He inherited a lot of money when my parents died. They were killed in a car crash last July, Sal.

I'm sorry to hear that. But . . .

The Fourth of July. He inherited everything they had. I was sure he would help me. He'd helped me before, you see.

Tried? I said.

He turned me down. I'm sorry, Sal. I tried.

No! Go to him again!

He'll refuse again. I almost knew he would, Sal. You see, God had already . . .

Katie, I don't want to hear about God! Just go to your brother . . .

It was God who revealed the way, Sal. I prayed so hard for guidance. And at last, He forgave me. Even before I got your letters . . .

Damn it, Katie . . .

. . . I knew I could forgive myself. God's will had become my will.

That same unsettling smile was on her face. This was now getting on seven-thirty, the lights had already come on in the park, the sky was beginning to deepen but she seemed to be staring into a blinding light, smiling.

I've forgotten the past, Sal. All of it. God has helped me do that.

No one can forget the past, I said.

I can, she said. I *have*. Pray to God, she said. Let him forgive you. Let him help you forget, too.

But I was *remembering*.

As she spewed all this religious crap, I was remembering everything that happened four years ago, on that sweltering night at the beginning of September. The noises of the night outside those French doors open to the river. The two of us in Charlie's office, alone with him. Charlie's obscene advances. Unzipping himself. Exposing himself to her. A young girl like Katie.

"You want this money?" Charlie asks again, and shakes the bills in Katie's face.

Does God have two thousand dollars? I said. To pay the man who's ready to break my fingers? My *fingers!* I said, and held up my hands to show them to her, waggling them in her face.

"Stop doing that," Katie says, and flaps her hands on the air in front of her, trying to wave the money away.

My livelihood, I said. My music, Katie! My *life!*

I'm sorry, she said.

"Cause that's the way it's gonna be. Either the little girl here sucks my dick, or you don't get paid."

Listen to me, I said.

Forget that night, she said. Pray to God and He'll forgive you, Sal. The way He's forgiven me. Believe me, Sal, God will *hear* you!

Fuck God! I said.

She gave a shocked little cry. Her hand went to her lips.

Call your brother again, I said. Tell him I'll go to the police. Tell him I remember it all, Katie. *All* of it! You hitting Charlie with the bottle, you shoving him in the river, *everything!* Go to him, I said. *Get* the money!

I can't go to him again, she said.

Then get it someplace else! I don't *care* where, just . . .

Sal, please. I'm a nun.

Then go to your mother superior, go to the *pope,* just get the fucking money. Or I'll go to the police. I promise you. I'll . . .

If *anyone* goes to the police . . .

Yes, *I* will, I said.

. . . it'll be *me,* she said.

I looked at her.

I'm a nun, she said.

It was very dark on that path. The sun was gone, there was not a breeze stirring.

A nun, she said.

The leaves in the trees were still, the night was still.

Don't make me do it, she said. You're the one who killed him, Sal. You.

No.

You alone. I'm a nun.

No!

You killed him because he was . . .

Shut up, I whispered.

. . . forcing you to . . .

Shut up! I shouted, and grabbed her by the throat.

16.

"IN THE END, HE BELIEVED HIS OWN STORY," BROWN SAID.

"EXACTLY WHAT HAPPENED," CARella said. "Same with her."

"Believed his story?"

"Believed *her* own story."

Both men were a little drunk.

"Each of them rewriting what happened," Carella said.

"Trying to change the past."

"*He* shoved Charlie in the river, *she* shoved Charlie in the river."

"*Nobody* shoved Charlie in the river."

"Charlie *jumped* in the river!"

Both men burst out laughing.

"Shhh," Carella said.

Teddy was asleep upstairs, the twins were asleep just down the hall. The clock on the living room mantel read ten past ten. The detectives had each been awake since six-thirty this morning, and on the job since a quarter to eight. It had been a long, long day.

"You think she really would have gone to the police?" Carella asked.

"Oh sure. She had God on her side."

"Didn't help her much in the park."

"She forgot to say 'Sweet Jesus, help me,'" Brown said, and burst out laughing again.

"Shhh," Carella said, and burst into laughter himself. Brown covered his mouth like a kid who'd uttered a dirty word. Carella cut his eyes toward the hallway. Both men were silent for a moment, and then began laughing again.

"Shhhh," Carella said.

"Shhhh," Brown said.

"You okay there? Let me freshen that for you."

"Just a drop. I got to be running along. Caroline's gonna start worrying."

Carella went into the kitchen, poured scotch into Brown's glass and Canadian Club into his own. Little soda in each. Fresh ice cubes. When he came back into the living room, Brown was standing at the bookcases, looking over the titles.

"You ever have time to read?" he asked.

"Not much. Except on vacation."

"When are you taking yours?"

"Two weeks from now."

"Where you going?"

"The shore."

"Should be nice there."

"Yes." Carella held up his glass. "Here's to golden days," he said.

"And purple nights," Brown said.

They drank.

"How did either of them ever expect to forget the past?" Carella asked, and sipped at his drink. "You want to know something?" he said.

"What's that?" Brown asked, and sank into the leather easy chair under the imitation Tiffany lamp.

"I'll be forty in October."

"Oh boy," Brown said.

"Forty."

"I hear you."

"Remember when we used to go out drinking after an important bust?"

"We're doing that right this minute, Steve."

"I mean in a *bar*. When we were young. When none of us were married. Remember that bar near the bridge? Just off Culver? All the guys on the squad used to go there and get drunk. Remember? After a big one? Kling was a patrolman back then. Hawes wasn't even on the squad. Remember?" He nodded, remembering, and went to sit in the easy chair opposite Brown. He took a long swallow of the drink, and then sat staring into the glass. "There was a cop named Hernandez I liked a lot," he said. "He got killed by a cheap thief who holed up in the precinct, remember? Do you remember a cop named Havilland? Roger Havilland? He was worse than Parker. Sometimes I think Parker *is* Havilland, come back from the dead. Remember the time that rich guy's kid got kidnapped up in Smoke Rise? King. Douglas King. Funny how you remember the names, isn't it? Remember the time Virginia Dodge came up to the squadroom with a bottle of nitro in her purse? Looking for me? Cause I sent her husband away? Remember? Remember the time Claire got killed in that bookshop? Kling's girl, remember? Claire Townsend. Remember the time The Deaf Man tunneled under that bank? I'll bet *he* never gets old, Artie, not The Deaf Man. Remember . . . Jesus, remember the *times?* I remember them all, Artie. I remember all of it, all of it. Every single minute. It goes by too fast, Artie. I'll be forty in October. Where did it all go, Artie?"

He looked up.

"Artie?" he said.

Brown was snoring lightly. Sleep softened his features, giving him the appearance of a much younger man. Carella went to him, stood watching him fondly, a smile on his face. He turned out the light then, and went to phone Caroline to say that her husband was exhausted and would be spending the night there.

SONNY GOT TO RIVERHEAD BEFORE DAWN. He parked the stolen car in an all-night garage four blocks from the Carella house, and then walked along Dover Plains Avenue toward the elevated train station, trying to look like any simple colored man shuffling to work on a Wednesday morning just like any other Wednesday morning. He walked past the steps leading up to the platform, and made a right turn into the street where Carella lived. He was a black man on foot in a white neighborhood while the sun wasn't yet up. He hoped no cop car would go rolling by, hoped nobody peering out his window would suspect him for a burglar instead of a man about to kill a police detective. This amused him. He laughed out loud, ducked his head as if somebody had read his mind, and hurried up the street.

The Chevy he'd been following for the past little while was parked in front of Carella's garage. This surprised him. He glanced over at the house. Not a light burning. He went straight up the grassy patch alongside the driveway, padding softly to the door on the side of the garage, between it and the house. This was the most dangerous part. This was when he could be seen from the house. But it was still dark, and he was still black—this amused him, too—and he picked the Mickey Mouse lock in nothing flat. Swiftly, he opened the door and closed it just as swiftly behind him. There were two cars in the garage, explaining why Carella had parked the battered police sedan in the drive.

Sonny took the Desert Eagle from his belt.

He looked at his watch. Ten minutes to six.

He figured in an hour or so Carella would be a dead man.

THEY WERE DRINKING COFFEE at the kitchen table when Fat Ollie Weeks called. Teddy and the twins were still asleep. The clock on the wall read 6:35 A.M.

"I figured you'd be awake," Ollie said.

"Been up since six," Carella said.

"I got a nun joke for you."

"Too late. We already cracked the case."

"Who's we?"

"Me and Artie."

"Artie?"

"Brown."

"Oh. Yeah. Brown," Ollie said.

"He's here right now," Carella said.

"What's he doing there?"

"We were celebrating last night," Carella said. "Like old times."

"But what's he doing *there?*"

"He slept here."

"He *slept* there?"

It was inconceivable to Ollie that any white man would allow a black man to sleep in one of his beds. Or pee in one of his toilets. Or use one of his towels. Inconceivable.

"Give him my regards," he said, making it sound like a curse. "Meanwhile, how do you like having a black dancing partner?"

"What do you mean?"

"Didn't Parker tell you?"

"No. What?"

"Sonny Cole's following you."

"What?"

"Sonny Cole. The guy who shot your father. He's been tailing you."

"If this is a joke, Ollie . . ."

"No joke. He's in a green Honda, watch for it."

"A green Honda?"

"Been on you the past two weeks."

"How do you know this?"

"He maybe dusted a dealer in Hightown. I caught the squeal."

"But how do you know he . . . ?"

"Eyes and ears of the world, m'boy, ah yes," Ollie said. "Give *him* my regards, too."

There was a click on the line.

"A green Honda?" Brown said.

"Sonny Cole driving it," Carella said.

"What's *he* fixin to do?"

"Guess," Carella said.

*   *   *

Watching through the paned glass panels on the side door of the garage, Sonny saw the kitchen door of the Carella house opening, and in that same moment he opened the garage door, and stepped outside, and yanked the Desert Eagle from his belt. He was swiftly walking the ten feet from the garage to the house, ready to drop Carella in his tracks the moment he came out onto the little porch outside the kitchen, when instead out stepped the big black dude who was his partner.

Brown was coming down the steps when he spotted Sonny.

He immediately reached for his nine.

Carella came out of the house a moment later and recognized Sonny from all those days sitting in the courtroom while Henry Lowell was letting him get away with murder, and he drew his own nine at once, so now there were three nines on this bright September morning, all facing each other with nowhere to go but murder. Three nines spelling the devil's own mischief upside down, nine, nine, nine.

"Get out the way, nigger," Sonny said. "I got no quarrel with you."

"I got plenty quarrel with you," Brown said.

Carella didn't know if he said the words or only thought them, but as he squeezed the trigger they were there.

Our father who art in Heaven . . .

And he fired.

And now Brown was firing, too.

And Sonny Cole fell to the ground.

He called Lieutenant Byrnes at home and told him that he and Brown had shot and killed a man named Samson Wilbur Cole who'd been waiting outside his house with a Desert Eagle in his hand. He asked the lieutenant to advise the local precinct, and also Homicide and Internal Affairs, and he told the lieutenant that he and Brown would be waiting here at the scene for them.

The shots had awakened everyone in the neighborhood and

they were all out in the street in robes and pajamas when first a patrol car and then several unmarked cars arrived. This was now
around seven in the morning. Some twenty minutes later, two
more marked police cars arrived at the Carella house and spewed
forth a glittering array of brass, all eager to talk to Carella and
Brown before the media got hold of this. Much of the day, in fact,
was spent downtown at Headquarters, with no less a worthy than
the Commissioner himself instructing the two detectives on what
they should say once the newspaper reporters and telecasters de-
scended en masse.

That evening, just as Carella and Brown were about to begin
regretting their own ten minutes of television fame, The Cookie
Boy was moving out of the spotlight and onto a 747 bound for
London, where he had relatives in the meat-packing business. At
six o'clock, while his plane was roaring down the runway for take-
off, a television journalist eager to turn the Sonny Cole story into a
big TV drama of black-white tension and family vendetta, asked
Carella how it had felt to kill the man once accused of murdering
his father.

Brown, taking the rap, said, "It was my bullet killed him."

Carella wondered exactly how he had felt.

The truth was he didn't know.

He guessed he felt all right.

ABOUT THE AUTHOR

ED MCBAIN is the only American to receive the Diamond Dagger, the British Crime Writers Association's highest award. He also holds the Mystery Writers of America's coveted Grand Master Award. His books have sold over one hundred million copies, ranging from his most recent, *The Last Best Hope,* to the bestselling *The Blackboard Jungle,* the screenplay for Alfred Hitchcock's *The Birds,* and the bestselling *Privileged Conversation,* written under his own name, Evan Hunter. He lives in Connecticut.